PRAISE FOR THE
THE LAYERS, DARL
AFTERTHOUGHTS.

"A beautifully written novel which feels fresh and timely. The way the story unfolds feels essential and organic to the narrative while also disrupting the expected. This is a novel with both a head and a heart. *The Afterthoughts* doesn't compromise on facing loss and hard truths, but it also reverberates with warmth and integrity."

– June Wentland, author of *Foolish Heroines*

"Reynolds has written a short yet layered reflection on the state of modern love, and the complexities of loving another person while maintaining one's own truth. A wonderful and perceptive novella, with many sentences demanding to be read twice."

– Susan Furber, author of *The Essence of an Hour*

"Reynolds' debut shouts a crucial message across the din of contemporary fiction, deftly and lovingly."

– Joe Bedford, author of *A Bad Decade for Good People*

"A beautifully written story. Reynolds' writing flows in a way which kept me glued to the page, needing to find out what comes next."

– Joseph A. Chadwick, author of *The Briarmen*

THE AFTERTHOUGHTS

STEPHEN REYNOLDS

The Book Guild Ltd

First published in Great Britain in 2024 by
The Book Guild Ltd
Unit E2 Airfield Business Park,
Harrison Road, Market Harborough,
Leicestershire. LE16 7UL
Tel: 0116 2792299
www.bookguild.co.uk
Email: info@bookguild.co.uk
Twitter: @bookguild

Typeset in 11pt Minion Pro

Printed and bound by CPI Group (UK) Ltd, Croydon, CR0 4YY

ISBN 978 1916668 652

British Library Cataloguing in Publication Data.
A catalogue record for this book is available from the British Library.

For Nanna Martin. Thanks for all the marshmallows.

PROLOGUE

The dream is lucid and fragmented. Chaos like spilt milk; rancid and cloying. A place where only useless panic obscures an acceptance as quiet and devastating as the end of everything. Time stops. But colours and screams and metal and skin, rush and bite and sob. And the pain. A pain beyond sense. A hopeless pain that dances on the broken bones of every repentant tomorrow. No embers, no afterthought, no meaning.

A lightning flash of something past. A sepia-tinged garden where my mother tends to roses that fade and scowl. Her eyes are a colour that lives inside me. Developmental. Vibrant and cognitive. She smiles as she sees me. A warmth that might be literal rises up in me to lace the pain with a sweet and yielding poison. A plastic cup with a tiger's face printed on it. Unforgotten now. Dormant all these years. Silently waiting for this moment, and only this moment, to resurface. The garden dissolves and I'm lying in a bed that was once my own. My father kneels beside me and gently strokes my hair with his giant hand. An action so tender it dilutes the pain with soothing resignation.

'Mummy's all better now, my boy. And in the morning, you can meet your new baby brother.'

'I want a story, Daddy.'

We are stood on a table, my brother and I, in a room of our grandparents' house. We're holding bowls of Neapolitan ice cream up to an electric bulb that glows a nostalgic orange. We stir frantically; a competition to see who can turn their desert into milkshake the quickest. We are the same, he and I. For this captured reel, we move and laugh and think as one. And then the mourners. So many. They age at triple speed as lines of sadness spread across their faces. Scars left by a silent whip that flogs us all. But in this scene, they are young and raw. My grandmother was the first of us to leave. The pregnant swirling clouds above us unleash and never really stop. Mingling with hot salty tears. *I want her back*, I think again, so many lifetimes later. I want my grandma back.

A chemical surge. Sweat and neon and the faces of friends who own a part of me long gone but fondly remembered. Tactile, messy, glorious and so willingly vulnerable. Innocent and exposed. Those halcyon days. And there she is; love of mine. All the warmth of an endless summertime. A beauty that boils blood and severs veins. Slowly the coldness creeps as we write our story. But our hands remain clasped together, even in the darkest nights. There are years in the wilderness, yes. Knots that will take us forever to untangle. But untangle them we will. We do. We did. And then life. Full and true and kind. And then her. Our girl. Our beautiful girl. Pure and untroubled, fact and fiction. The light that shines the way. The three of us, tired and happy and burning so, so bright.

And the pain. The dream is lucid and fragmented, and painful.

ONE

I wake with a start as the train lurches to an abrupt stop. There is nothing behind the glass of the window. Only night and its reflections. The light in the compartment is dim but warm. Like a childhood memory.

This is an old carriage, I notice. I must've fallen asleep as soon as I boarded. In the rush not to be late and the subsequent exhaustion, I hadn't noticed the décor of the compartment. It takes me back to my youth. The dusty, threadbare blues of the morning school commute. I thought they'd decommissioned all these old trains? The man sat opposite me meets my eye and nods genially.

'It's alright. A signal delay, I should think. I'd expect we'll be off again in a moment. Bad dream?'

'I can't remember.'

There's something old about him, too. Although he's not old. A few years my senior, perhaps? But there's something in the neatness of him. His trimmed moustache and creaseless suit. The hat and perfectly folded overcoat that rest on the luggage rack above his head. Or maybe it's his eyes. Yes, that's it. His hazel eyes are burdened. Weighed down by time he cannot feasibly have experienced. He holds out his hand.

'Percy's the name.'

His handshake is firm but also somehow intangible.

'I've finished with this, so you're welcome to it, if you like?' He picks up a newspaper from the seat beside him and offers it to me. The words on the page are blurred. I can't make them out and feel a sharp stab of pain behind the eyes when I try to do so. The pain feels strangely like a warning of some kind. I shake my head and muster a weak half smile.

PERCY

It was already the longest night of Percy's life. He'd never known cold like it. A cold that burned. A few hours ago, the men – himself included – had climbed from their ditch and began pacing up and down, their breath rising like smoke signals beneath the ghostly light of the star shells.

Captain Padfield had been spitting blood when he saw them and they were soon back in their shallow, frozen ditch. For frozen it was. As were their overcoats, so heavy and sodden with the endless rain and mud of this godforsaken place. Packed in like sardines, teeth chattering and their heads sticking out over the top so that Percy thought they may as well still be standing, for all the cover they had. And yet somehow, in spite of everything, a sleep of sorts had come then. They were all learning that the only thing capable of quelling the fear was the tiredness. And both would kill you in the end.

He woke with a start, like the jolt of a train abruptly stopping. He could still see nothing through the blackness of night. Would the dawn never come? Perhaps he was already dead? Were these the Plains of Asphodel? They certainly weren't the other one… what was it called? Where the luckiest souls, chosen by God, dwelt for all eternity. The souls resting in this spot may have been chosen, but not by God above, and lucky they were not.

The nervous whispers of those closest to him, as they lay in their open graves, carried on the still air of this endless night. Mutterings of despair, impatience and characteristically defiant jest. Young Tristram turned to Percy, his face as milky white and lifeless as the moon above.

'Perhaps the sun has gone forever, sir?'

'Perhaps, private. Although I'd been led to believe Asphodel would lay on some flowers for us to feast upon in our everlasting twilight. I see only mud and darkness.'

'Come again, sir?'

'The sun will rise, private. We can be sure of that, if nothing else.'

Time dragged on. Minutes like hours, hours like days. Percy allowed his mind to drift on the cold still air. Across the mud and mangled remains, over the unburdened ocean and onwards, to home. To the smell of the roses his mother tended to in their vibrant garden. The world used to be so full of colour and fragrance. All colour seems to have been washed away here, save for the ugly cherry red so liberally splashed across this loveless wasteland. And the less said about the smell, the better.

Percy thought of his mother and father and all his brothers and sisters, for there were many. Seated together around the family table on a quiet Sunday afternoon. The room dappled in sunlight. Warm rays filled with swirling dust. Heads bowed in prayer; be thankful for all we are about to receive.

He wondered if his father prayed for him now. If he'd sensed that his son needed watching over. Felt it somehow, across the unburdened ocean, through the mud and mangled remains. Percy searched for his father's prayer on the cold still air. But there was only the darkness.

'This must be what a condemned man feels like the night before the gallows.'

'Chin up, private.'

Percy looked again at his watch. Still over an hour to wait. He looked down the line at the men and found that he could make out something of their faces now; grey and cold and lost. Even the longest night has a dawn.

Distant birdsong broke the silence then. *How strange*, Percy thought, *that the birds still sing across this broken land*. Heralding a new day, as though the carnage around them meant nothing. As though every drop of blood spilled was for nought. Was it? No, Percy didn't believe that. Even if the last eight months had been the worst of his life. Of a thousand lifetimes. Even if they did say it would all be over by Christmas and here he was in March, lying frozen in a muddy ditch, waiting to meet his maker once again. An appointment he knew he couldn't *keep* rescheduling. He was a soldier. He loved his country and his King, and he would fight on for them. But if he was to die, then it would be for the family that sat together in a ray of sunshine, swirling like dust.

And then, the dawn.

An almighty noise shook heaven and Earth. The air was cold and still no longer. It punched Percy – and all the men that lay in their frozen ditch that dawn around Neuve Chapelle – square in the face. It was 7.30am and the artillery had begun firing. The noise was like nothing any of the men had ever heard. Tristram was shouting something at Percy, but he couldn't hear a word of it, though the milk-skinned boy was by his side. The blackness of their endless night had lifted and in its place: the fires of hell itself. Mighty bang after mighty bang rang out, as the guns fired over their heads and rained down burning death upon the enemy trenches.

Percy squinted to see through the flying mud and debris. Whole trees were being uprooted. The remains of houses and farm buildings were blasted into the sky, where they shattered into a thousand pieces. The air was full of barbed wire, sandbags and body parts. Whether new or old, Percy could not tell. Great columns of water were spouting up from the ground. Some of the men began to cry out. Not in fear or pain or dismay, but something else. Animal and savage. Beyond the ringing in his ears Percy heard Captain Padfield.

'Fix bayonets, prepare to move!'

And then Percy, too, cried out. The fear and tiredness gone. All thoughts of home, all thoughts of anything, gone. He roared and bared his teeth like a Leicester Tiger. The world turned an ugly cherry red and, like all the men that dawn around Neuve Chapelle, he left his frozen ditch and charged at the burning enemy lines.

TWO

There are three other passengers in the compartment, besides Percy and myself. They're all sleeping, apparently untroubled by the unexpected halting of the train. Although one of them, I only sense. She's sitting a few feet along from me. It is a she, I think. Each time I turn my head to look at her, I find it's impossible. A sharp pain behind the eyes again. She's peripheral: there – but only just. I turn towards the window but it's as though the glass is angled slightly. The reflection cuts out the corner in which she sits. *How black this night is*, I think to myself. Not even a suggestion of the world beyond the glass.

'It's alright.' That genial smile again. Oddly familiar now. 'It was a very sudden stop. You've pulled something in your neck, I should think. Best not to move it too much.'

'Where are we, exactly?' I ask.

'I've no idea, I'm afraid.'

The man beside Percy lets out a solitary snore; deep and growling with an accompanying nasal whistle to finish. I look at him properly for the first time. He's shaped like a teddy bear. A huge, perfectly round belly, rosy red cheeks and a set of bushy white whiskers that are both unruly and yet splendidly groomed. Like Percy, his clothes are wrong. Of another time. Although not the same time as Percy, not exactly. Is there some kind of historical society meeting taking place that they're both travelling to? A matching waistcoat and jacket with an ugly cherry red flower in the lapel. A bright yellow necktie and a slightly scruffy looking pair of trousers, pulled well up above the waist. In the luggage rack above his head lies a wooden walking cane and a straw boater.

As if sensing I'm staring at him, one lid lifts to reveal an emerald-green eye pointed in my direction. It rests on my face for a second or two before rotating to observe the rest of its surroundings. Sweeping and spinning as if independent from the body in which it sits. When it finds Percy, its partner immediately springs open and the whole rosy red and whiskered ensemble is all at once animated.

'Hello, Percy, my boy!'

'Hello, Algie.'

'How the devil are you? And how's that daughter of mine?'

'You can ask her yourself; she'll be along in a moment.'

'Splendid, splendid!'

Percy turns to me and there's a hint of something else mixed in with the geniality now. Apology, perhaps?

'This is my father-in-law, Algie.'

How can you enter a train compartment, sit down and fall asleep without realising you've sat next to your son-in-law? Perhaps he was already sleeping when Percy arrived? Perhaps he has dementia? His whole face smiles at me.

'Delighted, my boy.' The emerald-green eyes narrow then, and I have a sense of being dissected. 'My goodness,' he mutters before turning his gaze to the compartment itself. 'My goodness.' He turns back to Percy with eyebrows raised. 'When, do you think?'

Did he say when, or where?

'An unscheduled stoppage of some kind, Algie.'

They both turn to face me, and I have a sudden, almost overwhelming urge to leave this compartment. Instinctively, though, I know I can't. Not yet.

ALGIE

Algie considered it a splendid thing to be the centre of the world. And for those first five years of his long and eventual life, that's exactly what he was. Apple of the eye might be stretching it somewhat. But he was certainly the primary focus for his mother and father. Algie's father was a police officer. Or a mutton shunter, peeler or blue belly, as they were referred to in certain circles at the time. Unboiled lobster being Algie's own favoured colloquialism. Despite this, he was a mild-mannered, almost meek man. Apologetic and browbeaten. Which brings us to Algie's mother. She was a…

'Have you ever seen a Bengal tiger playing with its food? Some poor unfortunate infant water buffalo, having already had a great chunk of his hindquarters removed, is rolled around and pawed at until he almost musters up a hope that the ruddy thing isn't hungry after all. He gazes up hopefully at the great quadruped to be met by a cold dead stare and then… bang! Or rather, *roar*! The killer chomp is delivered, and it's lights out. Well, that was Mater. The Bengal tiger,

I mean. The infant water buffalo represents the general population at large. On official documents she was listed as Mrs. Martha Cordelia Boudica Knighton. To everyone in the real world she was known as the Snarling Tigress. Nobody called her that to her face, you understand? Not unless they wanted to be sitting on a cloud playing the harp with all the other infant water buffalo, that is. Oh no, to the face it was always ma'am or Mrs.Knighton. The grocer used to call her "Your Ladyship". She was no more a lady than I am, but you can bet your brass farthing she never corrected him. Anyway, that was my old mater.'

It came as something of a shock to Algie, therefore, when this oh-so-sweet set up changed forever with the untimely arrival of his brother. Master Leopold Thaddeus Ethelred Knighton was born in September 1872, just two days after Algie's fifth birthday. Algie did not consider this a welcome birthday gift.

As he stood beside his mother, looking down at this challenger to his throne, he instinctively understood that his life would never be the same again. In appearance, Leopold possessed the equine features of Algie's unfortunate father. But even at that first sight, Algie knew that what lay within was pure unfiltered Snarling Tigress. It was the eyes that gave him away. Those beady little windows to the soul. He was arching a disapproving eyebrow before he could even speak or sit upright of his own accord.

What a ratbag he was, thought Algie.

Sure enough, those first years of Leopold's childhood would shape a sibling rivalry that would last their entire lives. Or rather, Leopold's entire life. Which, as it turned out, wasn't all that prolonged.

9

He was killed in the Second Boer War, at the tender age of twenty-seven. Algie always knew his brother was destined for the military. Always so serious and disciplined. When Algie's mother heard news of her favoured son's death, she fell to pieces. She began a period of mourning that would last a thousand lifetimes. So many mourners, lines of sadness spread across their faces. Algie mourned his brother, too, in spite of everything. The line that separates love and hate can sometimes be a flimsy, paper-thin affair. And hate each other they did.

In 1879, during the summer that never was, Algie almost bested young Leopold in spectacular fashion. Almost. The bleak winter, it seemed to all, would never end. It was July but cloaks, knickerbockers and fur hats still adorned the flesh and bones of the long dead souls inhabiting this forgotten memory.

The Snarling Tigress and her two sons were gathered round the fireplace. Algie was picking his nose and Leopold was sat triumphantly atop his lavish new rocking horse, named Samuel.

A week or so before this wintery July scene, Algie's father had categorically stated that the family could not afford Samuel, but the Snarling Tigress had insisted. It had been so long since Algie's father had worn the trousers in his house that he could no longer remember what they even looked like, and so Samuel was duly welcomed into the Knighton coterie. Although, in a quiet show of defiance, Algie's father would silently scowl at Samuel every time he walked past him.

This evening, Leopold rocked back and forth in an eerily regimented fashion. His mother occasionally glancing up from her knitting to gaze adoringly at her miniature cavalryman.

In strode Algie's father, bringing a great gust of cold wind with him.

'This *bloody* cold!' he cried, clearly having not yet noticed the assembled family scene awaiting him.

'Language, Pater!' roared the Snarling Tigress.

'Ss-sorry, dearest.'

He emptied the pockets of his vast blue tunic onto the table before removing it and hanging it on the door behind him. He wandered sheepishly over to his armchair nearest the fire, his wife's eyes burning a hole in him all the while. He managed a brief scowl in Samuel's direction en route. The Snarling Tigress gave her lips a final purse before continuing with her knitting. Algie's father glanced down at him and gave him a lightning quick wink.

Something caught young Leopold's eye amongst the pile of pocket detritus now resting on the table. He dismounted Samuel and wandered over. Upon arrival, his eyes lit up and he squealed, 'Sweeties, Pater?!'

'What's that, Leopold?' answered Algie's father absentmindedly, already halfway through packing his first pipe of the evening.

The Snarling Tigress glanced up and upon seeing what her young darling had spied, she leapt to her feet and bounded over to the table.

'No, no! Leopold, dearest! Those aren't sweeties, my darling. Those are Pater's special tablets from Mr. Timkins, the pharmacist.'

'They're from America!' interjected Algie's father, with some pride, having misread the mood rather.

'That's not really relevant, is it, Pater?! They shouldn't be within reach of Leopold and Algie, should they?'

'No, dearest, you're quite right, of course.'

The mystery tin of sweets was hastily removed from view and the evening carried on as normal. Not another word was spoken regards the matter. Until the following day, that is.

During the afternoon, once the household duties had been completed and before she began her aggressive knitting ritual, the Snarling Tigress would often partake in a brief snooze. Algie had concocted what he deemed to be a fiendishly clever plan, to get one over on his young rocking-horsed foe. As soon as he was sure that his mother was asleep, he set to work. The plan relied on his father's general lack of organisational skills. Reasoning that – having hastily hidden the mystery sweets – he was sure to then forget to take them with him the following morning.

Sure enough, there they were, tucked down the side of the favoured armchair. As Leopold and Samuel galloped through some imaginary desert plain and the Tigress snoozed with mouth agape, Algie proceeded to wolf down the entire tin of sweets as quickly as he could fit them down his ample neck. They didn't taste much like sweets, truth be told. A vague minty aftertaste, perhaps. But it didn't matter, for Algie was now entering phase two of his cunning plan. He casually ambled past the young sibling atop his steed and dropped the empty tin on the floor beside them. Then – having adopted a look of earnest concern – he awoke the Snarling Tigress from her slumber.

'Mater, Mater! Please wake up.'

'Wha! What is it, Algernon?'

'Mater, Leopold has eaten Pater's sweeties even though you said he wasn't supposed to.'

'Sweeties? What are yo…' Realisation dawned across those formidable features.

'Oh, dear Lord no. Leopold!'

Algie was a little taken aback by her initial reaction. He'd been expecting an all-too-recognisable wave of fury, whereas what he actually got was more akin to, well, panic. Things only got more peculiar from there on in. His mother seemed positively terrified as she cross-examined the bemused Leopold. Algie was now becoming a touch miffed. If this had been him, he reasoned, it would've been over the knee, trousers down and brace yourself for twelve of the best.

'Do you feel alright, Leopold, dearest? When exactly did you eat the sweeties? Oh, my poor boy!'

After an hour or so of panicking – which included holding Leopold upside down and shaking him – Algie's father breezed through the door unsuspectingly.

'Whatever is the matter?' he enquired.

'You! You bloody idiot!'

He immediately turned tail with the intent of marching straight back out the way he'd come.

'He's eaten your bloody pills! The whole tin!'

'I have not!' protested a whimpering and, by now, terrified Leopold, for what must have been the hundredth time. Algie's father then joined in the cross-examination and as Leopold descended into uncontrollable sobs, Algie at last began to enjoy himself.

It was then, however, that he began to feel a strange sensation in his belly. As though something was moving around down there. Then came the noises. Like rolling thunder. Quickening in pace and increasing in volume.

'Erm... Mater... Pater?' he snivelled quietly. He didn't need to repeat himself any louder, for all three of them were now staring at him in slack-jawed amazement. Even Samuel had cocked an ear his way. The thunder was now reaching alarming volumes. And then... well, then it became abruptly and violently obvious who'd eaten Mr. Timkins' mystery sweeties. Which were, in fact, laxative pills. A new kind... from America.

Needless to say, Algie did not have a pleasant night. He was at least spared the customary beating from the Snarling Tigress. Indeed, she gave him something of a wide berth for a number of days. As did his father. Alas, the same could not be said for young Leopold, who spent the next three weeks following Algie around blowing raspberries at him.

THREE

'Can't you stay quiet for a moment, Algie?'

'Bessie, my love! You're awake.'

'Thanks to you, dear husband, yes.'

The woman beside Algie yawns and stretches like a character in a story. Or a cat. As if awakening from the deepest sleep. Like Percy, there is something familiar about her. Not a suggestion of previous encounters, obscured by the mists of time. But something. Something that I sense should unnerve me, but doesn't. Her attire is less obviously historical than her two companions. *There may be rumblings of disapproval at the society meeting*, I think to myself. Whispers of *try harder*. A knitted cardigan and colourless skirt. As difficult to date as the woman herself. She could be anything from fifty to eighty. Almost improbably generic. Or at least, she would be. Were it not for *that* face. A face that glows with the light of life itself. Kindness and wisdom. Forgiveness and strength. I am safe.

'Hello, Percy.'

'Hello, Bessie, old thing.' The two briefly stand and embrace before returning to their seats.

'Is our Clara not with you?'

'Yes, she is. She'll be along in a moment.'

'There must be news then, I…' She sees me then. And smiles. A smile that wraps around the space between us and cradles me like a babe-in-arms.

'Hello,' I say, resisting an inexplicable urge to stand and embrace this stranger myself.

'Hello, my love. And who might you be?'

'An unscheduled stop, my dear,' interjects Algie, as if this answers the question.

'Oh, yes. We're not moving, are we? How odd.' She looks at the black window and the strange scene it reflects. A flicker of something then. She almost turns to look at the figure in the corner but stops herself. I instinctively move to look at her myself but Percy cuts in.

'This is my mother-in-law, Bessie,' he says, apparently the host of whatever dream I've awoke to find myself in. There's no apology hidden in the inflection now. I detect something closer to pride. We're all safe now. 'Don't worry,' he continues, 'that's nearly all of us now.'

BESSIE

The sun that shines in the cornflower blue sky above is the sun of a child's drawing. Smiling and round and yellow.

'I could stay here forever,' Bessie says out loud, although she is alone. She's almost always alone. At least, whenever she can be. She has found the living to be almost unbearably tiresome from as far back in time as her memories will take her. The untended grass upon which she lies is fragrant and lush. It rises and curls above her as it sways on the gentle summer breeze.

I am safe, she thinks. She imagines it curling all the way across her body and burying her forever in this sunny and cheerful place.

She sits up and surveys the scene around her.

'That one.'

She takes out her paper and pencil, walks to the chosen stone and begins to rub. This stone is more weathered than the others she's rubbed today. The moss of neglect grows and spreads across its surface. Speckled and clawing. A badge that tells all who visit this place that the soul beneath is forgotten. Unmourned and alone.

'Don't worry,' Bessie says to the stone, 'it's nice to be alone. Nobody telling you what to do or saying silly and boring things at you.'

She cocks her head this way and that, as she concentrates on capturing all the words and not damaging the paper.

Here lies Mary Upcott. Born 1723, fell asleep 1787.

'There you are, Mary,' she says, looking down at the rubbing, 'now *I'll* remember you.'

And so, she does. She stands beside the moss-coated grave and remembers Mary Upcott, who died many years before Bessie was born. She remembers her as a cobbler's wife. For both Mary and Bessie were born into unenlightened times. But Bessie has a more enlightened mind than anyone before or since her, so she remembers that Mary Upcott had a sister. Mary's sister was a woman of independent means who lived a life of fun abandon in the city of… Bath. One day Mary Upcott ran away from her cobbler, who was boring and silly, and went to live with her sister in the city. For a time, Mary Upcott also lived a life of gay abandonment. But because she was Bessie's memory and because Bessie has a more enlightened mind than anyone before or since her, this wasn't enough for Mary. She remembers that Mary became a writer. She wrote books that allowed other enlightened minds to escape the confines of the boring and silly world they all lived in. Her publisher said she should change her name to that of a man, because people wouldn't read books written by a cobbler's wife. He – a colourless man with no redeeming features – suggested Thomas Reynard. But Mary refused.

'Good for you, Mary,' Bessie says. Then she folds the paper in half and places it neatly in her bag, with all the other rubbings she's taken this day.

Bessie's mother and father both worried about their daughter. Always wanting to be alone and spending so much time amongst the dead. All those rubbings, scattered over her bedroom. It wasn't natural.

'It's macabre,' said Bessie's mother.

'That it is,' agreed Bessie's father, although he didn't know what the word meant. It sounded a bit French to him.

They both feared she may never find a husband and would remain their burden until the day they both died. At which time, Bessie might take their rubbings and remember them a much more interesting life than the one they'd settled for. As it was, though, they needn't have worried. For Bessie had plans.

Here rests Jacob Fuller 1645 – 1700
And his beloved wife Mabel Fuller 1644 – 1708
And their beloved son, William Fuller 1668 – 1709.

'My goodness,' says Bessie, 'it must be awfully cramped.'

She couldn't think of anything worse than spending a moss-coated eternity in a small space with her hapless parents. What would they talk about?

'Poor William.'

She remembered William as a brave and capable boy. Forever a boy. She remembered him playing alone in the fields of his father. In a make-believe world of Roundhead generals and medieval knights. Far away kingdoms in magical lands. A sweet and innocent boy with a heart he always chose to wear on his sleeve. Uncomplicated by the world around him. True. She remembered him crouching on the ground and delicately correcting a beetle that had fallen on its back. Then she remembered him smiling as he sat and watched it scurry away. Unaware that it lived on thanks only to the kindness of a sweet-natured boy in the memory of a girl he never met. And the rest. For this was a memory within a memory. She knew it, had known it for as long as knowledge had existed. She became sad then. Just for a moment. Then she remembered that William and Bessie had met. Here, in this very spot. They played for hours amongst the unmourned and beneath the smiling, round and yellow sun. Then she folds the paper in half and places it neatly in her bag, with all the other rubbings she's taken this day.

Bessie's age is a tricky thing to pin down. It sways in the summer breeze like the untended grass that would one day grow around her own stone.

Here lies Bessie. She has plans.

This makes Bessie smile. People felt safe when Bessie smiled. This had always been the case, and always would be. And rightly so. On the evening of 4th October 1915, for example, Bessie smiled a smile that would make a girl, never to become a woman, feel safe for two long years. An angel of mercy who, to Bessie, was simply a plaything. But that was many years in the future. And many years ago, of course.

'Oh, do be quiet, Bessie,' Bessie said to herself, for there was no one else there, save for the dead. She'd confused herself again. She was always doing this. The past, the future and the great everything between. She was a girl, of uncertain age, taking rubbings of gravestones, as she did regularly. The next century – itself both the past and the distant future – could wait. Let it wait.

'She's touched, that girl,' Bessie's father would say. A boring and silly man, who she loved a great deal.

Here lies Bessie's father. 1845 – 1900. A boring and silly man who lives forever in this memory.

Bessie leaves the graveyard then and sets off down the old lane. The hedgerows are dotted with juicy berries of an ugly cherry red colour. She heads for a place that was once her home. A place where the dead live on and worry about her always. Bessie isn't like the others in this story. Remember that. She has plans.

FOUR

They fall in and out of sleep. It's unnatural. Sometimes mid-sentence. I'm unsure if I'm doing the same thing. Slipping in and out of consciousness. It's almost as disconcerting as the vast blackness beyond the windowpane. I have a sense of trying to grab hold of something but never quite managing it. Time and my thoughts are floating, never landing. I instinctively think of my daughter. I always do when the world around me stops making sense. The familiarity of both her and the act of remembering her gives me comfort.

Our darling, Annie. Named after my grandmother. I'd had to fight Ela on that one. Not because she didn't like the name, or didn't respect my wish to honour my grandmother, but she'd wanted us to name her Chakrika – Ela's mother's middle name. The raw potency of grief won the day. Neither of us could imagine her being called anything else now. Our beautiful girl. Pure and troubled, fact and fiction. The light that shines the way. I miss her, I realise. With an ache. *Odd*, I think. I was only with her… when? Today?

There are no outside sounds. No wind or rain, no distant hum of traffic. As though the external world had been paused. Frozen in time. An unscheduled stop. There are voices though, aren't there? Murmurs; inaudible but familiar. I take comfort in this. There are other people on this train. It is only a train. An old carriage, yes. The threadbare blues of the school commute. But that's not so strange, is it? And my fellow passengers, these three eccentrics. That's all they are, isn't it? Characters. But that's not quite all, is it? Because there are four people in this compartment besides me. She's peripheral. There, but only just. That's not... I mean, there's not a rational explanation for that, is there? Is there? Panic is rising now. All three of them wake up, at the same time. *Exactly* the same time.

PERCY

Several things register at once as Percy slowly opens his eyes. The noise; low guttural moans and hopeless aching sobs. The all-too-familiar sound of grown men weeping, calling for their mothers. Cognitive, developmental. Then the stench. Again, by now mechanically recognisable. Infection and rotting flesh. Death. And then, finally, the pain. A pain beyond sense. A hopeless pain that dances on the broken bones of every repentant tomorrow. No embers, no afterthought, no meaning. He tries to isolate it. To apply his reasoning mind.

Legs and head, he thinks. *Legs and head.*

But wait. Something *is* different, isn't it? Something else, something new. Beyond the guttural pleas and absent mothers, there are footsteps. Not tired limbs dragged through endless mud and mangled remains, but shoes on floorboard. Behind the godless stink of fading life there is something... clinical. Clean. Then it fades, or ceases to matter. Because he realises something else then. He's screaming. Odd, he thinks, that he hadn't registered this at first. Then someone is with him. Calming and clean and tender. Words spoken a thousand times. A place where a child's love for his mother can rest when his mother is gone. Is it Bessie? No, that's not possible. Even that thought isn't possible, is it? That's the future. Then she administers. Then nothing. Blissful and wretched. Painless and lost. The void.

'Perhaps the sun has gone forever, sir?'

'Private? Is that you?' Percy opens his eyes. Wood panel walls, reassuringly regimented straight lines. Windows. *Good Lord*, he thinks, *look at that... a window*. Sunlight spills in, illuminating clouds of swirling dust. Bedsheets. Nurses and doctors. Clean. Cleanness. Cleanliness. *Good Lord*. Pain, both his and that belonging to the faceless moaning figures filling the other beds. Still dancing, perhaps still hopeless, but at least it makes sense now. *Legs and head*, he thinks. Legs and head. He slowly moves his neck, turns to his right. A faceless rotting spectre where once there was a boy. He shuts his eyes as tight as he can then turns to his left and opens them again. Private Tristram, lying on the next bed, smiling his black-toothed smile.

'Welcome back, sir.'

Percy smiles back at the milk-skinned boy. 'Hello, private. How are you?'

'All the better for seeing you, sir. How are you feeling?'

'Legs and head.'

'Indeed, sir. Fritz gave us quite the bashing.'

'I'm rather afraid I can't remember.'

Footsteps on floorboard.

'Ah, sergeant, you're back with us, I see.'

A nurse. A girl, no older than the broken boys she cares for in this wooden panelled sanctuary. Although there's something unnaturally old about her. The eyes? Yes, that's it. Her pale grey eyes are burdened. Weighed down by things she shouldn't have had to experience.

'How are you feeling?'

'Legs and head.'

'Indeed. Can you cope or would you like something for the pain?'

'I can cope, I should think. Where am I?'

'Number ten, General, Rouen.'

'Good show, any chance of helping me up?'

'I'm afraid not. You need to rest, and those legs are taking you nowhere at the moment.'

Percy lets out a sigh. 'I suppose I'm stuck with this chap chattering on at me then.' He smiles and gestures with his eyes toward Tristram.

The nurse looks confused. Her pale grey eyes narrow.

'Are you sure you're alright?'

'Oh, fine. Don't you worry about me.'

Her gaze lingers on Percy for a second or two, then she gives a curt nod and walks away.

'A pretty lady, sir.'

'Indeed. A slightly odd one, perhaps. But then I'd expect I would be too if I had to deal with all she does.'

'I expect we'll all be a bit odd by the time this is over, sir.'

'Very astute, private.'

Percy tries to turn his body toward Tristram, but the pain won't allow it. 'What *did* happen, private?'

'You really can't remember a thing, sir?'

'Not a jot of it.'

'Bombs, sir. Lots of them. Almighty it was. Then gas.'

'Gas?!'

'Yes, sir. The Hun gassed us after the bombs. As we cared for the wounded men.'

'Devils.'

'Yes, sir.'

Percy had a sudden and acute sinking feeling then. Like falling. 'What of the men, private?'

'Most are dead, sir.'

Silence.

'Captain Padfield?'

'Dead, sir.'

Silence.

Percy tried to remember. But how does one *try* to remember? Either you remember or you don't. Nothing.

'You gave me your mask, sir.'

A flash of something then. A milk-skinned boy gasping for air. Ugly cherry red coughing. The walls of the trench collapsed. Bodies and body parts. Eyes stinging and streaming, ears ringing. The rancid air. Hell. It was hell. Crawling through the carnage with useless trailing legs. Consciousness fading in and out.

'Are you remembering, sir?'

Almost a surrender to the pain. To the void. But if Percy was to die it would be for the family that sat together in a ray of sunshine, swirling like dust. Say their names. Over and over. Keep saying them. They are the light through the darkness. Over and over.

'You *are* remembering, aren't you, sir?'

And then Tristram. Through the swirling rancid air. Gasping. Fading. Crawling to the milk-skinned boy, dragging those useless trailing legs through mud and mangled remains. Silent shouts. Shaking. Slapping. The ugly cherry red. Then the mask. Too late.

'You didn't make it, private. Did you?'

'No, sir.'

'I'm sorry.'

'I know, sir.'

'I tried.'

'You did, sir. You gave me your mask. You held me at the end. You could have done no more, sir.'

Time passing. Or not. Not exactly. Not in a way that makes sense. Passing but leaving nothing behind, no sense of itself. Birdsong. *How strange*, Percy thought, *that the birds still sing across this broken land*. Heralding a new day, as though the carnage around them meant nothing. As though every drop of blood spilled was for nought. As though the milk-skinned boy he held in his arms was never there.

'Private?'

'Yes, sir.'

'Did I make it?'

'Sir?'

'Am I dead?'

Silence.

'That is a very difficult question, sir. Is there pain?'

'Yes.'

'Then no, sir. You're not dead. Unless the pain is a memory, sir.'

FIVE

I think I'm having a panic attack. Or worse. This is all wrong. The compartment, my strange travelling companions and, perhaps most of all, the window. There's *nothing* out there. I've been on trains before. I've spent half my life on them. Even in the middle of nowhere, in the dead of the blackest night, you can still see... *something*. The compartment begins to spin. Perhaps it's a heart attack. All three of them are staring at me now.

'It's alright,' Percy says.

'It's not alright!' I wheeze back at him. 'They don't... they don't...'

'Spit it out, my boy,' says Algie.

'They don't use train carriages like this anymore.'

Bessie reaches across and takes my hand. She's looks me in the eyes and smiles. And I calm then.

'It's alright, my love.'

Her voice reaches inside me and soothes the child I once was.

'You're on a train and we've made an unscheduled stop. You're among friends. We'll get moving again before too long, you'll see. And then everything will make sense. I promise.'

'The window,' I whimper. 'There's nothing out there—'

'Out of interest,' Algie cuts in, 'when did they stop using carriages like this one, do you think?'

'What?'

'Roughly, I mean.'

'The nineties, I suppose. Wasn't it?'

Something passes between the three of them.

'My goodness,' Algie mutters.

Time passes. Or doesn't. Not exactly. Not in a way I can make sense of. It passes but it leaves nothing behind. No sense of itself. Bessie has gone back to sleep. I wonder if she dreams? Although, she may be pretending, as I am. The figure in the corner is… I don't know. Moving? No, not quite. Glitching. Percy and Algie are deep in conversation, but what they're saying makes no sense.

'The twentieth century has ended, Percy. The New Age is now history. The future came and went. We are relics.'

'We were already relics, Algie.'

'Yes, but… I mean to say. The nineteenth century died forever with us, or rather, with you. Your generation. To think that the twentieth will soon be beyond the memory of the living. The motorcar will be as was the cart. The television as was the telegram. Our times, our age, gone.'

'It's the way of things, Algie. Besides, our times were troubled, were they not? War and endless death. Perhaps the new century will be the utopia we were once told awaited us?'

'Poppycock, Percy! I've never understood your attitude on these matters. War and death, yes. As was the case for all times. But the *changes*, Percy.' He clenches his fists as he talks now. Animated and ruddy-cheeked. 'The twentieth century was history's great leveller. When mankind looked upon itself and decided there was a better way. Will the future remember? Votes for women, the technological age. The space age! The civil rights movement.'

'Spoken like a man who never knew war! And a man who died in the midst of the over-stimulated sixties! I saw a glimpse of what followed, Algie. And what of fascism? Of genocide? Of godlessness and depravity. Race riots, nuclear weapons and...'

I speak then. 'Stop it! You make no sense.'

I startle them both and they turn to face me.

ALGIE

A young Algie sits beside his formidable mother and one of her disapproving cronies, Mrs. Etherington-something-or-other, in their immaculately kept parlour room, one dreary afternoon. He's picking his nose and flicking the treasures therein across the room as the two women chatter enthusiastically on the subject of a Frenchman's death. A Frenchman of some note, Algie has absentmindedly ascertained. One of the Napoleons, he thinks. Living in Kent, apparently. Indeed, he'd overheard his unfortunate father and Mr. Pike, who delivers the milk, talking about the very same thing earlier that morning. He remembers, then, what the aged Pike's views on the matter had been and decides to offer them up as his own opinion now. He considers how impressed the two women will surely be with his in-depth knowledge of such a grown-up subject.

'He's a bloody Frenchy Niminy-Piminy, ain't he? Shouldn't ought to have bloody been over here and good riddance says I!'

It's true to say that Algie hasn't the first idea what he's just said. Not a single word of it, in fact. Although, his first thought is that he has indeed impressed the assembled cast greatly. A deafly silence ensues, as Algie smiles proudly at the two women.

'Stand up and turn away from me please, Algernon,' says Algie's mother, in a quiet and calm voice that sends a peculiar shiver down his spine.

'Mater?' he replies, in a cautious whisper.

'Do as I say please, Algernon.'

It's that word "please" that unnerves Algie. It seems most unlike the Snarling Tigress somehow. But he does as he is told and stands in front of his mother with his back to her. What happens next will stay with him for the rest of his days. She kicks him. Hard. In the posterior.

'Ouch!'

'If I ever hear you using language like that in my house again, I'll cut out your tongue with a pair of scissors, cook it in a stew and feed it back to you. Do you understand me?'

Algie is wailing and howling up a flood by this time, but his mother persists.

'Do you understand me, Algernon?!'

'Yes, Mater,' he sobs.

'Now go up to your room and stay there until your father gets home. At which point, he will administer to you the beating of your life!'

That kick rendered Algie's posterior a deep purple that remained well into his middle age. Or a good week or two at the very least. He sits in his room bawling his eyes out for what seems like an eternity until, eventually, there is a soft knock on the door and his father walks in.

'Are you going to beat me, Pater?' Algie quivers.

'No, I don't reckon I am, young Algie,' his father says kindly, as he sits himself down on the floor beside his young son. He's wearing his dark blue police tunic with shining brass buttons. It's several sizes too big for him and, as he crouches to sit on the floor, it seems to swallow him up.

'Mater kicked me, Pater.'

'Yes. I've been hearing all about it. Does it hurt?'

'Yes,' Algie whimpers, looking down at the ground.

'Now let me tell you something, boy. And you'd better listen good, alright?'

Algie braces himself for the onslaught.

'Life isn't too complicated if you've got your wits about you. Under this roof you do whatever your mater says. Which means, if you're going to 'bloody' this and 'bloody' that, then you'd better bloody well make sure it ain't in this bloody house.'

Algie looks up at his father to find him smiling down at him. 'You said bloody,' he sniffles.

'No, I didn't. And do you know *why* I didn't?'

There's a long pause as the two of them look at each other.

'Because you're in this house?' Algie offers, tentatively.

'Good chap. Now you sit here and if you don't tell your mater about it then I'll fetch you up some dinner, alright?'

Algie nods solemnly and his father clambers to his feet.

'Oh, and one more thing.'

Algie looks up at him nervously.

'Scream and wail a bit when I say so.'

'Pardon, Pater?'

He smacks the palm of his hand loudly on the bedroom wall.

'Now.'

Algie cries out as instructed, and his father smacks the wall again.

'Again,' he whispers, still smiling.

They repeat this back and forth a few more times.

'There you go, you've had your beating from me.' He winks at Algie and leaves the room.

From that day onwards he follows his father's advice and life in the family home is generally harmonious. Algie would often think of that day in the years to come. He would miss his father when he died. A kind and broken man, who Algie loved very much. Melancholy didn't suit Algie; life was a rich pageant of possibility, after all. A lark was always to be had. But on the rare occasions when sadness found him, it would always be whispering of the people gone. The lost.

SIX

'It's alright,' Percy says, with a predictability that's becoming maddening.

'No, it isn't. Nothing here is alright. Why are you both talking like that?'

'Like what, my boy?' asks Algie, in mock bewilderment.

'I'm not your boy! Like you're from the past. Is this a joke? You're freaking me out, so just stop it. It's not funny and you're both… weird. I should just… in fact, I will, I'm leaving.' I move to stand but the sharp stabbing pain behind the eyes returns and forces me back into my seat. I let out a whimper and put my head in my hands.

'It's alright.'

'And who is that?!' I point to the figure sat in the corner without looking at her.

The two men look at each other. Algie raises his eyebrows and leans back in his seat.

'All yours, Percy, my boy.'

Percy frowns at the older man and then turns to face me

once again. 'It's of the utmost importance that you remain calm.'

My eyes widen in fury at the incredulity of this statement, and I open my mouth to speak again but Percy holds up a hand to stop me.

'Where is this train going?' he says.

'What?'

'This train. You are on a train. So presumably you boarded with the intention of going somewhere, yes?'

'I...'

'Where are you going?'

'I say, Percy, old chap. I'm not sure this is the best way of keeping the boy calm?'

'Quiet, please, Algie.'

They both look at me expectantly.

'I... I can't remember. I suppose, home? I'm going home.'

'From where?'

'What?'

'If you're going home, where have you been?'

'I-I don't know, this is ridiculous.'

But he's right, of course. I have no idea where I'm going, or where I've been. I cannot remember boarding the train, buying a ticket or anything at all before I awoke as the train jolted to a stop. Where *am* I going? Where are my family? The two men read this realisation on my face.

'It's alright. Stop thinking about it now. Just remember that you don't know, alright? It's important to what I'm about to tell you.'

We stare at each other until the sound of a solitary snore breaks the spell. Unbelievably, absurdly, Algie has fallen asleep.

BESSIE

The scene is an illusion, Bessie thinks. Well, sort of. A memory of a memory. Neatly arranged tables, covered in cloth so white it glows. Ornate and delicate things. Silvers and embroideries. Of its time. This makes Bessie smile. People feel safe when Bessie smiles.

'Time,' she says to herself, although she's not alone. There are others, sipping tea and chattering inaudible words to recognisable rhythms. *Are we sharing this memory?* Bessie wonders. Or are these impressions of lives that never were? As lifeless as Queen Victoria, who rests above the unused fireplace, forever staring into the unseen distance. Regal, enigmatic and captured. The latter, she knows this. And the grasses. Arranged in wild displays that hang and sit and grow from every surface. Bessie is sure there cannot have been this many in the first edition. Far too elaborate for such restrained days. Those halcyon days. So willingly vulnerable. A girl on the cusp of womanhood. The clock ticks with a strange clarity that raises it above the chattering din of the ladies who tea.

And there she is. Odd, Bessie thinks, that this isn't the first time they met. Surely a more obvious choice? An endless daisy-strewn meadow where summertime lives forever and innocence blossoms into a beautiful and dangerous butterfly. But then, this day does have that special something about it, doesn't it? She stands on the threshold, across the space, both crowded and not. Bessie watches as she searches the room with those emerald eyes. They meet hers, and then the walk. That pulse quickening walk.

This is why it had to be today, Bessie thinks. If there was only this. Just this simple moment replayed for all eternity, that would be fine with Bessie. Bustle, volume, drape. Traditional in description. But not on *her*. The future lived in her, in that walk. The Naughty Nineties and the New Age. Strutting and defiant. The ladies who do not tea.

'Dear Heart,' says Bessie, rising from her seat.

'Beloved!' Smiles Effie. Bessie felt safe when Effie smiled. She takes her hand and kisses it. Definitely not first edition behaviour. The ladies who tea stare. Then Bessie remembers that they don't stare, and the two women sit.

'Have you been waiting for me for a long time?' Effie asks.

'Forever.'

'Oh, I am sorry, Beloved!'

She removes her gloves from hands that will never age. *If only she knew*, Bessie thinks. I have waited for all of time and more. I wait still, beyond time. We are *in* my waiting. Will never leave it. Perhaps, or perhaps those plans will come to fruition, after all. One of these days, that aren't days at all. And they speak. The words, lost now. Inaudible words to recognisable rhythms. Sometimes Bessie remembers that this is the day that the façade is finally dropped. Love declared; escape plans made. Flesh on flesh in a room suddenly emptied of all impressions that never were. Even Queen Victoria, regal and enigmatic, dissolves beneath the dancing cloth, so white it glows like skin. Other times she remembers that this is the day it all ended. Or rather, shattered. It never ended, never ends. But this is the day it stopped being a whole thing.

'There's something I must tell you, Beloved.'

Those words, sickly sweet and pleading for a forgiveness beyond all reason. Beyond Bessie's capability, even all these lifetimes later. Lacking the dance of the rhythm upon which they, and only they, speak words, lost now.

'I am to marry.'

A pain beyond sense. A hopeless pain that dances on the broken bones of every repentant tomorrow. No embers, no afterthought, no meaning.

'His name is Algie,' Effie says. 'You'd like him, I think.'

Like him?

'I know, I know. But you would. He's a lark. Full of joy and summertime.'

Like him?

'He isn't… I'm not… we always knew this day would come, Beloved.'

The ladies who tea, are we, are we, the ladies who tea, are we. Yes, Dear Heart. We always knew this day would come. Over and over. No escape.

But more often than not, Bessie just remembers that this is a beautiful day. Before the world exploded with ordinary things. Before she knew death, or war, or compromise. When tomorrow was a promise, not an apology. When Effie, her Effie, was young and true and strong and kind and enlightened. With a smile that makes her feel safe. They had plans; they really did. To the seaside. Sisters, that's what the world would be told. They aren't dissimilar, in many ways. And if there were those who sensed an untruth, or even a truth, then what of it? The entire world is both at their feet and a complete irrelevance. Silly and boring.

This time Bessie tries to remember something else. But how can one *try* to remember? Either one remembers or one doesn't.

'There is something I must tell you, Dear Heart.'

'What is it, Beloved?'

'I have plans.'

'I know you do, Beloved. I know.'

'Can I pour for you?'

'Why, thank you.'

Bessie pours, with hands that will grow old beyond the understanding of this day. This beautiful day.

Here lies Effie, my Effie. 1869 –

SEVEN

Chaos like spilt milk, rancid and cloying. A place where only useless panic obscures an acceptance as quiet and devastating as the end of everything. Time stops.

'Now then. Remember what I said? It's very important you remain calm. I'm afraid this is going to come as rather a shock.'

But colours and screams and metal and skin rush and bite and sob.

'I'm sorry to be the one to tell you this. Usually there'd be a direct… well, it doesn't matter now. An unscheduled stop, you see?'

And the pain. A pain beyond sense. A hopeless pain that dances on the broken bones of every repentant tomorrow. No embers, no afterthought, no meaning.

'I'm rather afraid you're dead.'

Screams that are a colour that lives inside me. Developmental. Cognitive. Sirens that crawl through the traffic and mangled remains. Say their names. Over and over. Footsteps on asphalt. Ugly cherry red. Too late.

'Did you hear me?'

The threadbare blues. *How odd*, I think. To fall asleep like that. In the middle of a conversation. These people are freaks. I really need to leave this place, to get home. Or wake up. And the window. Endless darkness. But not darkness, nothing. Endless nothing.

'I say, did you hear me? Are you alright?'

The compartment spins. A sinking feeling. Like falling.

'Bessie, wake up and lend me a hand, will you?!'

Too late.

PERCY

'Mrs.Alice Tristram?'

Her face immediately tightens. Percy had expected it to but that hadn't made it any easier to observe. To have one's fears realised does not diminish them.

'May I come aboard?'

She turns her back on him and disappears from view, into the darkness beyond the doorway. Tentatively, Percy steps from the riverbank onto the canal boat. As he does so, the cursed thing rocks back and forth on the water. He's never been at home on the water. He steadies himself, instinctively touching the wound on the side of his head. The walk along the Thames has tired him. Everything seemed to, nowadays. Legs and head.

Inside, the boat is cold, dark and all but empty. An unmade bed with a curtain half pulled in front of it, two bare wooden benches and what apparently passes for a kitchen area. Percy had been in dugouts with more home comforts than this.

'May I be seated?'

She doesn't answer but neither does she object, so Percy sits down on the nearest of the benches, resisting the compulsion to wince with the discomfort it causes his aching bones. Legs and head. She stares at him for a few seconds before seating herself on the other bench.

'I'm sorry to be troubling you, Mrs. Tristram. I'm here on something of a difficult errand.'

That stare again. Piercing blue eyes that seem illuminated in the gloom of their surroundings. She remains silent so Percy continues.

'I served with your husband.'

'How did you find me?' The suddenness of the question startles Percy. As does the thick cockney accent, although it shouldn't have, of course.

'Your sister-in-law, Joan, in Walthamstow. She…'

'You've seen my children? My boys?'

'Yes.' Tears fill her eyes then. But her chin juts forward in defiance and she composes herself in an instant. 'They are well?'

'I only met them briefly, you understand? But, yes, they seemed in fine fettle. They do you proud. And your husband, of course.'

'My husband?! What can you possibly tell me of my husband? He's been dead these past two years. Am I never to be left alone?'

As she says this, the boat rocks on the water. As though the river beneath their feet is in tune with her mood. A small wave of nausea rises in Percy's stomach. She seems to read his thoughts.

'What kind of a soldier goes green on a gently rocking canal boat?'

'Alas, this kind.' He offers a strained smile with the words and sees her face soften ever so slightly.

'He loved the river.' Her eyes glaze over at this. 'That's why you find me here, on this godforsaken boat. It was his. He'd planned to make it nice after the war. We were to float on this river, the four of us. Out of London and far away. To escape from the Tristram family and their *plans* for him.' She nearly spits these last words. The bitterness she feels towards her late husband's family is fiercely evident. 'He'd always loved this river. He'd tell me tales of days and nights spent sat in his old coracle, watching the dippers and kingfishers. The boy by the river. Always dreaming of faraway adventures. Well, he got one, didn't he.' It isn't a question.

Percy reaches into his overcoat and pulls out a grey cotton bag tied with string. Without another word he holds it out to her, reaching across the dark empty space between them. He watches as realisation dawns on her face. She takes it from him with trembling hands and holds it tightly in her lap. She looks down at it, as if trying to see through the cotton material to the contents inside.

'It's his belongings. His paybook and…'

'Were you with him when he died?'

'Yes.'

The heaviest of silences hangs in the air then. The boat is suddenly still. As if the river were holding its breath.

'Was he scared when he went, sergeant?'

'Percy, call me Percy. No. He thought only of you. Spoke only of you.'

Lies. He gasped and coughed an ugly cherry red. One of an endless number of boys with no last words.

'He made me promise to bring you his things. To deliver

them to you in person. I would have been here much sooner but, well, I'm…'

'You're wounded.'

'Yes.'

More silence. Percy again instinctively raises his hand to his head.

'Did he get his adventure then?' she says, with a coldness that seems to have risen up from somewhere deep inside her. 'What was it like over there? I would bid you tell me the truth, for it cannot be worse than I have imagined.'

Percy looks into her blue eyes, as if deciding something important. For a second, they remind him of Clara's eyes. Then he remembers that this cannot be so. The past, the future and all between. The familiar nightmare flashes through his mind for just a split second. Mangled remains and ugly cherry red.

'Hell. It was hell.'

She closes her eyes and breathes deeply. A breath that seems to unburden her of something. When she opens her eyes again, there's a new intensity in them.

'Look around you, Percy. Was his death worth it? I died with him. Do you understand that? And for what? Was any of it worth it? Am I free? Are you?'

Percy holds her gaze. Meets the challenge in those burning blue eyes.

'I don't know if any of us are ever truly free, Mrs. Tristram. And if you're asking me to justify the war itself then I fear my shoulders are no longer equipped to carry the weight of that assertion. But if you think your husband died in vain then I tell you that you are wrong.' He lets his words hang for a second before continuing.

'We did not start that war, your husband and I. But we played our part in ending it. He more so than I, having paid the ultimate price. There are generations of boys that will now not need to become men before their time. Because of us, the generation that did just that.'

But if he was to die, it would be for the family that sat together in a ray of sunshine, swirling like dust. He watches her as she stares back down at the package on her lap. Her body gently convulsing with silent tears. She is a broken thing. Just as he is. Just as it seems the whole world is now.

'He used to tell me stories of the river as well, you know?' he says quietly. 'I had to walk a long way beside it to find you. I feel something of him here. I think he is here with you.'

It's another lie. The first point at least. Tristram had never mentioned the river or this godforsaken boat. Percy realises then that he had hardly known the milk-skinned boy. There had been so many, after all. Bodies and body parts. Legs and head.

'I feel him here too. This river is as close to him as I can get now. I'm floating along this river until I reach the sea.'

'And then?'

'I don't know. Perhaps the sun has gone forever. What about you?'

'Me?'

'What will you do now? With your peace?'

'I've re-enlisted. It's all I know now.' Percy hesitates for a second and then continues, 'Go and get your children, Alice.'

She looks up at him. Her face a thousand things.

'Go and get them, fix this place, and go where the river takes you. Or go home and rebuild your life. Your sister-in-law seemed to me a kindly woman. She was worried for you and would see you reunited with your children in a heartbeat. She misses you, as they do. Find the peace that your husband died to give you. It is God's will.'

'God?'

'God, Alice.'

'You believe in God? You believe in war and freedom. You believe in many things, Percy. Faith in the face of all you have seen.'

'If I did not believe, I should think the darkness would swallow me whole.'

The void. As these words travel across the no-mans-land between them, they grow in their meaning. Gain a greater significance than Percy had originally intended.

'Thank you for bringing me his things. I know it cannot have been an easy journey. Though now I must ask you to leave.'

The boat rocks once more. Percy stands.

'I apologise for speaking out of turn. It was not my intention. I merely wished to make good on my promise.'

'And you have done so. I wish you well, sergeant.'

Percy climbs back on to the riverbank, instantly feeling better for being on dry land. He walks then. Away from what remained of Mrs.Alice Tristram and towards what remained of his own life.

'I did my best, private. I pray she may find her peace in the end.'

'I know, sir. You could have done no more, sir.'

EIGHT

I hear them before I see them. Before the threadbare blues reassemble. Before this stationary scene lurches on. This nightmare.

'Why didn't you wake me, Percy? It was far too soon.'

'I'm perfectly capable of explaining our predicament, Bessie.'

'Clearly!'

'Now, Bessie, old thing. Be fair. The boy had overheard us, and Percy did what he thought was best.'

'Oh, do be quiet, Algie.'

'Right you are, dearest.'

'I notice you left it all to your son-in-law, although I feel confident in assuming it was your dulcet tones that brought about the situation.'

'Bessie! I was as a church mouse. Was I not, Percy?'

'Well…'

I open my eyes then. A few seconds pass before they notice. I stare at the strange trio and am alarmed when an involuntary feeling of, not only familiarity, but also affection, washes over me.

'What do you mean I'm dead?'

The three of them turn to face me. It's Bessie who speaks.

'There you are, my love. You had us worried.'

'Why would you tell me I'm dead? I'm not dead.'

'I'm sorry, my love. It was… remiss of us to break it to you in that way—'

'Indeed,' cuts in Percy. 'I hadn't intended to be so forthright. I apologise.'

'But, I'm not dead.'

'Dead isn't the word I'd have used, my love. It's very final. It suggests the end. As you can see, it's not the end.'

'But I don't…'

'You're somewhere different. That's all, really. And you're not technically you, but we can get to that in good time.'

I stare at her. Time passes. Or doesn't.

'You're all mad. You realise that, right?'

Algie lets out a loud and booming laugh at this.

'The boy's got the measure of us there, eh!'

Bessie smiles and I feel safe.

'I am sorry, my love. It must be a shock for you. There would usually be someone you recognise to walk you through all this, of course. But, well, you're an unscheduled stop, you see? There are things we don't yet understand.'

I stare at her.

'No, I don't suppose you do see, do you? The thing is, there's obviously a gap between us—'

'Rather a large gap, by the sounds of it,' interjects Percy.

'Yes, indeed,' Bessie continues.

'A couple of generations at least, maybe more,' adds Algie. Familiarity.

'You really *are* all mad, aren't you?'

'Can you remember anything at all of what you were doing before you woke up and found yourself here with us, my love?'

Colours and screams and metal and skin, rush and bite and sob.

'Flashes. But they make no sense.'

They nod at me in comical unison. There is sympathy and something else. Something in their burdened eyes. Something *parental*.

'But, I mean, this is ridiculous. I obviously got the train, didn't I? I'm on a train... so, I obviously...'

'But you don't remember getting on the train, or where you're going?' adds Percy.

'I've been very tired recently.'

'And it's a train you say they don't use anymore,' he continues.

The threadbare blues of the school commute.

'And you can't get up and leave this compartment. And the three of us are clearly...'

'Alright! Stop, please.'

'Take your time, my love,' says Bessie. Soothing and safe. 'You must have many questions. We'll endeavour to answer them all. Whenever you're ready.'

I'm so tired, I think. I want to cry and laugh and sleep, all at once.

'Who's that?'

I point at the figure in the corner, but don't look.

Nobody looks. Not even a glance. She is both seen and

unseen. All three of them shuffle uncomfortably in their seats and then Bessie speaks.

'Are you sure that's your first question, my love?'

'Yes.'

ALGIE

As we already know, melancholy didn't suit Algie. Life was a rich pageant of possibility, after all. For this reason, there is much Algie doesn't remember. He remembers his sepia-toned childhood with a vividness that's both questionable and true, to varying degrees, depending on how you choose to measure these things. Storybook characters and farcical scenarios that revel in the uncomplicated happiness of life. And quite right too. But then there's a gap. A period of time that Algie has no use for now. Where despair and loss and guilt are locked safely away forever and ever. You may think that Algie's schooldays would be full of enough high jinks, mischief, and tomfoolery to warrant their own story. Or a chapter or two at the very least. And you would be right, they certainly had their moments.

'Which one of you did it?!'

'Please, sir, it was Algie, sir.'

'Algie! Answer me this: should I simply engrave your name on this cane, boy?'

'Well, I don't think so, sir. A little butter upon bacon, don't you think? And it's not mine, after all. Unless it's a gift, sir? In which case…'

'Silence!'

But it's all too tangled up, you see? The darkness always smothers the light, in the end. And so, Algie doesn't remember.

Collateral damage. The greater good. There is always a lark to be had. So, we move from knickerbockers and endless summers, to love. Sweet and innocent, magnificent and pure. Bessie. His Bessie. Just a girl then, of course. On that crisp spring morning that heralds a new dawn. She is standing, he remembers, by a gravestone. Taking a rubbing of it, in fact.

'Good day.' Algie lifts his hat.

She turns to face him, startled at first but then something else. A tilt of the head, almost imperceptible. A deep kind of sadness, Algie thinks.

'Got the morbs?' he says, enthusiastically.

She stares at him in confusion.

'Sorry, I mean, upset? Did you know her?' He nods in the direction of the gravestone.

'Yes,' she says, in a voice Algie thinks probably sounds the same as a harp does, when plucked upon by an angel. Or should it be a cherub? 'She was very dear to me.'

'I'm sorry.'

And he is.

As he looks upon the most beautiful face he's ever seen, he feels it entirely unfair that this world should conspire to bring sadness to such a face. She smiles then. And Algie feels safe. It is the most extraordinary thing. A warmth that might be literal rises up in him.

'May I take a look?' He gestures toward the rubbing in her hand.

A faint flush in her cheeks. *She really is amongst the very jammiest bits of jam*, thinks Algie. But she folds the paper delicately and places it into a satin chatelaine.

'I'm Algie.' He lifts his hat again, suddenly feeling rather ridiculous.

Something passes across her face at the mention of his name. It might be fury, he thinks. But this makes no sense. It doesn't fit this memory, so he remembers that nothing passes across her face. That face. Except perhaps for a smile. Warm and safe.

'Good day, Algie. I'm Bessie.'

'Ahoy, Bessie!'

They speak of many things then. On that crisp spring morning that heralds a new dawn. Of family and friends and falling stars, of sunshine and moonlight and battle scars. Of the future and all things past, of hopes and dreams and promises that never last. Of language and science and the brave New Age, of memories rewritten with every turn of the page. After perhaps an hour or more, or less, a silence falls between them. The first of a lifetime together. Some would be comfortable, others awkward. Some hostile, others full of an unspoken tenderness. This one is harder to label, as it is the first. Algie searches his mind for something to say. He feels as though the next words to leave his mouth will be the most important of his life. She loves me, she loves me not. He creases his brow in deep thought, in deference to the magnitude of the task before him.

'I say, would you like a game of I spy?'

Bessie laughs at this and as she does – in that very moment – Algie falls in love. And from that very moment until the very moment he dies, on a forgettable day somewhere near the end of the brave New Age, he will always love Bessie. And then, after the very moment he dies, he will go on loving Bessie, forever and ever. Never for a single second, in this life or the next, will his love falter. From that very moment onwards, the darkness will never again smother the light. Sadness will occasionally find him. The place where the memory of his father lives, or things yet to come. But the light will always triumph. For she is the light. And isn't that wonderful? Because life can be very long, can't it? And so, even at the end, when faced with eternity, to want only the one you love. To remember only the one you love, well... isn't that wonderful?

NINE

'That is an Unremembered.'

There is a sadness in Bessie's voice. I again feel a compulsion to reach across to her. All three of them look down at the floor, like repentant schoolchildren, caught red-handed.

'An Unremembered?' I echo.

'I say, would anyone like a game of I spy?'

'Oh, do be quiet, Algie.'

'Right you are, dearest.'

'What's an Unremembered?' I ask.

Silence. Then a long, tired sigh. Bessie's eyes meet mine and she smiles at me with a melancholic warmth that lingers in the air between us. But it's Percy who eventually speaks.

'An Unremembered is someone who has passed away and remembers someone into being here, but has no one to remember them.'

'Oh, I see.'

'Do you really?'

'No, of course not! Nothing you're saying makes any sense.'

'Alright, let me think a moment.'

Percy closes his burdened hazel eyes and gently strokes his neatly trimmed moustache.

'Alright. Take myself, for example. When I died, my mother remembered me. I think. Although I can't remember where she is now. Anyway, that's how I got here. Originally, I mean. I remembered Clara, but she wasn't dead at that time, but the memory gets stored and then when she passed away, up she popped.'

I stare at him, blankly.

'Stop,' I think, or say out loud. I'm no longer sure.

'I'm not explaining at all adequately, am I? Alright. We're memories, you see? When we die, someone needs to remember us in order for us to be here.' He gestures to the compartment around us. 'Likewise, we get to remember one person and—'

'Percy!' Bessie cuts in. 'My head is spinning, so goodness knows how this poor boy is feeling.' She lets out another long sigh. 'An Unremembered is a soul that cannot pass into the afterlife. It is trapped between two worlds. It needs to wait for the right person to die, so it can be recognised, at which point it will arrive fully into this world, with us.'

I realise something then: I'm crying. Odd, I think, that I hadn't registered this earlier.

'No!' I shout. 'I am not dead. You are all insane. This is a dream, a nightmare. I have a daughter, and… and… I am not dead!'

Colours and screams and metal and skin, rush and bite

and sob. And then the door of the compartment opens. And I see, then, that I am dead.

BESSIE

Tears fall from Bessie's eyes onto the paper. She rubs too hard, and it rips. A year has passed, she remembers. Though the details of it are entirely lost. She supposes she drifted, her only intention to forget. Time had left no trace of itself since they were last together. Since her love had announced she was to marry. And then she had died, her Effie. It was as though Bessie had lost her twice. Although, it was many more times than that, of course. Bessie had lost her over and over again and would continue to lose her forever and ever. For there was no yesterday, no today and no tomorrow. She knew that. Understood it now. And yet, she had plans. Though they escaped her sometimes, it was true. She must remain vigilant. She must remember. She hadn't been to the funeral. She *knew* that, rather than remembered it. For, how can one remember absence? She could not, could never, bear the idea of it. Of watching and listening as the mourners, so many of them, and their solemn-faced plus ones, spoke in turn. Effie the daughter, Effie the sister. Effie the fiancée. But not Effie, her Effie. Only she knew her Effie. And maybe somewhere, not entirely out of reach, there was a memory where they did it. To the seaside. Tables and chairs on the promenade. Forever young. A place where summer is the only season and tomorrow never comes. She tries to remember. But how can one try to remember?

'Good day.'

Bessie turns, startled by the sound of a voice both new to her and so familiar that she almost wakes. A man, a boy, really. His hat aloft, a smile full of joy and summertime, but a sadness in those emerald eyes. Her gaze lingers on those eyes. *How like Effie's they are*, she thinks.

'Got the morbs?'

The spell broken, replaced by a furious irritation. An unwanted interruption, a moment lost.

'Sorry, I mean, upset? Did you know her?'

Did she know her? More than anyone has ever known anyone. And perhaps not at all.

'Yes. She was very dear to me.'

'I'm sorry.'

And he is, Bessie thinks. This boy, this fool, this strange apparition. He is sorry.

'May I take a look?' His eyes, her eyes, are looking at the torn rubbing in Bessie's hands. Never. Never may anyone see this final impression of her. This afterthought. Bessie folds the paper and puts it away. Forever.

'I'm Algie.'

You'd like him, I think.

Bessie's eyes widen. A fire rises and threatens to burn away everything she ever was.

I know, I know. But, you would.

Bessie screams then. A howl that shrieks and writhes and wails. The scene dissolves, the sky burns. She is animal. She runs at him with claws that slash and tear. Flames dance around the two ethereal figures as she rips Algie, her Algie, her beautiful, kind and loving Algie, to shreds. Less than shreds. Embers. Dust. She rips through skin and flesh and bone. She devours him, erases him. Until he isn't there.

Until he was never there. Save for his eyes. His emerald eyes. These she spares. She lifts them from the ashes. The dust that was once the boy who would become the man she loved. And who would love her for a thousand lifetimes and more. Forever and ever. She wipes the blood and dust from those emerald eyes and places them tenderly into her satin chatelaine.

'I'm Bessie.'

'Ahoy, Bessie!'

He speaks of things then. In that way that he does. Full of mischief and wide-eyed innocence. She cannot remember what he says. The words are lost in the pain and confusion of that day. Dreams, she supposes, for her husband is a dreamer. Bessie has plans, Algie has dreams. It will always be so. They walk. She allows him to take her arm. She cannot honestly say why. On this day, and perhaps many more into the future that is also the distant and unreliable past. It is probably the eyes. A piece of her, in this boy.

You'd like him, I think.

He was to be to her all that Effie could never be. Would never be allowed to be, for these were unenlightened times. Did she make up her mind on that day? No, she remembers; she didn't. But there was a moment. When a silence fell between them. The first of a lifetime together. A strange silence. Expectant and extraordinarily heavy. Pregnant. It felt as though the whole world waited in the corners of that silence. As though everything depended on what happened next. Every possibility, past, present and future; waiting for the words. He looked nervous, she remembers. She remembers and remembers and remembers.

'I say, would you like a game of I spy?'

Bessie laughs then. She remembers that this was the moment he fell in love. Her stupid and kind boy. She knows that he never loved Effie, her Effie. Not really. This cheerful mourner. But those are conversations they will have in days yet to come. Forgotten days. She holds the knowledge but not the memory. And what of Bessie's love? Was this the moment she fell in love? She laughs at the thought of this. No, that moment was many, many years away. But it would come. For love, Bessie thinks, is a world with many oceans. Different and the same. This wasn't even the moment she fell out of love. That moment may one day come as well, but not in this life. For memories are being rewritten with every turn of the page.

TEN

My grandmother was the first of us to leave. And the mourners. So many. Those who knew her and their solemn-faced plus ones. Endless rain on a summer's day. Recovering the satellites. Strangers who can never be strangers, no matter the distance travelled. Old grievances on hold. United now, in sorrow. 'Do you remember when?' Ships adrift on life's stormy seas, called to shore by her lighthouse on this, our darkest night. Pain, regret and, most of all, love. So complicated and yet such a simple thing, really. We carry each other, all of us, on this, our darkest night. Words spoken, and those not. Hands held, arms linked, we face the storm. Tears that fall in her name, and never really stop. *I want her back*, I think again, so many lifetimes later. I want my grandma back.

A young woman's head appears through the gap of the opening compartment door. Handsome and angular. The star in a silent movie, tied to a train track. Or a beautiful stranger staring back at you in a black and white photograph from the 1920s. Cocktails in nightclubs and stories lost forever – or captured forever, in the pages of tattered copies of F. Scott Fitzgerald and P.G. Wodehouse, on the shelf of a waiting room somewhere in the distant future, beyond the New Age. She smiles at us all with thin but shapely lips. Distant echoes of safety and warmth but laced with something more exciting.

'Hullo, all!'

'Clara!' my three companions cry at once.

'Percy, my darling love, I have someone here who wants very much to see you.'

She opens the compartment door fully and enters, hand-in-hand with another woman. She's older than Clara. She looks terrified and excited and a thousand other things.

Percy stands. Tears that fall in her name, and never really stop.

'Hello, Daddy.'

The three of them embrace, weeping and laughing. An outpouring of emotion so raw and true that it stops time. More than that. It erases time. There is only this moment, has only ever been this moment. This love.

'Let me look at you, my girl.' Percy holds his daughter, who is at least thirty years his senior, at arm's length. 'My goodness, Annie. *Look* at you. As perfect as the day I saw you last.'

'Oh, Daddy.'

'Do you understand where you are?'

'Yes, Mumsy has explained everything. But wait, where is he?'

She looks around the compartment and sees Algie and Bessie for the first time.

'Grandpa and Grandma!'

'Hello, my girl.'

More tears as they embrace. All five are standing now. Only I am sitting. Me, and the Unremembered.

'But wait, he must be here.'

She looks around again and finds me. All these lifetimes later.

She is as she was when I was a child. Neapolitan ice cream and bedtime stories. Kind and strong, greying but not yet grey.

'I drew you a picture, Grandma.'

'Oh, thank you! Let me have a look then.' Glasses on a chain, perched on the end of her nose.

'It's a Mr. Men.'

'Well, of course it is. It could be nothing else. Is it Mr. Stretch?'

I giggle, delightedly. 'No, silly. It's Mr. Tickle.'

'Of course, it is! And we all know what Mr. Tickle does, don't we?'

Gentle hands, tears of laughter. A laughter uncomplicated by all that life has yet to bring. Pure and safe and innocent. She is as she was when I was a child. Because she is *my* memory. I remembered her. And I see, then, that I am dead.

A sepia-tinged garden where my mother tends to roses. I walk towards her, my arms outstretched. Tears roll down my face and I'm surprised to realise that I can taste them. Salty and wet. A memory within a memory. She turns towards me, and I remember that time slows down then. Or stops. Because I am outside of time now, aren't I? I see her face as I remember it. Every curve, every line. The first face I ever knew. Full of love and devotion and kindness and truth. Her eyes are a colour that lives inside me. Developmental and cognitive. The whole world in one face. Eyebrows crease in concern, lips form words of endless compassion. Everything I understand in one single face.

'Oh, what is it, my darling baby boy?' Running and falling into those arms. My protective blanket. Warm and safe. I am safe forever and ever. Sobs that seek only *her* reassurance. Unconditional love called to heal, a tap that drips forever. Through time and memory and a thousand lifetimes. I remember and remember and remember. A slip, a fall. A grazed knee, no more. No pain, no ugly cherry red. Because that isn't the memory. *She* is the memory. My mother. My mum. My mummy.

'Show me, baby boy. Let Mummy kiss it better.' She kisses my knee, gently rubs away the pain that isn't there. Conspiratorially whispers, 'Shall we go inside and have a chocolate milkshake?'

I smile then, I remember. Not for a milkshake, but for her. Because *she* is smiling. She carries me in her arms. I remember the garden, although my eyes are shut tight. Surrendering everything to her embrace. Savouring it. Pink and yellow paving slabs and muddy wellington boots. Freshly cut grass and wriggling worms. The pond my father built, with its ripples and reeds. The glass patio doors where the world inside and the world reflected back at us merge and blur into one. Fuzzy around the edges, like faded film projected over empty seats.

'Here we are, honeypie. In your favourite cup.'

A plastic cup with a tiger's face printed on it. Unforgotten now. Dormant all these years. Silently waiting for this moment, and only this moment, to resurface. She sits beside me, a protective arm resting on the sofa cushion above my head. Faded greens and oranges and yellows. My feet don't reach the edge. Contented curling toes inside Spiderman socks.

'There we go, all better now?'

I look up into the kindest eyes I'll ever know and smile. Chocolate smeared around my gap-toothed grin.

'What a brave boy.'

I nod. I accept the only reassurance I crave. Hers.

And as the scene dissolves, I fall asleep in her arms. Sinking into a love that each of us can only know once in our lifetimes. Her belly is swollen. Inside, my baby brother sleeps soundly. Unknowing and safe. She keeps us both safe in this memory, outside of time. Her boys. Forever her boys. In her arms, in her belly, both in the memory of her dead son.

CLARA

'Absolutely not!' cries Algie.

Clara rolls her eyes. 'Oh, for heaven's sake, Pops!'

'You can roll your eyes all you like, my girl. I'm your father and I absolutely forbid it.'

Clara has just delivered the news that she intends to accept a position she's been offered in Kenya. Working as a nanny to the children of a British officer stationed there.

'It's really the opportunity of a lifetime, Pops. You must…'

'It's nothing of the sort! It's dangerous, it's on the other side of the world and it's full of bloody foreigners—'

'Algie!' Clara's mother cuts in.

Clara's heart leaps. She's been waiting for this. For all of her father's bluster, it's her mother who will have the final say. It was always so. And she will surely speak up against this tyrannical teddy bear and all his unenlightened overprotectiveness. Her mother has a more enlightened mind than anyone before or since her.

'Sorry, my dearest, I didn't mean to use foul language, but really, you must see...'

'Your language is as foul as your prejudice, Algie.'

'Thank you, Mother. I knew you'd support me on this.'

'I'll do nothing of the sort.'

'What?!' Clara cries.

'I agree with your father, you mustn't go.'

'Ha!' exclaims Algie.

'Oh, do be quiet, Algie.'

'Right you are, dearest.'

'Mother. I have to say, I'm really rather aghast. I had considered you to be a modern woman. Perhaps you would prefer I find myself a husband and give up on my dreams entirely? A clerk, perhaps? I can have piles of ugly children and get fat.'

'Spare me your righteous indignation, Clara, darling. And your misguided snobbery. I do not want you to go to Kenya because I do not wish my daughter to be complicit in the oppression of an indigenous people, whose property, land and basic rights are being stolen from them,' explains Bessie, with a smiling and deceptively calm steeliness.

'Ah,' says Clara, her shoulders slumping as she senses a lost cause.

'Eh?' says Algie, his brow furrowed in bewilderment.

Enlightenment has its drawbacks, Clara thinks. Her mother was entirely different to every other mother she'd ever met. For the most part, this was a splendid thing. After all, how many ten-year-olds were taken to a suffragette rally?

'Mother, won't you think of Women's Sunday? Or Black Friday?'

'My darling Clara, you wish to become a nanny to a wealthy general's children. Emily Davison, you are not.'

'Eh?' says Algie.

Curiously, Clara can't remember how she finally convinced her parents to let her travel to Kenya. On various go-rounds, she remembers different scenarios. In one, she persuades her mother to let her go by hinting at how delicious a scandal it would be if she were to fall in love with and marry a native. But this doesn't sit right. Her mother did not court scandal. She did not proclaim equality for all, regardless of race, gender or class, simply to be controversial. She wholeheartedly believed in every cause she spoke up for. While Clara was no Emily Davison, her mother, given the right circumstances, wouldn't hesitate to throw herself in front of the proverbial racing steed.

In another, Clara remembers that she convinced her father by suggesting she was almost certain to bag herself a well-to-do officer who would ensure his daughter lived a care-free life of luxury. But this was so unfair to her beloved Pops that she only remembers it once and then never again. Her father doted on her and wouldn't see her marry for any other reason than love. And his own laissez-faire attitude towards money simply didn't lend itself to any notion of marrying up. Her parents were better people than she understood at the tender age of eighteen.

Really, that's what made the whole business of filling in the gaps so cursedly tricky, wasn't it? How can one ever really remember anything with any semblance of truth? How can we ever be more than uncomprehending onlookers in our own memories? Why was it scenes, rather than emotional capability or intellect, that were stored for posterity? Clara didn't attempt to answer these questions, of course. Indeed, she wasn't really conscious of even asking them. She didn't remember the memories within a memory... that way madness lies. She was not her mother, after all.

In most cases she would settle on some vague idea that she had convinced her parents to let her go to Kenya by appealing to their spirit of adventure. It lacked detail, but it had the ring of truth about it. For her parents were adventurers both. Her father had dreams and her mother had plans. Two pieces of a puzzle one could complete on a lazy Sunday afternoon that oozes through time and space like melting butter on crumpets.

Yet, it did frustrate Clara that she couldn't remember. What was the purpose of this memory if not to lay the foundations of what was to come? As a young woman, Clara danced and laughed beneath a golden moon. Jazz and cocktails and the faces of friends who owned a part of her long gone but fondly remembered. Tactile, messy, glorious and so willingly vulnerable. Innocent and exposed. Those halcyon days. All that would truly define her was yet to come, she understood that. But she would've liked more than one captured reel from those careless and carefree days and nights. Endless summers, so lost now. Faces with no names, laughter with no joke. Why this memory? Incomplete and inconsequential.

'Stop saying "Eh?" like that, Algie. You sound like an ignorant buffoon.'

'Eh?' says Clara's father, but this time with a mischievous glint in his emerald eyes. Her mother holds his gaze and then, inevitably, she smiles. People felt safe when Clara's mother smiled.

'Oh, come here you great big lump,' her mother says, before the two of them wrap each other in a tender embrace. Clara rolls her eyes.

'Oh, please!' she cries. 'This is important!' But they appear not to hear her. She turns to leave the room, full of a comfortable and secure youthful indignation.

But then she remembers that before leaving the room, she turns to look at her parents. Time peels away then. Two pieces of a puzzle she knows so well. A warmth that might be literal rises up in her. *Love is such an uncomplicated thing*, thinks an eighteen-year-old Clara. The love she feels for them both, the love they both feel for her, and their love for each other. Captured so perfectly in this moment, and only this moment. This reel. A memory that gives a girl her understanding of love. Because that's all there is, really, isn't it?

When the sun sets on the endless summer. When the golden moon is finally lost behind the swirling clouds of the forever night that waits for us all. All any of us will remember, if we're lucky, is love.

ELEVEN

In the middle of nowhere, amidst the endless blackness of a forever night, there is a train. Ordinarily it speeds along in the empty darkness. As much as a train can speed along, when it has no track to speed upon and no landscape to speed through. Motion, like time, reason and destination, is an affectation here. Mostly. Nevertheless, speed along it does. Every once in a while, as is the case now, it will make an unscheduled stop.

Have you ever been on a train that's ground to a halt in a tunnel? Silence, and the night that isn't actually the night at all. There will be a reason, of course. Some passengers will already know it, some will find out eventually and the others will never know. So is the case for our train. Although, our train doesn't really carry passengers, as such. Our train carries memories. And the memories within those memories. It may be the only such train, or it may be one of an infinite number. All speeding along in the forever night that isn't really night at all.

Certainly, our train only carries the memories of one line. Not a bloodline, you understand? Ugly cherry red and so devoid of any meaning, when you really think about it. But more of that later.

No, our line is a line of memory. A strand that is both fragile and true. For what are memories if not truth? Our own truth. Perhaps not authentic, if you're so inclined to argue that point. But truth in the truest sense. The truth of our memories is the closest any of us will get to love, I think. And that's all that really matters in the end, isn't it?

There are many compartments on this train of ours. Each one a single light that shines out into the void. Warm and orange, like a childhood memory. Only one compartment, our compartment, is responsible for the unscheduled stop. Only one compartment ever can be. For, even outside of time, a line is a line.

There are doctors and thieves, grocers and lamplighters. Landowners and chimney sweeps, knights and herbologists. Or perhaps none of those things. Is what we do who we are? For some, I suppose. There are lovers and in-laws, mothers and uncles. Husbands and nannas, partners and sons. I suppose the train is endless, like the darkness in which it stands. Anyway, all of these fathers and wives, sisters and grandfathers, they are memories. Each other's memories. They sit and talk, laugh and argue. And they remember. Some sleep. Those who need to make sense of it all, even now. To apply some kind of order to things. Others move between the train and the things they remember in less definable ways.

But why am I telling you this now? Well, I think it's the right moment. Even though I don't know any of it myself at this point. I've only just come to the realisation that I'm dead, after all. But, as we've already discussed, time isn't really a *thing*. Besides, I don't want you to confuse the setting with the destination. Not from here on, anyway. Our train might not be going anywhere, as such, but our story is. Well, it might be. Goodness, what if it isn't? Anyway, I'm telling you this now because I don't want things to be too confusing. The setting is important, very important. But there's more.

ANNIE

The two of them stood there, green-faced and miserable, watching as the endless ocean rolled and crashed. Stretching all the way to the horizon in every direction was only water. Annie had the sensation, not for the first time, of being lost in this incomprehensible new world. It felt as though everything she understood had simply been rubbed out. Erased. Trees, buildings, people and animals, all gone. She wondered briefly if they'd ever been there. If the world as she understood it had been no more than a pleasant dream she'd had. But that couldn't be true, of course. Because she hadn't slept a wink since stepping foot on this awful boat.

Neither had her father, who stood beside her now, bent over the edge of the boat, retching and heaving. Annie could only just see over the edge and when it was her turn, her father had to lift her. There had been accidents. Lots of accidents. When the two of them needed to be ill at the same time. Annie had decided that, all things considered, she didn't care for the sea very much.

The sun had set and taken with it the only colour there was in this new world. Everything was now once again grey and dull. Her mother would be in the ship's bar by now. Drinking one of the horrible drinks that both Mumsy and Daddy liked but that Annie thought tasted like tummy medicine. The retching stopped and her father slumped down beside her on the sodden and slippery wooden floor. He wiped his mouth with the back of his hand and let out a quiet moan.

'Daddy?'

'Yes, my sweet.'

'I want to go home.'

He reached across and took her hand in his.

'I know, my darling. But we *are* going home, and it will only be a few more days now.'

Annie didn't understand this. Her mother and father had explained that they were going to England. Annie had never been to England, so how could it possibly be home? Her home was the place they'd left behind. The only home she'd ever known. Where palm trees lined the busy streets full of cars tooting their horns and bicycles ringing their bells. Big tall buildings of different colours and bright blue skies full of fluffy white clouds. Where Annie played for days that never ended, in their beautiful garden where her mother tended to roses. Where Judith (whose secret name – Makena – only Annie knew) made her cucumber sandwiches and combed her hair.

'That's a funny name.'

'In my home, it means "One who brings happiness".'

'Why is it secret?'

'Oh well, because here I am called Judith and far away, in my home, I am Makena.'

'But this *is* your home?'

'One day you will understand, little one.'

When Annie had been told that Judith, whose secret name was Makena, wouldn't be coming with them to England, she had cried for a thousand years. Or so it seemed. She ran to Judith, whose secret name was Makena, and fell into her arms. She begged her to come with them. It had always been the four of them for as long as Annie could remember. A family.

'Don't you like us anymore?'

'Oh, my little one, of course I do. One day you will understand.'

They held each other then, and they both cried. Annie remembered. A memory within a memory. Their tears were different to each other's somehow, although Annie couldn't say how exactly. Perhaps one day she would understand.

Annie's tummy began to roll and crash again, like the endless waves.

'Daddy?'

'Yes, my sweet.'

'I think I need to be poorly again. Can you lift me over the edge, please?'

'The gunwale, my darling. Do you remember I told you what it's called?' her father asked, in an exhausted monotone.

'Gunwale,' Annie mimicked, lifelessly.

Percy lifted his young daughter and held her in his strong arms, leaning over the edge of the boat. Annie remembered his arms; the fine black hairs and his brown leather-strapped wristwatch. She remembered feeling safe, even happy, in spite of everything.

The boat was white and slightly blurry around the edges.

It was missing bits. She couldn't remember their cabin or the bar, or what her mother was wearing. She couldn't remember boarding or alighting or any of the other passengers. She was also aware of not really experiencing the sickness. The illness was a memory and lacked depth and detail. She was aware of these missing things, if not entirely conscious of them. Or the other way around, perhaps. She understood that she was not *in* time, but outside of it. Things both moved forward and didn't. Her thoughts, for example. She was a child and not a child.

Conversely, all that she did remember was vivid and detailed and bursting with the vibrancy of newness. It was too vivid. It reminded her of going to the Imax cinema with Billy and the grandchildren, in a lifetime far away, beyond the New Age. She had something of her grandmother about her and, as such, instinctively didn't fight against these strange and confusing contradictions.

Annie was not easily unnerved. She remembered her father most of all. Not just how he looked; big and strong. Neatly combed moustache, big, dimpled smile, and sad, burdened eyes. But also, his soul and his heart. She remembered his love for her. Unconditional and unbreakable. She remembered his kindness. She let it flood through her and a warmth that might have been literal rose up and bathed the memory in light. She realised that this was her memory of him. That was its purpose. To her, he was forever this moment. Both her protector and, as a child at least, the only person who understood exactly what she was going through. Peas in a pod. That was love, Annie remembered. This memory was the love between the two of them.

TWELVE

'Do you really not remember anything?' asks the memory of my grandma.

A hopeless pain that dances on the broken bones of every repentant tomorrow.

'I remember… the pain, Grandma. That's all really. What do you remember?'

'All of it, I think. The hospital. That horrible nurse with the birthmark shaped like a billy goat. And your dear old grandad, of course. Sat there day and night. And your dad and stepmum… you all visited, didn't you? You and lovely Ela. And your brother. He was with that awful girl with all the piercings.'

I laugh at this. 'Tammy.'

'That's the one. He's not still with her, is he?'

'No. They split up years ago.'

'Good. He told me once that she didn't like dogs. Never ever trust anyone who doesn't like dogs.'

She is just as I remember her. As though no time has

elapsed. In truth, though, that isn't the strangest thing about this conversation. The one I'm having with my long-deceased grandmother, having just realised that I myself am dead and that neither of us are real. I'm calm now. That's the strangest thing. I'm a worrier by nature. I panic easily and am usually riddled with anxiety about something or other, or everything. Fight or flight. I fly, every time. And yet here I am, a dead man on a ghost train, outside of time.

'So, then. I'm afraid I'm going to need you to catch me up on what's been happening with everyone,' she says, with an excited twinkle.

'Well, you have a great-granddaughter named Annie.'

I watch as her eyes mist over. She retrieves a screwed-up tissue from her sleeve and wipes a solitary tear from her cheek. The action is so familiar to me that I'm almost overcome with emotion myself. She takes my hand and places it in hers.

'You always were my favourite.'

A wry smile, a long-shared joke. But I know that it's the truth.

'What else would you like to know, Grandma?'

'How's your grandad?' Her smile fades and her face is a thousand things. Love and kindness, worry and regret. The deepest sadness and the tenderest love. 'I'll never forgive myself for leaving him on his own.'

'He's doing well. Things were tough for a while but, you know him. He's a fighter. He mastered the washing machine after three years of failed attempts. He had to buy a whole new wardrobe after he managed to shrink all his trousers and dye his shirts pink.'

She laughs at this.

'He misses you, Grandma. We all do. But he's OK.'

'And your dad?'

We spoke like this for an hour, or a lifetime. I told her how everyone was doing, and we even talked about her funeral. Outside the window the darkness is resolute. Algie sleeps, Bessie is there then not there. Fading in and out of sleep as she remembers. Percy and Clara can't stop gazing at my grandma, their daughter. They sit arm-in-arm and stare adoringly at her like proud parents watching their child delivering their lines in the school nativity play. The Unremembered glitches and crackles in the corner.

'Poor thing,' my grandma says at one point, almost looking at her.

'Shouldn't we have started moving again?' I enquire.

Percy looks at the window and frowns. 'I'd expect we'll get going in a moment.' He smiles at me reassuringly. But I sense he's unsure. He fears something is wrong.

PERCY

Lost forever in the swirling rancid air. Gasping. Fading. The piercing ringing in his ears, almost loud enough to drown out the screams. Young men crying out for their mothers as they slip from this life into the forever night. Ugly cherry red through the smoke and dirt. Broken bleeding fingernails digging into the muck. Crawling to the milk-skinned boy, dragging useless trailing legs through mud and mangled remains. Silent shouts, the ringing is a dagger that stabs and cuts.

'Private!' Shaking. Slapping. 'Tristram! Come on, man!'

The ugly cherry red. Then the mask. Failing fingers

uselessly fumbling. Too late. Too late. Tears, sobs and the dying of the light.

'You did all you could, sir.'

Percy wakes with a start and instantly clutches his stomach. From one nightmare to another. The tiny windowless cabin rocks violently and he dives for the bucket by his bedside. He retches and heaves. A banging on the door.

'Lieutenant!'

'What is it?'

'Your alarm call, sir.'

'Very well, I'll be along shortly.'

Percy wonders if there was ever a time before he boarded this blasted ship. If the world as he remembers it is no more than a pleasant dream he'd once had. But he knows this can't be true because his dreams are not pleasant. He washes his face in the stagnant brown water and looks at his reflection in the rusting shard of mirror that hangs by the thinnest thread. He is running away, he knows that. And with equal clarity he knows that it is useless. You cannot run from your own memories. You cannot run from sleep.

He makes his way along the sodden deck. The sun is white in the pale sky. The sea is rough, and the world is lurching from side to side and up and down. It takes all his strength not to turn back or run to the gunwale and continue his retching. Although there can be nothing left in him now. There are people all around him, although their chatter is drowned out by the wind that howls. Civilians. He is the only military man on board. The scene has a drunk dream-like quality and he briefly wonders if he's still sleeping in his prison cell of a cabin.

When he boarded the previous night, the decks were empty and the details of the vessel obscured. *Good Lord, only last night*, he thinks. He has so many days of this ahead of him.

The sepia-tinged dining room is absurd in its pomposity. A vulgar mix of modern sleek, symmetrical, sharp angles and the lavish elegance of the previous century. As though this were a grand ocean liner rather than a derelict vessel still somehow afloat, as Percy considers it to be.

It was jammed in the ice, but I saw in a trice it was called the 'Alice May.'

He chuckles to himself at this.

He's ushered to a table and left to wait in the hope that what's presented to him will be something he can keep down. Tristram sits three tables along, his tattered uniform coated in mud and smatterings of ugly cherry red. They nod at each other and the private lifts his glass in cheers.

And then, both suddenly and predictably, from nowhere and exactly as he remembers her, there she is. A girl from another world who's set to become his entirety. Elegant and youthful, handsome and angular. The star in a silent movie. Cocktails in nightclubs and stories captured forever in the pages of books he's not yet read. Skin like pearl and eyes that Percy could lose himself in. Does lose himself in. Distant echoes of safety and warmth but laced with something more exciting. Their eyes meet then, and she smiles at him with thin but shapely lips.

He is both aware and not. He is forever in this moment, with its rush and gooseflesh, and outside of it; an observer from another place.

His heart quickens, finds its new rhythm, for it is hers now. He can only see her. The ship, this blasted ship, and all the chattering passengers are gone. Even Tristram, forever tethered by death and circumstance, has faded into a distant and indefinable light. It is said we all die twice. Perhaps Percy will not think of him again in this life. The life he is both about to live and will never live again. No more or less than a circling congregation of moments.

For the first time, he sees the future, not the past. No mud or mangled remains, but hope and beauty and a lifetime shared. Hands clasped together through the longest nights. Tender kisses and steely strength. He sees the girl and the woman, the intellect and the mother. He sees her strength and her frailty, her truth and her lies. He sees an old woman, still handsome and angular, surrounded by family, forever the matriarch. He sees it all except the ending.

Thank goodness, he thinks, *thank goodness I go first.*

This is his first happy memory, he realises. The mud and mangled remains had wiped from his mind a childhood lost to him forever. His mother and father are whispers he cannot quite hear. Faded names on a moss-coated gravestone. All his brothers and sisters, for there were many, are satellites that float beyond his orbit. He wonders for a fleeting second if they remember him. If he lives on in the memory of those he loved but can no longer see. And then, again, he only sees her. And she wipes away the melancholy of memories lost. The mud and mangled remains could never be entirely erased, but they fade and sit quietly forevermore in a darkened corner of his long dead mind.

He stands and walks across a room that is now only light and colours. His stomach no longer rolls or crashes, and neither do the waves. He is no longer a soldier running away. He is hers. Clara. His Clara.

'Hullo,' says the handsome and angular girl.

THIRTEEN

'Unless...' He lets the thought hang in the air between us. A flicker of something in those burdened eyes. But then it's gone and the smile returns.

'So, you're my great-grandson?'

'Yes, I suppose I am.'

'And my great-great-grandson?' adds Bessie.

All of a sudden, all eyes are on me. All save for Algie, who still snores contentedly. As if enjoying a carefree snooze after a Sunday roast.

'My little Annie, a grandmother!' adds Clara, looking adoringly at my grandma.

'So, tell us all about yourself,' says Percy, in a manner that gives me the uneasy feeling of being at a job interview.

'Well... erm... what would you like to know?'

'Everything!' he answers, with a smile.

'Why don't you start at the beginning?' says my grandma, gently squeezing my hand in encouragement.

'Yes, what year were you born?' asks Percy.

'1978.'

'Good Lord.'

'So, we would have met?!' says Clara.

'Yes, you met each other many times,' my grandma chips in, looking between the two of us in surprise.

'Don't either of you remember?'

We look at each other and shake our heads.

'He's my Charlie's son,' Grandma adds.

'My goodness! Little Charlie, I'd forgotten all about him!'

'You had?' My grandma looks crestfallen at this.

'Don't worry,' Bessie says. 'This place… it's funny like that. Memories aren't… we aren't…'

'We aren't whole,' Algie proclaims, as he opens his emerald eyes and surveys the scene. 'What's happening?' he enquires.

'Are you married?' asks Clara.

'No. But my partner, Ela, and I have been together forever, and we have a daughter. Your great-great granddaughter, I suppose.'

'Living in sin!' says Clara, with a wry smile.

'Good for you!' adds Bessie, with a warmth that makes me feel safe.

Percy creases his brow. 'Why aren't you married?' he asks.

Clara and Bessie look at him disapprovingly.

'Well, it just wasn't what either of us wanted, really. I don't believe in God, for one thing.'

An uneasy silence falls throughout the compartment at these words. Then, after what feels like an age, Algie lets out a loud and explosive laugh. And then they're all laughing.

Even my grandma can't stop herself from chuckling as she squeezes my hand by way of apology.

'What's so funny?'

'I'm sorry, my boy,' chuckles Algie, struggling to control himself. 'But you must admit, it's a touch ironic given your current circumstances, don't you think?'

This seems to set them all off again and I find that I'm struggling not to join in, although I don't really understand what's happening.

When the laughter finally subsides, I tell them more about my life. Percy and Clara are overcome with emotion to hear that my daughter is named after theirs. The strange thing is, as I try to answer their questions, it slowly dawns on me that I don't remember a lot of it. As though it all happened centuries ago. Or to someone else. Bits are vivid, almost unnaturally so, but great chunks of my own story are missing or obscured. I find that it's easier to answer questions about the world in which I lived than about my own place within it. I try and fail to explain the internet and global warming.

'The world is dying?'

'Yes. Well, no. Kind of. We're damaging it in a way that will make it uninhabitable.'

As I stumble clumsily on, the world as I remember it becomes a more and more terrifying place. I am a messenger from the future, and I bring bad news. My travelling companions stare at me open-mouthed as I regale them with tales from beyond the New Age. The ashes of a fire that once burned brightly. Pandemics and populism, social media and a war on terror. I'm speaking to people who remember the Boer War, cholera outbreaks and the horrors of the trenches. Their lives sprawl across so much history and social change. From votes for women to man on the moon. The Holocaust to the national health service. And now further, because I'm just another among their number now. Somehow this makes it easier. The darkness lifts slightly and I remember other things. The fall of the Berlin Wall, gay pride, a man of colour in the White House and the Good Friday Agreement. Algie, in particular, is enthralled. Hungry to hear of the world beyond his years. He is uninterested, however, in economic crises:

'Been there, done that, my boy.'

Or global pandemics:

'Spanish Flu. It happens, my boy, always has always will. Tell me about flying cars, robot computers and space! Tell me about the new century!'

ALGIE

'A new century!' proclaims Algie to his assembled cast, with loud drunken gaiety.

'He's off again,' mutters Figgy Figgins.

'It is almost upon us!' Algie continues. 'Can you imagine such a thing, you rabble of feckless old fustilugs? We are witness to history and the future!' He holds his hands aloft in triumph and is met by utter indifference.

'Just show us your cards, Algie,' pleads a weary Rascal Rogerson. The table, around which the five men sit, is lit by a single bulb that glows a nostalgic orange.

The Red Lion Inn has long since closed for the night, but our clandestine protagonists have a long-standing arrangement with its ruddy-nosed proprietor.

'What's that?' replies Algie. 'Oh, yes, right you are, young Rascal.' He turns over his cards and lays them on the table, with a twinkle in his emerald eyes.

'Oh, for the love of… you blaggard, Algie!'

Algie chuckles as his crestfallen cohorts mutter and swear in frustration. 'Pay up, good sirs, if you please.'

Outside, the night is black. Nothing beyond these four walls is visible through the glass of the windowpane. But a storm is raging and the howling wind rattles the wooden frames. Rain falls this night. Captured forever like snowflakes in a globe. The men begrudgingly pay Algie his money, one by one, until it's Figgy Figgins' turn.

'Thing is Algie, I'm penniless, old chum.'

'Come now, young Figgy. You know the rules. You've not been drinking water all evening, eh?'

'I've not got even a farthing left, Algie. But fear not, old friend. For I can pay you with something better than coins.'

'Is there such a thing, young Figgy?' asks Algie, as his friend disappears from view. He rummages around in a bag by his seat and reappears with a small bundle of blankets. He gently pulls back a corner to reveal a tiny puppy, skinny and shivering.

'Has that been down there all night?' asks Rascal.

Algie looks at Figgy in disbelief. He's about to launch into a full-volumed and expletive-laden tirade at the sheer audacity of the fellow when he glances into the eyes of the pitiful puppy. It whimpers as it looks up at him. And then… Algie melts. He's smitten. For only the third time in his life, Algie is in love. It's with a cracked voice that he replies.

'Alright.' He clears his throat and gathers himself. 'Very well, young Figgy. Never let it be said that I'm not a generous chap. Hand over the little fellow and we'll say no more about it.'

Sometime later, maybe an hour, maybe less, Algie and the ruddy-nosed proprietor are sharing a final nightcap. The others have long-since departed, swallowed by the endless storm.

'They're good ratters, them Jack Russells.'

'My thoughts exactly. Always useful. Otherwise, I'd have insisted on the money, of course.'

'Your Bessie won't be too pleased though, Algie.'

'No. You could be right there, my man. Do you have any ribbon?'

'Ribbon?'

'Yes. Preferably pink. I have an idea.'

As Algie makes his way home, the storm rages on. He cradles the whimpering puppy, still wrapped in blankets and now also in his large woollen overcoat. In these rain-soaked moments, as the wind howls through his bones, Algie shows the animal more love and care than it has ever known. A love and care that he will continue to show his beloved puppy for the next seventeen years. Never again will it go hungry. Its whole world will be one of love. Its own recollection of its beginning will soon fade and all it will understand of the world is love. On this night, in this storm and in this memory, it is saved. Algie has tied the pink ribbon into a bow around its tiny neck. The pair arrive home, one drenched to the bone, one warm and snug. Algie places the puppy gently down on the front step, then he raps loudly on the door, runs and hides behind the rose bush in the front garden.

Lights come on; familiar irritated footsteps pound the wooden staircase. The door swings open.

'Algie you—' Bessie stops mid-sentence. There's no one there. And then she sees it. It opens its eyes and looks up at her. It cocks its head and wags its little tail. And… she melts. For the fourth time in her life, Bessie is in love.

She picks up the beautiful bundle and smiles down at it. The dog instinctively feels safe when Bessie smiles. Algie appears from behind the bush, his arms aloft in triumph.

'Bessie, my love! Look what I got for you, what a beauty, eh?'

'Algie, you fool. Come here, you great lump.'

The three of them embrace on the doorstep, as the rain slows.

'What shall we call him, my love?' asks Algie.

'We should let Jack decide. Now, come on in, and keep your voice down or you'll wake him.'

Bessie turns and carries the puppy into its new home. Algie freezes for just a second. His brow furrows.

'Jack. Our little Jack. I'd… forgotten.'

'What's that?' whispers Bessie from somewhere nearby.

'Eh? Oh, nothing, my love. Good thinking, we'll let the boy decide.'

Time slides away then, and all at once it's the next morning.

'Dropsy,' says their little Jack, as he jumps up and down for joy.

'Dropsy?' say his mother and father in unison.

'Dropsy.'

'I'm not sure that's… how about Scamp?'

'Dropsy.'

'Or Trigger?'

'Dropsy.'

'The thing is, my sweet, that means… well, it also means…'

'Dropsy.'

Algie and Bessie look at each other and smile a resigned and contented smile.

'Dropsy it is then,' says Algie.

The boy screams in delight and strokes the puppy excitedly.

'Gently, my sweet. He's very delicate.'

Algie looks at his son. His son, Jack. This isn't a memory of Jack, Algie knows this. This is a memory of Dropsy, the dog that meant… that means so much to him. It's a memory of the moment Dropsy and Bessie meet. The three of them on the doorstep in the storm. How can a father forget his son?

'I don't understand,' he mutters.

'What's that, Algie?'

'Eh? Oh, nothing, my love.'

As we already know, melancholy doesn't suit Algie; life is a rich pageant of possibility, after all. For this reason, there is much Algie doesn't remember. He remembers his sepia-toned childhood with a vividness that's both questionable and true, to varying degrees, depending on how you choose to measure these things. Storybook characters and farcical scenarios that revel in the uncomplicated happiness of life. And quite right, too. But then there's a gap. A period of time that Algie has no use for now. Where despair and loss and guilt are locked safely away forever and forever. Except that some gaps are too big to simply lock safely away, aren't they? You can't run away from your own memories. And you can't always simply choose to not remember.

'Jack. Our little Jack.'

FOURTEEN

Algie wakes with a start. I've been watching him sleep; all restless limbs and worry lines. He looks different somehow. The jovial teddy bear of a man is gone. Replaced in a dream by someone I haven't yet met. Melancholy doesn't suit him. Bessie has been watching him too. She gently holds his hand with a tenderness I've not seen between them up until now. She shushes him as though speaking to a child. No, not quite that. As though she's been expecting this change in mood. As though she knew it was coming before he did. She whispers a solitary word in his ear. He nods solemnly and they embrace.

'He should be here, Bessie, my love.' Such sadness in those words. Overwhelming in their broken resignation.

'I know,' Bessie says, as tears roll down both their cheeks. They are as one in this.

'We should have remembered him here and we didn't.' He's struggling not to descend into sobs now.

'I know.'

There are cruelties, even here, I think to myself. What if the light is an illusion and the tunnel just goes on and on? The others are sleeping, save for the Unremembered. I sense that sleep may never come for her. I watch my grandma lightly snoring by my side. How many times have I wept for her? Once the numbness subsided, I sobbed for a thousand lifetimes. How ugly a place the world seemed then. How useless words and memories were. Yet it seems they're all that remains in the end. Strange, I had thought it would be love. I think of Ela and Annie. Will I see them here one day? I have reason to hope so. But I cannot wish it, can I? What use then, is love?

Bessie looks into her husband's emerald eyes. 'He is remembered, my love. We remember now, in this moment. And this moment will come again, and again.'

I stare once more at the blackness beyond the window. What of nature, then? What of rolling hills and babbling streams? Of jagged cliffs and lapping waves? Or animals? Insects and birds? Soaring gulls and delicate butterflies? Can it really just be us, in the end? All sat inside a machine remembering each other. Suddenly it all seems vulgar and miserable. Unnatural.

BESSIE

Here lies Jack Algie Knighton, forever our baby boy.

The sun in the sky is lifeless, Bessie thinks, as she holds the paper over the stone. It's just hanging there. White and dull. She put it there, of course. She wonders, then, if it was quite so lacking on the day itself. *Memories are so selective,* she thinks. Her cheeks are damp but the tears that made them so are of another world. She remembers Algie on the train, his broken sobs, and she almost does shed a tear then. Because she knows that *he* won't remember and that before too long, in this place outside of time, he will lose his baby boy all over again. Guilt and loss, round and round forevermore. She looks all about her, at the vagueness of it all. The peripheral details of a memory that was only ever about a mother's grief. Was this ever even a real place? The trees that line the graveyard do not gently sway in the breeze. They are not in summer bloom or turning autumnal red. There is no nature here, only loss. The names on the other stones are blurred or random or retrospectively added by Bessie on some other go-round. The stage set of a play with one actor and no audience. Forevermore.

She sits down on the wet grass beside her son's gravestone. She remembers the wetness but when she touches it, lets the blades of grass brush between her fingers, it's dry and dead. She thinks of her Jack. Of all he never was. She remembers and re-remembers. She remembers that he didn't die on that lifeless summer morning. That he lived and grew to be a caring and sensitive soul. Happy and enlightened. She remembers that he was a pilot. A farmer. A soldier. A cricketer. A writer. Yes, that's it, a writer. He wrote of enlightened things. She remembers how proud of him they were and how good to them he always was. Always there for Sunday roasts. A moustache, a beard, cleanshaven with his wavy blonde hair. Or darker, because it always goes darker with age, doesn't it? Did he marry? Yes, he married, for love and love alone. No children, though, too much to remember. But his wife, her daughter-in-law, was a fine, goodly woman. Strong and true. No housewife or mother but her own woman. Our Jack would want it no other way.

But it crumbles. Or never takes. Because there isn't enough, is there? His life was so cruelly short. He is forever unformed. Unremembered. He is their love, no more or less. Is that enough, in the end? *Where are the birds?* she thinks. And thinks. This can't go on, can it? She has a plan, after all. She makes a decision then, and the lifeless sun in the motionless sky dissolves. The trees that never sway, with their leaves that never fall. The stones with no names and the wet grass, as dry as sand. All of it disappears.

She is at home. In the place where they are a family. She smells logs burning and a winter stew in the pot. A warmth that might be literal rises in her. She turns to see her young son sat on the rug. He is laughing uncontrollably as the puppy grips the corner of the rug in its tiny teeth, attempting in vain to pull it along the floor. The animal's little tail wags hysterically. Dropsy and Jack. Jack and Dropsy. It can only be one winter, for there was only one they shared. The light glows a nostalgic orange. She sits down beside her son.

'Jack, my darling boy.'

He looks at his mother, still laughing. He points at the crazed mutt in delight as it wriggles its posterior with the effort of its impossible quest.

'Silly Dropsy,' Bessie says. She looks into her young son's eyes and smiles. Jack feels safe when his mother smiles. 'You are the most beautiful boy I've ever seen. And I love you now and always, with every breath in my body.'

There is a whisper of confusion on the boy's face, but no more. Because he only feels love and trust, and safety. Nothing else of the world is known to him.

'I just want you to hear that from me one last time, my darling boy. Because this is goodbye. Not for you, you will only ever know this beautiful moment, that both never was and will always be. But for me, this is the last time.' She brushes her son's wavy blonde hair as gently as her dead fingers will allow. 'I never forgot you, Jack. And neither did your father. He thinks he did, but he's wrong. It's that place, you see? We loved you; we love you. Forevermore.' She leans over and kisses his uncomprehending chubby face. 'Goodbye, Jack.'

And then this scene, too, dissolves. The never-eaten stew and forever burning fire. Bessie takes the piece of paper from her pocket and unfolds it.

Here lies Jack Algie Knighton, forever our baby boy.

And finally, she weeps.

FIFTEEN

'Why does everyone always look to me for answers?' says Percy. 'I haven't the foggiest, I'm afraid.'

My grandma has just asked the question: what happens when the compartment is full? At which we all instinctively turned to Percy.

'It's because you're so frightfully clever, dearest,' replies Clara, with a mischievous glint in her eye as she links her arm through her husband's. 'But as it happens, I know the answer to this one myself, Annie, my darling—'

'We get to eight passengers then start a new compartment,' interjects Algie.

'Oh, Pops! You beast!'

'Well, there are eight seats, aren't there? Not rocket science, is it?'

'No, but I was trying to sound clever.'

'Ha! Bad luck, old thing. You got your brains from your old Pops and your looks from your mother.' He glances adoringly at his sleeping wife.

'Yes, well. Small mercies, I suppose,' says Clara.

'So, what happens if you're remembered by someone in a compartment that already has eight people in it? You end up in a compartment on your own?' I ask to nobody in particular.

'Ah, well, now you're being interesting,' says Algie, leaning forward. 'It's all theoretical, you understand, but I have a theory.'

'A theoretical theory, Algie?' adds Percy, with a smile.

'Indeed. I think you can be in more than one compartment at once.' He sits back at this, puffing out his chest as though he's just solved a riddle and is awaiting the plaudits.

'There must be more than one train,' says my grandma.

'Yes, that's what I think,' adds Percy. 'I feel sure I will have been remembered by my parents, or brothers and sisters. So, I think there's another train out there.' He gestures towards the black window. 'Somewhere. And I'm on that one too. We'll all be on more than one, I should think—'

'That's what I'm saying to you,' cuts in Algie.

'But what if the others aren't trains?' says Clara, her eyes lighting up. 'What if there are buses and aeroplanes. Or flying carpets!'

Clara, Percy and my grandma all laugh at this.

'So, this train,' I ask. 'Everyone on here is from the same... what? Bloodline?'

'Blood! Pah!' cries Algie. 'Blood has nothing to do with anything.'

'But...'

'I'm not blood-related to my wife, am I? Or to Percy. I've never understood the preoccupation with blood. Take Bessie, for example. She was adopted.'

'Was she, Pops?! I never knew that,' says Clara.

'Of course you did, my girl. You just forgot. Happens a lot here. Anyway, she was adopted and I happen to know for a fact that her mother and father are in the next compartment along. Or they were at some point, at any rate. Queer sorts, they always were. My point being, they aren't blood-related, but they're on the same train.'

'Then what is it? Why are we here?' I ask.

'Family, my boy. We're family. It's got nothing to do with blood or name or any such nonsense. We're family and that's all there is, in the end.'

'Can I change compartment?'

A stunned silence follows my question.

'Sorry, I didn't mean that how it sounded. I just mean… well, I'm an unscheduled stop, right? So, how's it going to work now? The timeline's messed up, isn't it? My grandad, my mum and dad, and my stepparents. My brother… and then Ela and Annie. Where will they all go? I'd obviously get to be in a compartment with my partner and child, wouldn't I?'

'Do none of you remember?' The question is Bessie's, now awake and looking disbelievingly at the assembled cast. 'Not one of you?'

We all look blankly at her. She lets out a long sigh.

'Yes, we move. The four of us: Algie, Clara, Percy and myself. We were in a different compartment before the stop. Then we woke up in this one. This is the third compartment Algie and I have been in.'

'Good Lord,' says Percy. 'I do remember. We were with Doris and Leslie.'

'And their awful twins,' adds Clara.

'This is giving me a headache,' says my grandma.

The conversation continues. We move when we move. Don't overthink it. Couples stay together, apart from when they don't. We forget and remember and forget again. *We are so little, really*, I think to myself but don't say out loud. We sleep and we wake. We are here and not here. And still the train is motionless. Are there others? There must be, I suppose. An infinite number. Out there in the forever night. A library of memories. We are books in a library. Or passengers on a train going nowhere. Either way, I'm lost. I accept that with neither joy nor despair. It could be worse.

'The most important question,' says Clara. Handsome and angular. The star in a silent movie. 'Is does this train have a bar?'

CLARA

'Oh, darling, you mustn't go!' Daisy flutters her long lashes imploringly as she brings the glass to her lips.

Clara arches an eyebrow in the direction of her inebriated chum. 'Daisy, dearest, at least half of that lurid concoction is pooling at your feet.'

Daisy looks down and both women snort with laughter.

'And besides.' Clara gestures towards the smoke-filled dancefloor, where Jimmy and Teddy are lurching around absurdly with only the loosest acknowledgement of the tune being played. 'I think you'll be fine!'

'Oh, but dear Jimmy will miss you so much, you know how he feels, darling. And it will be ghastly over there in...'

'Kenya.'

'Exactly… hot and smelly and positively bursting with savages.'

'Big, strong, exotic savages?'

'Clara! You are wicked.'

The pair descend into giggles once more.

'But why, darling? Why?'

'The adventure, Daisy. Think of it. A new world.'

'Ghastly.'

'Lions and elephants and giraffes.'

'Awful.'

'Snow-topped mountains, rocky deserts and lush tropical valleys.'

'Simply terrible, darling.'

'And the colours, Daisy.' Clara absentmindedly fingers her string of pearls. 'The Maasai warriors… and do you know, they drink a spirit called Chang'aa that's so strong it's not allowed in this country?'

'It sounds appalling, darling.'

'Oh, Daisy.'

'Ahoy!'

Jimmy and Teddy have staggered over, arm-in-arm, for support rather than comradeship.

'We've had it with dancing, do you two fancy The Blue Lagoon for a nightcap?'

The Blue Lagoon, unlike the grandiose pomposity of Rectors, was cavernous, almost clandestine. It represented the end of the night. The end of the party. And on this night, Clara remembers, it represents the end of *all* parties. Well, no, that's not true. Rather, the end of a chapter. Those halcyon days, so willingly vulnerable. In her memories at least, it was the end of the girl and the beginning of the woman.

Kenya had been a great adventure, hadn't it? Just not the one she'd expected. How quickly her innocent naivety had slipped away. It could be gay enough when she allowed it. But, in the end, she is her mother's daughter. Enlightened in unenlightened times. She wept as many times as she laughed, boiled with fury as often as she stared in wonder at that beautiful land. She was ultimately impotent, however. So, perhaps not entirely her mother's daughter. Colonial guilt would be a lifelong albatross, rather than a clarion call to action. Silent and brooding and, in the end, locked away.

No, the great adventure was to be something entirely unexpected. She left a wide-eyed young girl, eager to see the world. She would return a wife and mother.

'No. Wait. Let me rephrase that. I would return a woman, with a handsome husband and a beautiful daughter.'

But all of that was the future, of course. On this night, on this final page, Clara the girl was with her wonderfully useless friends. They were, and in this memory, would always remain, the centre of the world.

'Hanky-Pankies all round?' asks a jubilant Teddy.

'Naturally, darling,' slurs Daisy.

Jimmy leans over and talks quietly into Clara's ear. No longer capable of a whisper, but as discreetly as the hour will allow. 'I say, Clars, what about it? Cancel this Africa tish-tosh and hitch up with me.'

'Are you proposing, Jimmy?'

'Why not? I've got a pile of cash and no desire to spawn any offspring. Sounds pretty Clara-compatible.'

'It's tempting, sweetness. But what of love?'

'Pah! I adore you. Will that not do?'

'I'm afraid not, old thing.'

'Oh well, suit yourself.' He smiles and raises his glass. 'A toast,' he says. 'To Clars! May her adventure be all she hopes for.'

'And may she not get eaten by lions!' chips in Teddy.

'Or ravaged by exotic savages,' adds Daisy.

'To Clars!' Glasses clink, music plays, and laughter sounds out across the last memory of youth.

Of all the memories, Clara supposes, those of our youth are the most dangerous. The pull of freedom and abandon. A time before we are truly ourselves and yet also the moment above any other when we are at our most self-assured. No lessons have yet been learnt and yet there will never again be a time when we feel such an understanding of the world around us. Such a part of things. So capable and yet, in truth, so gloriously naïve. A moment when the world belongs to us and us alone. A moment that cannot be trusted.

There is a line that separates memory from nostalgia, isn't there? And it's never less distinguishable than when thinking of youth. It's the newness of it all, Clara supposes. In part, at least. But as she remembers it again now, its potency is dulled. It will forever be a part of her, long gone but fondly remembered. But that is all it is.

What happened to Daisy and Teddy and Jimmy? Are they on a train, remembering this night? Is it even significant to them? She thinks she remembers that Daisy and Teddy married. She tries to remember what happened to Jimmy. But how can one *try* to remember? They are ghosts, and so is she. They are here, in this reel, in this montage of her life, as an expression of youth. No more, really. She thinks of

Percy. Two pieces of a puzzle. She thinks of Annie, young and old and everything between.

And she understands then. Why they are her forever. They are the memories she can trust.

SIXTEEN

Are we souls? Perhaps. It sits easier than memories, doesn't it? It does with me, at least. If we are souls then we are still quintessentially ourselves. Bodiless but still the same entity as in life. That feels important. If we are souls, then we simply left our bodies at the point of death and are now all sat around remembering our lives. That almost makes some kind of sense. Logic and order are still in there somewhere. It isn't random, it isn't chaos. If we are memories, and memories within memories, then we are… what? Nothing, really. We are not ourselves. The things we remember, the lives we are replaying, are not technically our own. They belong to something now dead.

There is also the possibility that this is all a dream, isn't there? It seems utterly improbable but how can I not at least consider it? I have had some kind of accident. The dream is lucid and fragmented. So, what if I'm lying in a hospital bed? In a coma. This could all be my dream. Well, it could, couldn't it? The problem with all of this, with these possibilities, is that they create a need for resolution. An expectation that these questions will be answered. But how can they be? Even in death, I'm not about to discover the meaning of life, am I? There will be no resolution to these questions. Not now, not ever.

'We are the afterthoughts,' says Bessie.

'We are not all that remains in the end. We are all that remains *after* the end. The end has passed. We are beyond the end.'

'Embers,' muses my grandma.

'No,' replies Bessie. 'Embers still burn. Even cold ashes evoke the fire that once burned. We are none of these things.'

Silence then. Silence and the forever night.

'Are there cavemen?' I ask.

'Pardon?' says everyone.

'On this train. Is there a compartment on this train full of Mesolithic man, carrying rudimentary spears? Just sat around chatting. Remembering the good times.'

Clara and Algie both laugh at this.

Percy leans forward. 'I don't know. I've never been that far along.' He pauses. 'Why have we never investigated this?'

'We probably have,' says Algie.

'Well, let's do it now,' suggests my grandma.

We all look at each other. Bessie smiles and we all feel safe.

'This is more like it!' she says, rising to her feet.

My grandma squeezes my hand and we both stand. As do the others.

Are we souls? Perhaps. Are we memories belonging to something now dead? Maybe. Are we the afterthoughts? Probably. If anyone would know, it would surely be Bessie.

An enlightened mind amongst the forgotten. But whatever the truth; we can still think. We can still converse. We can learn. If we are not ourselves then let's be something else. Something new. It's Bessie who pulls back the door of the compartment. I look at my grandma. The first of us to leave. I remember that pain. I feel it. She looks at me.

'Let's go and find ourselves a caveman.'

ANNIE

Annie lightly drags her fingers along the smooth plastered wall. The dark green carpet is dappled in afternoon sunlight. She can hear her parents' voices, happy and excited, coming from another room of the house. From every room, perhaps. Beyond the pane of the window, a sparrow sits atop the neatly preened hedge that separates the garden from the lane. It cocks its tiny head to one side as it registers movement behind the glass.

The air is thick with evocative smells. Honeysuckle, cut grass and orange marmalade. The smells of her childhood. Annie lived in many houses throughout her life. This is one of only two that she would forever think of as home. Even on this day, the first time she'd ever seen it. She remembers. A memory of home. Where summertime lasts forever, and life is as simple and joyful as wellington boots splashing in muddy puddles.

She closes her eyes and brushes her fingers along the mantelpiece. She remembers the photographs in frames that will adorn it over the next forty something years. From the sepia-tinged images of her grandparents and the solemn faces of people she'd never met, and never thought to ask about, to the wedding photos – her parents' and then hers. Two splendid portraits, decades apart, of people in love.

She moves to the corner where the Christmas trees will stand and can almost smell the pine. No, not almost, she can smell it.

Her father, proud as can be, dragging a giant tree through the house as Annie and her mother shriek with laughter and excitement. Needles in the soles of feet through joyous spring and into endless summer.

She walks through the kitchen that will change only once in all the years her parents live here. From white and bare wood to garish lime green Formica.

She pauses for a moment at the entrance to the dining room. A thousand things. Sunday roasts and birthday parties… but other things as well. A bed where her father will lie. The slow fade from life. Scrunched up handkerchiefs spotted with ugly cherry red. She remembers Charlie, her Charlie, sat at the foot of the bed listening to an old soldier's tales.

'Why does Grandad live in his bed, Mummy?'

She remembers Billy wheeling the television set through from the living room, so that the whole family can crowd around her father's bed and watch a man walk on the moon.

She glides silently through the hallway, where one day soon a telephone will sit, in pride of place. She can hear her mother's affected voice and it brings a smile to her cold lips.

'Westbury 4291, the Clayton residence.' From the handsome woman with the movie star looks to the frail elderly lady, hunched over her frame.

All of life is in this house. And it is good, she remembers. Love and happiness echo through these walls.

She slowly climbs the stairs, remembering more photographs adorning the walls. A family gallery of smiling faces in their Sunday best.

Her parents' voices are close now, but she moves beyond them, to the empty square room that will be her bedroom. Teddy bears and secret diaries, bedtime stories and teenage tantrums. She smiles a smile that tells of a lifetime as yet unlived. A smile of love and loss and the knowledge that the endless summertime will pass. Winter will fall.

Her parents are there then, by her side. Her mother wraps an arm around her shoulders. She almost breaks at the warmth of it, the smell and the feel of her mother. But then, she remembers, she's just a little girl. And it's moving day. Their new home.

'What do you think, my darling? Should this be your room?'

A foreign thought flutters breezily through her mind then. What if she said no? Could she change the life as yet unlived?

'Yes, Mummy, I want this one.'

What if she turned to her young and handsome mother and told her of all the things to come?

'It's beautiful.'

That night, the three of them set up camp in the living room of their new home and they are as one. They hold each other in the dying light of their new dawn. Percy tells stories of faraway lands and swashbuckling adventures. Clara sings songs that sooth her darling daughter. Lullabies beneath a full moon that shines just a bit too brightly. The three of them dream of all that is yet to come.

Annie remembers the feeling but not the words. The smells and the overwhelming sensation of belonging. And the foreign thought flutters away. Why rewrite happiness? If all that's left in the end is to wallow in the warmth of all that was good and beautiful… well, that will be fine, won't it?

SEVENTEEN

I wake with a start. The threadbare blues of the morning commute. Only Bessie is awake. Her face is something different and the sight of it unnerves me. No smile to keep me safe. Eyes unfocused. Fear? No, not quite that. A quiet despair and... calculation.

'No free will,' she says, but not to me. 'Not here, at any rate. That settles it then.'

'Bessie?' I whisper. She glances at me, then at the Unremembered and, almost imperceptibly, shakes her head. And then they're all awake. Sudden and unnatural. My grandma squeezes my hand.

'What happened?'

'I don't know, Grandma.'

'Wha... eh? What's that?' Algie blusters into consciousness. 'Did I miss something?' he says. 'Weren't we just...'

'Oh dear,' says Percy. 'That's rather disappointing.'

'I'm confused, Percy, darling. Did I pass out?'

'No, my love. I fear it's the same for all of us. We left the compartment and then we woke up to find ourselves back inside it.'

'How?' I ask, already knowing that there can be no answer to the question. Percy shakes his head.

'Can anyone remember anything beyond walking through that door?' my grandma asks. We all look at each other and shake our heads.

'Do you think we've forgotten what happened or that nothing happened?' The question is from Clara. 'I mean, did we go exploring and then return, fall asleep and forget? Or did we just get… *put back* in here as soon as we left?'

'By what?' I ask. Again, knowing there can be no response.

Algie reaches for his daughter's hand. 'The former, must be. We're always forgetting things here, aren't we? Nothing more sinister than that, I should think. Yes, we just forgot.'

'All of us,' says Percy, but it's not a question.

'So… we're stuck here then? In this compartment… or, whatever compartment?' says Clara.

'It doesn't matter,' cuts in Bessie. And she's smiling again. The hopelessness gone, the eyes twinkling once more. 'It really doesn't matter. Whether we forgot or never left. It's not important. This place isn't important.' Her warmest smile and we all feel safe. 'There is another way.'

I look up into my father's kind and tired eyes. He's kneeling beside his young son's bed, gently stroking his hair with a giant hand. An action so tender it dilutes the pain with soothing resignation.

'Mummy's all better now, my boy. And in the morning, you can meet your new baby brother.'

I slowly calm as sobs fade into whimpers. Optimus Prime looks down at me from the ceiling above. The Incredible Hulk is poised for action on the curtains that hang behind me. The moonlight shining through them is that of a film set, or a dream. It illuminates our scene but renders all beyond it invisible. We are the only two figures in the forever night. I had never seen my mother in pain before this day, had never understood even that she could be in pain.

'I don't want a brother.'

My father smiles at this, gently touches my cheek. 'Why's that?'

'Because he hurt Mummy.' My eyes begin to mist again at hearing my words out loud and my father holds me.

'It's alright. Ssshhh. It's all alright now. It wasn't your brother who hurt Mummy. And she wasn't hurt anyway. Not like when you fall over. It's different, my boy.'

Somewhere beyond this embrace, that lasts a thousand lifetimes and forms so fundamentally my understanding of fatherhood, a part of me smiles. How can my young father explain to his son the pain of childbirth in a way that doesn't leave its mark? And yet, he did. He must have, because the words that followed are lost now. This memory is of a father's love. Gentle and strong. A blueprint of masculinity that shapes and moulds a young boy's understanding of the world. Over the years, there will have been discipline and rebellion, disapproval and distance. But none of it remains as the final breath is expelled. There is only the love.

I pause time then and lay there in his arms; cradled and safe. Protected from everything that ever was and ever will be. Safe in a way I would never feel again.

'I want a story, Daddy.'

From deep in the embrace, I cannot see him smile but I feel it. His face muscles change, and I feel myself smiling too, at the knowledge of it.

'Well, that's good, my boy. Because I have a magical story to tell.'

The world dissolves and there is only my father's voice.

'Once upon a time there was a happy little boy named… what shall we call him?'

'Optimus.'

'OK then, there was a happy little boy named Optimus. One day Optimus was playing in his bedroom with his teddy, who was called…'

'Uncle Bruce.'

My father laughs at this. 'Uncle Bruce it is. Optimus and Uncle Bruce were playing happily when Uncle Bruce had an idea. "*I know*," he said.'

'Why doesn't Uncle Bruce have a voice?'

'Sorry,' my father replied before affecting a deep baritone. '"*I know*," he said, "*why don't I take you to the magical kingdom to meet all of my friends?*" And Optimus said…'

'Yes!'

'And Optimus said "*yes!*" So, the two of them shrunk themselves with their special shrinking guns and walked into the magical kingdom, which was under the bed.'

'Did it take them long to get there, Daddy?'

'Oh, quite a while. They had to hike across the bedroom

carpet, after all. And because Optimus wasn't always very good at tidying his room, there were lots of things in the way that slowed them down.'

'Like monsters?'

'Well, maybe. But mostly colouring books and Transformers. And Uncle Bruce had to go to wee-wee behind a Castle Grayskull.'

My father's son laughs at this.

'But then, finally, they made it to the magical kingdom. "*Follow me*," called Uncle Bruce. At first it was dark and a bit scary in the magical kingdom. But very soon, all the lights came on. Purple and orange and green and blue. A magical world where the sky was pink and the grass was blue.'

'And the trees were red?'

'And the trees were red and could burp. And there were houses made of Coco Pops and cars made of cheese and Marmite sandwiches.'

'And strawberries made of feet.'

'And giant strawberries made of big smelly feet.'

'And a train made of fishes.'

'And on that train were all of Uncle Bruce's friends. There was Paolo the Polar Bear and Henry's Cat. Tommy the Tractor and Susan the Sausage.'

'And Skeletor.'

'And Skeletor. And they were all happy to see Uncle Bruce and even happier to meet Optimus. And Uncle Bruce and Optimus had the most fun they'd ever had. They played colouring-in and spaceships and they ate only chocolate. Because chocolate was good for you in the magical kingdom, you see? And they sang songs and had a dance.'

'I don't like dancing.'

'Well, that's good news. Because I forgot to say that, in the magical kingdom, dancing means something different. It means...'

'Erm...'

'It means...'

'Lego?'

'That's right! They sang songs and played with Lego. They made a Lego swimming pool filled with Lego jelly and ice cream and all went swimming. Then, when they got sleepy, they had story time. And each of Uncle Bruce's magical friends, who were now all Optimus's magical friends as well, took turns to tell a story. Paolo the Polar Bear told a Christmas story and Tommy the Tractor told a funny story. Susan the Sausage told a story about going to the seaside and Skeletor, well, he tried to tell a scary story but he had the hiccups so it just sounded silly and everyone laughed. Especially Henry's Cat, who laughed so much that his shoes fell off. And then it was Optimus's turn to tell a story, and do you know what story he told?'

'He told a story about his mummy and daddy.'

'That's right! He told a story about his mummy and daddy, and it was such a lovely story that everyone clapped and said that they would really like to meet Optimus's mummy and daddy. But Uncle Bruce was sad because he knew that Mummy and Daddy couldn't get to the magical kingdom and he told Optimus this and this made him sad too. But then, Optimus had an idea. Do you know what his idea was?'

'To go to the seaside!'

'Well, it *may* have been that. Or it could have been to take all their magical friends back to Mummy and Daddy's house?'

'But Mummy and Daddy are at the seaside.'

'Of course they are! Well, that's that then. Everyone packed their suitcases full of Monster Munch and aeroplanes.'

'Real aeroplanes.'

'Real aeroplanes.'

'Not toys.'

'Nope, real ones. And they all went to the seaside in Susan the Sausage's story, to see Mummy and Daddy.'

'On the train?'

'Nope. They flew there on their magic carpets. The train stayed in the magical kingdom.'

'Why?'

'I can't remember. Why do you think?'

'Because the seaside was the magical kingdom.'

'Oh yes, that's it, well remembered. The seaside is the new magical kingdom and the old magical kingdom was actually a train station, just outside Gooseberry village, where all the people who don't like pizza have to live forever. You see, it was all of Optimus's and Uncle Bruce's friends that made it a magical kingdom. When they left it was just a boring old train station and the seaside was now magic instead.'

'Daddy?'

'Yes, my boy?'

'I'm not sleepy.'

'No. Me neither.'

PERCY

Percy paces nervously. He clutches his cap in his hands, his thumbs rubbing at the cloth, kneading it like dough, or a stress ball from another time. The midday sun is relentless. The air is thick and sticky like honey or boiling flesh. He averts his eyes from the ugly cherry red lotus flowers that pepper the garden. Another scream rings out. He pauses, the noise passes, and he continues his pacing. He stares absentmindedly at a ray of sunshine, captured beneath the overhang of the veranda. He remembers his father then, a memory that swirls like dust. A father and son from another place and time, sitting side-by-side in a windowless room, awaiting news.

'Will it be a boy or a girl, Daddy?'

'I don't know, my son. I hope for a boy, of course.'

'Why?'

'It is good to have sons and heirs.'

'Why?'

'To keep the family name alive and to ensure it prospers.'

Percy had since seen something of what happens to sons and heirs. Mud and mangled remains. Lambs slaughtered and left to rot on the fields of Flanders. He wonders if his father's opinions on such matters had changed. When the first of the letters were delivered, perhaps? No, Percy was in no need of a son and heir. He secretly prayed for a daughter. A princess that he could provide for and protect from the world. An unenlightened man with good and kind intentions and a head full of ghosts that cry out for their mothers in the silence of the night.

How long had it been now? Too long, surely? He wrings out his cap with palpable tension, as though it were a dish cloth. He's conscious that what he's feeling is not excitement. It is terror. His beautiful young wife is in pain. This is not England, and it is not uncommon for women to... flashes of ugly cherry red. No. He must not think of it. And he must get rid of those blasted flowers.

'Oh, but they're so gorgeous, darling. So alive.'

Percy loves his wife with an intensity he sometimes struggles to process. His love for her is the kind of love that buckles knees and stops clocks. It could paint smiling faces on the yellow sun and pull him into its warm embrace from the very depths of his darkest nightmares. It was a lot. He sometimes wonders if she even knows it. How he feels. Outwardly he is such a sensible sort. Strong and true, dependable and reasoned. Perhaps that's a good thing, he thinks. The fires that burn within are perhaps best left concealed. Although that was a difficult proposition at this precise moment in time. Time. What part of him is it, he thinks then, that is aware of things yet to come? How can a memory be sentient? Yet, there it is. He not only remembers his wife's beautiful eyes beneath the veil, but also those of the daughter he's yet to meet.

'If she's a girl, can we name her Madeleine? I've always wished my name was Madeleine.'

'Certainly not.'

'And whyever not, Percy?!'

'Because her name is Annie.'

'Oh yes. Of course it is, how silly of me.'

Perhaps they could return to England now? Percy didn't want to raise a family here, after all. It had been an adventure. Had it? He wasn't sure. For Clara, yes absolutely. But for him? It had meant to be an escape, of course. But you can't run from your own memories. In a sense it had been a mistake. Yet, he owed this land everything, didn't he? He would never have met her and all that was to come; all of his life that was good and happy, would never have happened. Our decisions mean so much, he thinks. So many possibilities. But he yearned for England. The England of a memory. Cricket and tea on the lawn. Sunday service and roast beef. That he was more likely to find all of those things in this foreign slice of England did not occur to him. There was the heat, of course. He'd had enough of the heat. There were days when Percy needed to feel the winter in his bones. The cold winds of home. And the pace of everything in this place. It was too fast. Too chaotic. And, perhaps most of all, the sense of foreboding that seemed to course through every aspect of daily life here. That quiet unspoken suspicion that trouble lay ahead. That they were all on borrowed time. That was no atmosphere to raise a child in. He would have to talk to his superiors as soon as possible.

Surely, it's been too long now? His pace quickens. Another scream. Pause. Resume pacing. He both knows and doesn't know that it will all end well. He both knows and doesn't know that his daughter will live a long and happy life. He wasn't sure about her Billy on first meeting. A head full of big ideas. Percy wasn't keen on big ideas. He longed for small things now. An Englishman's castle and perhaps a little village shop to run. A faithful hound and a crossword puzzle. But he'd warmed to the boy. He had a steadfastness about him that Percy respected. A clever so-and-so too. Young men would always be difficult for Percy. He couldn't stop himself imagining them wading through mud in a trench or lying lifeless across barbed wire in no-man's land. All his life he'd do this. He'd make a macabre wager with himself as to whether they'd have survived it or not. He thought Billy would have. Nothing to do with any particular capability. It was all so random. It was just an instinct.

A birdcall shook him from this impossible train of thought. Some exotic creature. He'd never learnt the names of the species out here. Although he knew the names and habits of all those in England. It was about connections. He needed this world to remain transient. Rootless. But all that was about to change, wasn't it?

'Sir.'

'Judith!'

'You have a daughter, sir.'

The girl smiles at him with such genuine warmth that he finds he has to swallow down a sob. He follows her back inside the house, his legs jelly beneath him. And then her. Their girl. Their beautiful girl. Pure and untroubled, fact and fiction. The light that shines the way. The three of them, tired and happy and burning so, so bright.

He kisses his beautiful young wife, whose tears are of both pain and a happiness so full that it obscures every darkness there's ever been in this world. They look down at their daughter. This perfect thing that they have done. And the light that shines on the three of them is that of a movie set, or a dream. Percy remembers that he is happy. That from this moment until his last, he is complete.

'Hello, my darling. You are going to be quite, quite exquisite.'

EIGHTEEN

There was an experiment conducted at a university – Warwick, I think – where a group of adults were shown doctored photographs of a hot air balloon trip. Images of them as children were edited in and they were told the trip had actually happened and that the photographs were taken from the albums of family members. All of which was untrue. Over half of them, when shown the images, said they could remember the experience. Some of them in great detail, recounting who they were with on the day itself. Our memories define our sense of self, don't they? But they can't be relied upon. They are truth for us, but they aren't the truth itself.

Although it's difficult to pin down, I have a handle on things, I think.

'It's all quite toxic, really, isn't it?' I say.

'How do you mean?' asks Bessie.

'Well, if I understand this: we sit here and we remember. Moments of our lives. A selective, finite number of episodic memories that just endlessly repeat.'

'Yes, I think so—' she replies.

'Although,' cuts in Percy, 'it's difficult to say for sure that they're repeating, isn't it? I mean, I get a sense of that, but it's not clear.'

'I don't think they're repeating,' adds Algie, with the sigh of a man burdened with an unsubstantiated knowledge. 'Time isn't passing, you see? So, they aren't repeating as such. They're just… always there. We are always remembering all of them. And then forgetting them again. Or sometimes, at any rate. If you follow me?'

'That's a remarkably intelligent theory, Algie,' says Bessie.

'It really is, Pops,' adds Clara.

Algie's already rosy cheeks darken further. 'Well, thank you, my dears. I flatter myself that I have been known to—'

'It's not true though,' cuts in Bessie.

'Right you are, dearest.' He visibly deflates as Bessie continues.

'You see, they *do* repeat. I know this to be true. I've been on several go-rounds and—'

'Well, whatever,' I interrupt. 'But it's essentially all just nostalgia, isn't it?'

The compartment falls silent.

'I mean, nostalgia is toxic. Or it can be. And incredibly unreliable. It's not a healthy thing to spend all your time looking backwards, is it? To wallow in all that once was. To rose tint it all. It's kind of perverse. In fact, it's my idea of hell. Which got me thinking, you see?'

'Yes, well, I think we should—' my grandma tries to cut in, but I keep going.

'Are we in hell?'

Silence. A silence that hangs thickly for a long while.

It's Percy who finally breaks it. 'An interesting question from someone who doesn't believe in God.'

'I really don't think—' my grandma begins, but I interrupt her again.

'I mean, why not? We're dead. This is… what happens next. And we're not… well, this isn't exactly *paradise*, is it? I mean, think about it. We can't leave this compartment. We are forced to sit here forever, thinking about a life we can no longer live. Of people we can no longer be with. So, what if…'

'This isn't hell,' says Bessie, with an authority that immediately silences me. We all wait for her to speak again. To follow up on this definitive statement. She closes her eyes for a long moment, during which Algie falls asleep. 'And besides, we *can* be with most of those people we're remembering. We are with our loved ones on this train. No, this is not hell. Or heaven. This is a puzzle.'

'A puzzle?' we say as one.

'A puzzle. And sometimes I think I'm close, but then it slips through my fingers. The answer is right there in front of us, and yet always just out of reach. But I have plans. You see if I don't, Effie. I can re-remember. That much is certain now. Information that's stuck and been stored for future use on the next go-round. But it's not enough on its own. I'm missing something.'

'I say, Mother. Are you alright?' Clara and Percy look worriedly at her. I feel a peculiar nervousness as well. My grandma holds on to my hand. The threadbare blues blur and begin to fade into sepia.

'What's that? Oh, yes, I'm fine, my dear. Don't worry.'

Bessie smiles and we all feel safe. Or nearly. A fragile safety that rests on the uneasy knowledge that if Bessie loses grip, we are all doomed. I don't understand any of that, but I know it to be true.

They fade away then, and I look out of the window. Maybe it's like one of those Magic Eye things from the nineties. If I just look hard enough. But there is only blackness. I see a flicker of something in the very corner of the glass. Where the Unremembered would be reflected, were the window not so strangely angled. For the briefest second, so fleeting as to be unreal, I know a truth. But then it's gone. I stop myself from turning to face the glitching creature that we all ignore, as though it were the most normal thing in the world. But then, we are not in the world, are we?

Algie snores and I find that I'm smiling at him affectionately. This man I should never have met. Did never meet. I see traces of others in him. My father and brother perhaps. Is that a natural thing in an unnatural place, or is it because he's not real? I don't know. I will probably never know. Does it matter? We are the Afterthoughts, this is a puzzle, and Bessie has plans.

ALGIE

Algie sits staring into the roaring open fire, from his usual seat, at his usual table, deep in the cavernous belly of the Red Lion.

He will often stare long into the flames as they leap and crackle. They hold no secrets, no answers or enlightenment for him. He just finds a peace in their seductive dance. On occasion, his focus will be such that certain other details of this home-from-home will alter slightly. A missing table, an ornately framed hunting scene on the wrong wall or a patterned carpet that belongs in some other place or time. He doesn't notice these things for a long while. Many lifetimes perhaps. Or, at least, he notices them but chooses not to register them. Even now, when such a choice is no longer open to him, Algie doesn't trouble himself. The walls of reality are no great shakes. What does a fellow really need, when you get down to the nub of the thing? The love of a buxom beauty, a few chums to indulge in and a belly full of beer and beef. What else can there be, in the end? Reality be damned.

Dropsy yawns contentedly and repositions himself in Algie's ample lap.

'Oh, and a faithful hound, of course!' He looks down adoringly at the snoozing mutt.

'Algie!' comes the cry from the unseen ruddy-nosed proprietor. 'You can't sit there all day without a bloody drink!'

'Patience, my good fellow. My drinks will be arriving shortly.'

And indeed, they will. For, on this particular day and this particular memory, Algie is waiting for someone. He returns his gaze to the flames, although their spell has now been broken. He thinks of Bessie, and her disapproving scowl sends a shudder through him. But she is wrong, and he is right. It may not happen often, but it had been known on occasion. And once in a while, dash it all, a fellow must stand firm.

'Even for you, Algie, this is a preposterous idea. You cannot in all good conscience make the boy travel across the world simply to quench your ample thirst.'

'Now, my dearest, I'm afraid I will not be moved on this. If Clara expects me to give my blessing to this union, having never met the fellow, well… I shall not.'

'We are to meet him, Algie, as you well know. They are to marry in England!'

'Not without my say-so they aren't! And the fellow must ask my permission in person. Man-to-man. A fellow cannot let another fellow whisk away a fellow's daughter without that fellow having first shared a beer with the fellow… by which I mean me… in the fellow's public house of choice. It is the way of things.'

'It is nothing of the sort, you gibbering fool. You cannot make the boy travel from Kenya to buy you a drink at the Red Lion. It will take him weeks, Algie. He will have to obtain leave from the military, at great expense. It is absurd!'

'Maybe so. But it is happening, and that is the end of it! Our Clara is worth all the expense in the world and if he wants to marry her, he will jump on the ruddy boat without a moment's hesitation. I will then look him dead in the eyes and get the measure of the man. And if he is a blaggard, you will thank me for it!'

Quite so, thinks Algie. *Quite so.*

The bell above the door of the Red Lion rings out, as a young man enters, hitting his head on the low, crooked frame of the door as he does so. The ruddy-nosed proprietor narrows his eyes in suspicious appraisal.

'What'll it be?'

The man, rubbing his head and looking generally dishevelled, walks towards the bar. 'Good afternoon, I'm looking for Mr. Knighton.'

'Who?'

'Erm… a Mr. Algie Knighton?'

The ruddy-nosed proprietor lets out a small snort of amusement. 'He's out the back… you'll want a pair of tankards.' He proceeds to pull two pints of beer as the young man stands, smiling awkwardly.

Algie has all but dosed off, as is his habit, when the young man finds him.

'Mr. Knighton?'

Algie wakes with a start and looks up at the man. Dropsy, also rudely awakened, lets out a low growl and bares his tiny teeth.

'I'm Percy.' He smiles nervously, places the foaming tankards on the table and holds out his hand. Algie surveys him for a moment before standing and pulling him into an embrace. A most unexpected one, as far as Percy is concerned.

'Call me Algie, my boy.'

Reality be damned. Algie both knows the boy and doesn't. His daughter's happy life with this young man plays out in his mind like a moving picture.

'Now, then. Let me look at you, my boy.'

A handsome young man with a neatness so at odds with Algie's comfortably haphazard appearance, as to make the pair of them look like a music hall comedy double act. A precisely trimmed moustache and sensible haircut. A well-fitted suit that brings to Algie's mind his bank manager and a pair of shoes so shiny that the boy may as well have been wearing his uniform. The eyes though. Those tired, hazel eyes. They are burdened, aren't they? Too old for the boy that stands before him.

They sit down, Dropsy leaping back onto Algie's lap, and raise their tankards to each other.

'Cheers!'

For a time, they speak of small things. Percy tells tale of his journey, omitting the many hours he spent bent double with seasickness. Algie gives him a potted history of the Red Lion and tells a few tall tales of his own adventures therein. Algie remembers that he slowly begins to get the measure of the man who would be his son-in-law. But it is only a memory, because Algie also knows that he already has the measure of this man. That this man is the finest of men.

'There is something I must ask you, my boy.'

'Please, go ahead.'

'The war.'

Silence falls as the two men stare at each other.

'Yes,' replies Percy, tentatively.

'I know something of it. Thankfully not too much and not first hand. But enough to know that it's left its mark on many a man.' He looks at Percy intently, with a grave seriousness that ill-fits his jovial face. 'Has it left its mark on you, my boy?'

Percy doesn't respond immediately. He takes a moment. The directness and perhaps even impertinence of the question may, in any other circumstance, have angered him. But he understands what is being asked. And why. Why this man needs to know if his daughter would be sharing her husband with the ghosts of Flanders.

'*You did all you could, sir.*'

He takes a deep breath and meets Algie's gaze. 'For a while, yes. Some things seen cannot be unseen. But I carry it with me no longer. Not since I met your daughter, actually.'

Algie holds his gaze for a moment longer and then nods, as if that is the end of it. 'Well then, that's all…' Algie breaks off as Dropsy leaps from his lap and struts confidently towards Percy. He stops at his feet and looks up at him, his head cocked to one side.

Both men look down at the creature, Percy in nervous anticipation and Algie with a keen curiosity. Percy senses that what happens next is of greater significance than he can fully appreciate. After a few seconds in a state of suspended animation, the mutt wags its tail and jumps up into Percy's lap.

'Splendid! Splendid!' declares Algie as whatever remaining tension there had been evaporates. The two men speak freely then. Of things past and yet to come. But although the thing was decided, after a time, Algie reminds Percy why they are there.

'So, then, my boy?'

Percy looks at him uncomprehendingly.

'I think you have something to ask to me?' He raises his eyebrows at the young man and understanding finally dawns on Percy.

'Oh yes! Of course.' Percy straightens his back. 'Algie… Mr. Knighton, sir. May I have your permission to ask for your daughter's hand in marriage?'

In the brief silence that follows, Algie attempts to look stony-faced. But a broad smile soon spreads across his rosy cheeks. 'Of course, my boy! I will be honoured to welcome you into the family.'

'Thank you, Algie. The honour is mine.' He lets out a sigh of relief and smiles at the man who would become his father-in-law.

'Same again?' Algie enquires, glancing at his empty tankard.

'Yes, thank you, that sounds good.'

Another silence follows as Algie continues to glance between his empty tankard and his future son-in-law.

'Well, off you go then, my boy. The bar's where you left it.'

NINETEEN

Was I a good man? How can I know? I can't remember enough of myself. If this is hell, then there's my answer. I could be a killer. Or a politician. Or both. I could be a serial killer politician who brutally murders his own constituents. Or perhaps just those who write him angry letters about residents' parking and inadequate cycle lanes. I could be anything at all. I could be famous. Although, probably not, I suppose. Statistically, I probably work in an office, in a job I hate. I probably drink a bit too much and don't do enough exercise. And when the lights go out, I probably lie awake for a while and think about where it all went so wrong. What happened to the dreams I once had? Where did all the love go? Yes, it's probably that. It sounds right, doesn't it? Although, I do remember my family. I have a partner who is beautiful and kind and intelligent. I remember those things. Or, I remember that I think those things. We have a daughter. A daughter who I love so much it physically hurts. Why do I feel a tremendous and overwhelming sadness when I think of her now? Loss, I suppose. They always say the worst thing is for a parent to lose their child. Although, I don't suppose they had this exact scenario in mind.

I hope I made others happy. I hope there is someone, at least *someone*, who thinks the world is a poorer place for my absence. Is that a selfish want? What will my legacy be? I don't know. I can't remember what I did to earn one. How pathetic that is. What an ending! All that effort. Or perhaps all that shameful lack of effort, for all I know. And I can't remember. Is that funny or infuriating? Both. What is it all for? Is the only point of any of it to accumulate enough memories that you'll have something to think about when you're dead? And why aren't we moving? The lack of motion is… claustrophobic.

'Why aren't moving yet?' I ask to nobody in particular.

'You're an unscheduled—'

'Yes, yes, I know. An unscheduled stop. I shouldn't be here, I get it. But I'm here now, aren't I? I've been here for long enough. What are we waiting for?'

Bessie looks at me then, as if I've said something significant. But it's Algie who speaks.

'I say, here's a thought. I have this memory, where I meet you, Percy, for the first time. The details are hazy. But you're there. So, my thought is this… *are* you there? Or rather, are *you* there? As in, the you I'm looking at now. Or is that fellow just my recollection of the you I met the first time? Originally, in life, I mean.'

'Pops, my head is spinning,' cries Clara.

'Do you mean, do I remember being in your memory?' asks Percy.

Algie ponders this. 'Don't know, my boy. When you say

it like that it sounds like nonsense. I've lost track of it now. Nope… forget I spoke.'

'But it's a good question, isn't it?' says my grandma. 'I mean, do we inhabit each other's memories? If so then—'

'The answer is no,' cuts in Percy. 'I don't remember being in Algie's memory. That memory isn't… I mean, I don't remember it here.'

'But do you remember it at all?' I ask. 'Meeting Algie isn't one of your memories here, but do you remember meeting him?'

Percy closes his eyes, trying to conjure the memory. But how can you *try* to remember?

'No, not really. I'm aware of it, I think. It's helped shaped what I know of Algie… but I can't see it. I can't remember it. No.'

We're all silent for a time as the magnitude of this realisation sinks in. We, none of us, really even remember who we are.

'At the moment of our death,' begins Bessie, 'they say our life flashes before our eyes. That's true. But what's actually happening? A collection of memories. Those moments that you've subconsciously chosen to revisit, at the last. Some are moments selected for practical reasons. To sooth and calm you at the end. Others are simply too emotive to be left out of the final reel. In some accidental way they are the moments that define us. For whatever reason, they then become all that remains of us. In this place, they are all we have left. All we are. The only connections to what once was. The Percy that appears in your memory, Algie, isn't real in any sense. It's just a replay of your mind's interpretation of what once happened.'

At Bessie's words I feel the sensation of being water, circling a plughole.

'Annie's question, on the other hand,' Bessie continues, 'as to whether we inhabit each other's memories, is a pertinent one. But it needs fine tuning. We don't inhabit each other's memories, that's clear. But can we? That is the question.'

Was I a good man? How can I know?

BESSIE

Bessie wakes with a start. The compartment is dark velvet blue and rich mahogany. The stage-managed luxury of an era now beyond living memory. *Living* memory. They are moving fast through open countryside in the dying embers of a day with no details. A setting sun that never shone on high. Sitting across from Bessie is the pretty young thing for whom this memory exists.

Bessie knows how this goes. How it has always gone. 4th October 1915. A young nurse on her way to war. An angel of mercy. A chance encounter that will lead to... what? Letters hidden in drawers. The reawakening of a truth buried for so long, laid to rest with her dearest Effie. And then, in the end, loss. More loss. Two long years of secrets and fears and empty promises. Schemes that would shatter all she held dear into a thousand pieces, were they ever to have been realised. A smile that would make a girl, never to become a woman, feel safe for two long years. But two years only.

She is glancing at Bessie with those glassy eyes. Deeper and darker than the velvet blues and rich mahogany. Her pale skin is ghostly white, even now. *She is a china doll,*

Bessie thinks. Ethereal, illusory and breakable. And then she asks herself a question. What is the purpose of this memory? It is not love, for in truth, she never knew this girl. Despite those desperate declarations sprawled in spidery ink. Not passion or lust either, for this is the only time Bessie will gaze into those dark glassy eyes. What of truth, then? A memory to remind Bessie of the truth she buried for so long? No. Life is not such a simple thing as all that.

Her life was not a lie but a beautiful and complicated train ride. Happy and sad, truth and lies, repression and expression. There is only one alternative path Bessie mourns, and this is not it. This girl is not the one who got away.

Guilt, she thinks. The purpose of this memory is guilt. A lifetime of love and loss, of all the riches and goodness that family brings – and this horrid memory of guilt made her final reel? To be relived for all of time and space? No. *No*.

And so, Bessie re-remembers. She does not return the gaze of the pretty young thing, who she will not name. She does not comment on the ugly cherry red paint that adorns those full and shapely lips. They do not smile and laugh and talk of things past or yet to come. They do not meet, on this day, in this memory that is now an escape route.

Instead, Bessie turns away from the girl and looks out of the window. She remembers the landscape into being. This green and pleasant land. Hedgerows and dusty lanes, dancing rivers and vast wooded valleys. The setting sun glows a nostalgic orange and floods a place that never was with warmth and a safe familiarity. Bessie smiles and this whole world feels safe. When she turns back to face the compartment, she remembers that it's Algie sitting across from her. A young Algie – too young for this memory that now unravels like the final second of a dream.

'Good day.'

He lifts his hat to her and his emerald eyes twinkle.

'Got the morbs?'

She smiles at him.

'Hello, Algie, you silly old fool.'

He stands then and holds out his hand.

'Fancy a dance?'

She takes it, as the compartment dissolves. And then, as they embrace in a spinning swirl of colours and light, he is Effie. Her Effie.

The scene reassembles and they're dancing in a beautiful hall that is both empty and full of tables with smiling diners and couples dancing all around them. The music that plays is the music of youth and promise.

'Beloved,' Effie whispers and Bessie remembers the warm breath in her ear. 'Have you been waiting for me for very long?'

Their eyes meet.

'Forever.'

And they kiss then. Bessie remembers this kiss, the feel of it, of her lips and skin, both tender and savage. Bessie and Effie, Effie and Bessie. The two of them, with their plans. They dance as the music of youth plays on. The night is endless until it ends.

'Effie?'

'Yes, Beloved?'

'Are you... *you*?'

'I am yours, Beloved.'

'Are you really here?'

Effie smiles sadly at these words. 'Of course not, Beloved. Look around you. How could I be here? In this place that never was?'

'Then what is the use? I can never find you.'

'Don't give up, Beloved. For I'm certain that somewhere I am searching for you still.'

'But where, Effie? Where?'

'We must look in the place where we will be.'

The music stops, the scene dissolves into colours and light.

Bessie wakes with start. The compartment is dark velvet blue and rich mahogany. The pretty young thing is staring at Bessie, concern mixed with curiosity.

'Bad dream?' she says, through those cherry red lips.

'We must look in the place where we will be,' Bessie whispers.

'I'm sorry?' the girl says. Bessie looks at her then, meets her eyes for the first time. This girl she never really knew. This hollow secret. This innocent young thing who will die before the world knows peace again. A young life, with *so* much she never knew.

Is she somewhere now? On a train with people who love her? Is Bessie a memory of hers? Was she young enough to mistake this for love? Bessie wonders if someone held this girl, at the end, just as someone held her. Someone to squeeze her delicate young hand as the light of life fades out. A life unlived but full of horrors beyond its years.

'Oh, nothing,' Bessie replies. She gives the girl a curt smile and the girl feels safe. Bessie turns her head to look out of the window, at a world that never was, and she remembers. She remembers something new, doesn't she? She remembers something for the first time. A new memory. She has changed the reel.

'We must look in the place where we will be.'

TWENTY

Colours and screams and metal and skin rush and bite and sob.

'It was a car accident,' I announce.

'Oh… no!' says my grandma, in an exasperated, almost reprimanding tone that I recognise from life. As though I've spilled my cocoa on the carpet, wet the bed or drawn a moustache on my baby brother in permanent marker pen. All of which, I suddenly realise, I almost certainly did. I feel moved to explain that I didn't do it on purpose but, as if reading my mind, she clasps my hand in a consolatory manner.

'What was?' asks Clara.

'How I got here. My death.'

Algie leans forward, suddenly animated. 'Really?! Was it a flying car?'

'It was a Ford Fiesta.'

'Fi-es-ta.' He rolls the word around in his mouth as though he's tasting wine before a meal. 'Sounds exotic. Could it go under water?'

'Oh, Pops, please!' Clara cuts in. 'I'm sorry, my dear, do please ignore my insensitive father and go on.'

'I can't remember the accident itself. Or where I was going or anything. I just remember a figure leaning over me. Talking to me. But I can't remember what he was saying, or I never heard him. I remember the broken glass and the red of the car. An ugly cherry red. All twisted and… I couldn't move and the pain was… like nothing I've ever known.'

My words are met by a reflective and sombre silence. My grandma again squeezes my hand.

'I died peacefully in my sleep. Just nodded off,' offers Algie.

'Oh, Pops. You really are…'

'Cancer,' says Percy, almost absentmindedly. 'I died of cancer.' His burdened eyes glaze over. 'Funny, really. When you think about it. All the times I dodged a bullet, so to speak.'

'Bessie was cancer too,' says Algie, placing a delicate hand on the knee of his sleeping wife. 'Far too young.'

'She *was* seventy-one, Pops,' says Clara, but softly now.

'Well, too soon then. Too soon for me. I never imagined I'd outlast the old girl. And she never mentioned it, of course. So, the whole thing felt so dashed sudden.'

'Yes, it was heartbreaking. It was my heart that gave up in the end, of course,' adds Clara. 'A moment's pain, no more than that really.'

'Mine too,' says my grandma. 'Although, now I think of it, it was rather a protracted affair.'

'Oh, my dearest.' Clara leans across and takes my grandma's hands in hers. 'You were always so very brave.'

'Fearless,' adds Percy, his face full of love and fatherly adoration. Then he turns to me. 'Do you remember anything else?'

'Like what?'

'Oh, I don't know.'

I look at him then and I think I catch those burdened eyes glancing in the direction of the Unremembered. Involuntary and almost imperceivable.

'I'm just thinking that the reason we haven't got going again yet might be in that memory somewhere?'

'Like a puzzle?' I say, and we all instinctively look at Bessie, sleeping soundlessly. I wonder for a second, not for the first time, if she's actually sleeping or just pretending.

'Perhaps,' Percy continues. 'Or perhaps not. I don't know.' He sighs and looks out into the vast empty blackness beyond the window.

'So,' begins Algie, 'tell me more about the flying cars of the New Age, my boy. I'd expect they can all get to the moon, eh? Do you have to wear a space suit when you're driving them?'

'I never got used to it,' says Clara, ignoring her father. 'Death, I mean. Losing Mummy, then Pops. And then you, Percy, my dear. I never felt quite whole again. Each loss took away a part of me that could never be restored. With each loss I was lesser somehow.' She stares vacantly at the wall behind me for what seems like many moments. Then the spell is broken and her face breaks into a broad and soulful smile. 'So, you see. I'm really rather pleased with how things have worked out. Here we all are. I've no real wish to escape this place.' Her eyes widen, as if she's only just realised she's speaking out loud. 'My goodness, this is sounding rather like a confession, isn't it? It's true though. If this compartment is my eternity, then so be it. I'm with all of you. I'm whole again.'

CLARA

Clara was never whole in Kenya. It had been an adventure. Had it? At first, certainly. And it had given her everything, after all. Percy and then, of course, her darling Annie. Her memory of childbirth is, and she finds this interesting, decidedly foggy. A pain like nothing else she's ever known. Sweat and screams and poor young Judith, wide-eyed in fear. But the girl was a rock, that day and every other. She remembers it, but it isn't in the final reel. It flashed past at the very last, but no more than that. Strange that that should be so. The happiest day of her life, holding her tiny helpless child in her arms for the first time. But it's blurred around the edges. Colours too vivid and shapes unformed. More like a dream than a memory. Percy's tears of happiness; had that been the first time she'd seen him cry? Now that she thinks of it, most of the time she spent in that faraway place is unclear to her now. When she compares it to the vividness of the years that followed, at least. Strange that that should be so. Such an adventure. Was it? Or was that what followed? The three of them, their gorgeous old home and the village corner shop. Small things, she supposes, but doesn't really believe.

On this particular morning, for example, she remembers everything. Every detail. In the final hours of a fragile peace, in her own corner of a world she thought she understood.

'Westbury 4291, the Clayton residence.'

She hears the clipped voice of the operator and then the changing tones of a connection being made. The feel of a new rug beneath her stockinged feet. Her daughter's distant calls from above and the cherry red curtains that conceal her from the outside world. She'd loved those curtains, although in this memory, they now seem somehow ugly. A Saturday, she remembers. No school for Annie, Percy already at the shop. The world beyond the curtains is awaiting an announcement from Mr. Chamberlain. The world inside the house is busy planning the day ahead. A day of small things. Happy things. But plans change and the curtains must eventually be opened. The sound of wind then, carried down the line from some other place, in the world that waits beyond. A fierce and angry wind. And then her father's voice.

'Clara? Can you hear me?'

She already knows, doesn't she? Somehow. Those five words and the strain she can hear in them.

'Pops? Is that you? Where are you?'

'Worthing.'

'Pardon?'

'The seaside. Your mother, she wanted… oh God, Clara.'

'Pops?! Pops, what is it?!'

'She's gone, Clara. She's gone, my love.' Ordinarily such a booming voice, Clara remembers. But not then. So small and fragile, like a child, really.

Can she re-remember this moment? The moment the peace ended? 2nd September 1939. A day early. No, this moment is too big for that. It cannot be rewritten. Not even, she suspects, by her mother.

She falls to her knees then. She doesn't faint, doesn't drop the phone, but her legs can no longer carry her. As if the news has hit her limbs the hardest. As if the blow is physical. She asks questions and her father answers them. But it is a reality now and no new information can change that. When her father, so small and fragile, hangs up, she sobs and wretches and howls into the abyss of the empty phone line.

'I still don't understand why she wanted to go to Worthing, Algie? Of all places.'

Twenty-four hours later and four wretched and sleepless figures sit on a bench, on a windswept and all but deserted promenade. The angry lapping waves are all that moves in a desolate, colourless landscape. So much seems to be missing from the world. The question is Percy's, although they've all asked it many times, even young Annie.

'She just said she needed to be here at the end. I didn't understand it. Still don't. It's all been so blasted quick.'

But her father was wrong about that. It hadn't been quick at all. The cancer that killed her mother had taken many months to do so. Perhaps even longer. They knew that now, had been told it by nameless medical professionals at some point during the darkest nightmare Clara had ever had. How or why her mother had kept the truth of it from them, they did not know.

Clara wonders if her memories are obscuring something here. Something unpalatable that she cannot face. Knowledge. They'd known she'd been ill; they must surely have recognised on some level that it was serious. That their beautiful matriarch was not long for this world. For her part, Clara simply couldn't comprehend a world without her mother in it. The very idea that either of her parents could possibly die was so absurd as to not warrant a second's thought.

'It feels significant, doesn't it?' she says. 'This place, I mean.'

'As though we're meant to be here,' Percy replies.

'Yes, exactly,' Clara continues. 'As though we're... linked to it, somehow.'

'It's very cold,' says Annie.

'Yes, it certainly is,' agrees Algie. 'Come on, let's get back to the hotel.'

But Clara remembers that she doesn't leave the bench then, not straight away. She remembers watching the three of them, all she had left in the world now, walking away from her. One of Annie's hands in Percy's and the other in her father's. She remembers wondering how her father would cope now. How any of them would? And then she remembers thinking about her mother. An enlightened woman in unenlightened times. Strong and loyal and tender and kind. The first face she ever knew, the first soul she ever loved. Everything she knows of womanhood, of the strength it takes to raise a family, to run a business and remain full of joy and love in this uncaring world, comes from her.

She mourns and will mourn forevermore. She mourns her mother for all that she was and she mourns the part of herself that only her mother knew. With every fibre of her being she feels that she is her mother's daughter at this moment. Her little girl. Lesser somehow, but with a love that runs deeper than ever.

And through it all, she senses that this is not the end. She feels deep in her long dead bones that she will see her mother again. She knows it, of course. Somewhere deep down. The future is a book she's already read. But she remembers that feeling now, of *knowing* against all logic, that her mother would never leave them like this. That this place she has led them to means something. That somewhere, somehow, her mother has plans.

TWENTY-ONE

We all wake with a start. Violent, like that sense of falling as you rouse from a dream. The whole compartment had been sleeping when the noise rang out. There *had* been a noise, hadn't there? A knock on the door. A thousand butterflies flutter. A wave of something like panic washing over us all. We're all here. Nobody is missing. A moment of dumbfounded silence and then the knock rings out again. It's Percy who answers.

'Erm… hello?'

'Refreshments?' comes the reply. We all stare at each other, open-mouthed. Percy begins to speak again but Bessie stands and pulls open the door in one swift and decisive movement.

'Any refreshments for you, my lovely?'

Standing in the doorway, beside a trolley that sparkles silver, is an elderly lady with the kindest face I can ever remember seeing. And remember it I do. She has blue rinse hair, thick-rimmed cat eye glasses and pale blue eyes that twinkle in the grey light of the corridor beyond the compartment.

'I… erm…' Bessie is evidently speechless as the elderly lady continues to smile sweetly at her.

'None for you, deary? How about your friends?' she asks, and then more loudly so that the whole compartment can hear. 'Any refreshments for any of you in there, my lovelies?'

We're still sat in stunned silence. Well, most of us.

'What do you have today, my dear lady?' Algie enquires, with an enthusiasm usually reserved for flying motor cars.

The lady steps into the warm orange glow of the compartment. She's wearing a bright puce dress and a thick white woollen cardigan. She seems delighted by Algie's question.

'Well now, my lovely. We have both pink *and* white for you today.'

Algie looks up at her kindly smiling face, utterly nonplussed. 'Come again?'

'Marshmallows,' she replies, as if it's the most obvious thing in the world. She gestures towards the sparkling silver trolley, which is indeed filled with bowls and bags of pink and white marshmallows.

'Erm… *only* marshmallows, is it?' Algie tentatively enquires.

The elderly lady looks at him and frowns, cocking her head to one side in appraisal. 'Well, I'm not hiding a leg of lamb in my beehive, my lovely. It's a bit thin for that these days I'm afraid.'

Algie's eyes widen and he lets out a jubilant and booming laugh. 'Ha! Well then, a bag of your finest pink and white marshmallows, if you please, my good woman.'

As the lady shuffles to the trolley to retrieve the goods, my grandma leans in to me and says quietly, 'Don't we know her?'

And we do. I suppose nothing should really be a surprise, given the circumstances.

'That's Nanna Martin,' I reply, at a volume that should have only been loud enough for my grandma to hear, but as soon as the words leave my lips, Nanna Martin whirls around to face me. Her face conveys a thousand things: surprise, joy, understanding and then, eventually, a strange kind of sorrowful warmth.

'Hello, sweetheart. I thought it must be you, though I hoped I was wrong.'

'Hello, Nanna Martin. How are… I mean, I don't…'

'Come along then.' She holds out her hand, still smiling, and I take it without a second's hesitation. As she leads me from the compartment, I can feel the others' eyes on me. Save for Algie, who's now enthusiastically tucking in to his refreshments.

'Yes, I thought it must be you,' she says as we walk past the trolley and down a grey and shadowy corridor.

'Nobody else would've remembered me like this, you see?'

The large windows that stretch along one side of the corridor are black and lifeless. As with the window in the compartment, they offer no hint of a world beyond. We're passing other compartments now, too, but I can't quite seem to see in through the glass of the doors. Vivid colours and unformed shapes.

'It was the marshmallows that really gave it away.' She chuckles to herself. 'My Jennifer – your mother, I mean –

always said I gave you too many of the things. Oh, how I miss that girl of mine.'

Ethereal whispers bleed through the walls. I strain to catch the words but they're snowflakes, melting before they hit the ground.

'Ah, yes, here we are.' She stops outside an empty compartment and ushers me inside. It's exactly the same as the one we've just left; threadbare blues and nostalgic orange.

She sits me down beside her and I'm conscious that the space around us isn't quite right. Or rather, things are the wrong size, aren't they? I'm looking up at Nanna Martin, but I must be a foot taller than her.

'Right then, sweetheart.' She looks intently into my eyes. 'It's good to see you, my lovely. You always were a handsome little fellow.'

'It's good to see you too, Nanna. Although, I can't really… I do remember you, of course, but it's this place. It's difficult to…'

'Say no more, sweetheart. I understand. You were ever so young when I shuffled off. Let's get straight to it then, shall we? Why am I here?'

'Sorry?'

'Here. As a guest, on this train. Your guest, my sweet. Must be. I'm here to see you… I knew it must be you.'

'I'm sorry I don't… how did you know it must be me?'

'Well, look at me! Do you think I'm spending eternity as a ninety-three-year-old woman in my slippers?'

I glance down to see a pair of fluffy lilac slippers.

'Carrying around a lifetime supply of marshmallows? No, only you would remember me like this. And as I'm a guest here, it's your rules, you see?'

There's a pause before I answer. 'No.'

'No?'

'No. I don't see, Nanna. I've no idea why you're here. Or even where here is.'

'Oh dear. I assume that lot have explained that you're… well, that you're no longer…'

'Yes. Yes, I know that. But only that really.'

'They must be Charlie's lot?'

'Yes.'

'Funny sorts. And I don't mean funny ha-ha.' She contemplates this. 'Apart from the big chap, he seems like a sweetie-pie.'

'Algie? Yes, he is. They're all very nice… and my grandma's there.'

'Annie? Oh, my goodness, I didn't notice. As you say, this place is funny like that. Do send her my love, won't you?'

'Of course.'

'Why aren't we moving?'

'I'm an unscheduled stop.'

'Well, naturally.' She holds my hand in hers. 'Far too young. But, so what? You're here now, you've had things explained to you, you say? So why aren't we moving?'

'I don't know.'

'Well, I'd expect that's why I'm here then.'

'What do you mean?'

'You need some help and I've been sent.'

'By who?'

'Well, if you don't know that, sweetheart, then perhaps you need more help than I can give.' She smiles warmly at me. This woman from a childhood I can only partially remember and that might not even be my own. A distant and loving figure, with a walking frame and a bag of pink and white marshmallows. A memory, unforgotten now. Laying dormant and waiting for this moment, and only this moment, to resurface. A kindness that flowed through my young life. Moulding me in ways I would never consider, let alone understand. A love that asks for nothing in return. I think of her and I remember then. She died when I was young. Very young, I think. She never saw her great-grandson in school uniform. She was like a mother to my mother, but was her grandmother really, I remember. But she was everyone's Nanna. I think of my mother then, and I cry.

'I want my mum,' I say to this woman who knew and loved her as I did. And then I sob. For my mother and for myself. I sob because I'm dead. I've left them all behind and I'll never see my daughter again.

'Oh, my sweetheart. Come to Nanna.' She folds me in her arms and I'm a child again. Tiny and lost. I weep in her embrace for all of time.

'I'm sorry,' I say, many lifetimes later.

'Oh now, don't be sorry. This might be why I'm here.'

'What?'

'Well, everybody needs a good cry, sweetheart. Perhaps the train will getting moving again now. Perhaps that was all that was needed.'

'I don't understand.'

'What's to understand? Nobody gives hugs like your Nanna Martin. If hugs and marshmallows are what was needed in order for you to let go then, well… who else were they going to get?'

I laugh at this and we sit side-by-side, waiting for the sound of an engine firing into life. Time that isn't really time at all passes.

'Unless,' Nanna Martin says. I look at her, waiting for her to continue.

'Unless what?'

'No. No, probably not. So, tell me, how's your mother?'

'She's... wait, what were you going to say? Unless what?'

'Oh, it's nothing, I should think. But there was an Unremembered in that compartment with Charlie's lot, wasn't there?'

'Yes.'

Something grave passes across her face. A seriousness that doesn't suit this memory. 'Well, I'm sure it's nothing, but find out who's it is.'

'Who's what is? The Unremembered?'

'Exactly. Poor things. We had one once, turned out in the end it was our Doreen's first husband, George. Things got more than a bit uncomfortable then, I can tell you. Mind you, I liked George. A quiet and dignified man. Much nicer than that Harold of hers, if you ask me. Always running his mouth off. The empty barrels make the most noise, I've always said as much.' She looks at me over her cat-eyed glasses and smiles. 'Yes, well. Never mind about that. I sense that it's time for me to leave, sweetheart.'

'Leave?! But I...'

I wake with a start. Threadbare blues and empty windows. Was that a dream? A dream within a dream. Can the dead dream? I look around at my fellow passengers for some kind of acknowledgement of what's just happened, but find none.

They talk and sleep, sleep and talk. Motionless and outside of time. I look at Algie and at the closed door. No trolley, shining silver, or remnants of pink and white marshmallows. It never was, I realise. Or it was but not here. Some other place in this hall of mirrors. A new memory. Nanna Martin, sweet and kind; a memory beyond the final reel. How cruel, I think then, that so much is beyond that dying breath. Water circling a plughole, but the sink is all but empty. How many others are out there? How many people I loved are lost to me now? Dormant and out of reach, travellers on trains I've no ticket for. I look around at my fellow passengers for some kind of acknowledgement, but find none.

'Do you remember Nanna Martin?' I ask my grandma, much, much later.

'Yes, I remember her. A lovely lady. Always feeding you marshmallows, wasn't she?'

'Yes.' I smile and close my eyes. 'She sends her love.'

My grandma looks at me, surprised at first but then accepting. Nothing should really be a surprise here, I suppose.

'Well, send her mine back, won't you?'

ANNIE

Just before the dawn, there is a dullness to the world. As if everything is in the background; starless and grey. Still asleep but no longer dreaming.

They are the only sound in this washed-out hush. The clip-clop of their shoes on the uneven surface of the deserted lane. The pre-chorus hedgerows sit silent and their breath hangs in the air and then fades away, as the last warmth of home is extinguished.

She knows this hour and is comfortable where others might be restless. She likes the anticipation of its silence. The day is a blank canvas and the night is old and tired. Many years ago, on what may have even been the first time she accompanied her father on his daily deliveries, she asked him what would happen if the sun didn't rise. If the nothing hour never ended.

'The sun will rise, my girl. We can be sure of that, if nothing else.'

Sometimes the moon still hung in the colourless sky, as if trying its luck. Hoping no one would notice if it stuck around to watch the world erupt into light and song. As if it craved the sunlight and the hope it brought. Other times, like this morning, the moon was nowhere to be seen. The Earth, an abandoned planet with no light or stars. The nothing hour may never end, on mornings like this one. *There is a clear-headedness about it*, Annie thinks. A place with no room for the past.

It's her mother who accompanies her today; they're laden with trays of eggs and rolled up newspapers.

'Now then,' her mother says, consulting the delivery note her father had given them. 'Ah yes, here we are. 24 Mill Lane; half a dozen and the Gazette. Oh, this is the new family, from London.'

News travels fast in a country village. Even faster if your family happens to run the corner shop. And Londoners moving in to a run-down residence on sleepy Mill Lane is a juicier headline than anything printed in the Gazette.

'The Murrells,' her mother adds, as Annie opens the gate and walks up the garden path.

She places half a dozen eggs and a newspaper on the

doorstep and as she does so, the front door swings open. Startled, Annie looks up, still bent over the delivery. And there he is.

'Oh, hello there,' calls her mother, from behind the gate. 'Eggs and Gazette,' she says, before adding by way of an explanation, 'delivery from the corner shop.'

'Hello there,' replies the tall, thin young man standing in the doorway. But he isn't looking at Annie's mother as he speaks. He's backlit by the orange glow coming from the house and, to Annie at least, this gives him a distinctly angelic appearance in the dullness of the nothing hour. She lets out a little gasp as she looks up at his long handsome face.

'Do stand up, Annie, dearest,' calls her mother from somewhere that may as well be a thousand miles away. She stands to face the man, who she now sees is not much more than a boy; a year or two older than herself, no more than that.

He smiles a smile that melts Annie's insides.

'Billy Murrell,' he says, in a voice she's sure she recognises.

'Who is it, Billy?' comes a call from inside the house.

'Delivery from the corner shop, Mother.'

A stern but attractive-looking woman appears next to her son in the doorway. She glances at Annie, then spies her mother, smiles and heads off down the garden path. As the two women introduce themselves and speak of things Annie has no reason to remember, she stares into the eyes of the man she will one day marry.

'Well then,' he says, still smiling at her. There's a question in there somewhere and Annie suddenly realises she hasn't said a word.

'Oh, sorry. It's Annie. Annie Clayton.'

'Hello, Annie Clayton.'

'Hello, Billy Murrell.'

They speak then, of trivial things. Clumsy at first.

'Eggs, eh? I make rather a fine omelette, as it happens.'

'I'd like to try that sometime.'

Realisation, a flush of red.

Those few minutes, on a doorstep, in the nothing hour, whose silence holds so much anticipation, are captured forever. And by more than one of those present. For the love that would shape the lives of these two young souls is a mutual and faithful love. Passionate, yes, but – as has been said so many times before – it's what remains once the passion fades that really matters. Loyalty, trust, patience and companionship.

Annie feels all of this as she stands on the doorstep in the moonless world. In that sense, she supposes, the memory is inauthentic. But then, aren't they all? And besides, she is smitten by this dashing young thing. The future can wait; books on a shelf, their spines unbroken.

He's wearing his RAF uniform. That can't be true, of course. But in some corner of her mind, he is always wearing that uniform. So handsome; her young love. She sees in his face the things she saw that morning. He is both confident and nervous. She loved that about him; *loves* that about him. For true love doesn't die with flesh. Quick to embarrass but never shy. Strong and vulnerable, forthright and guarded. And he loves her, doesn't he? Already. Even at this moment, as she stands on his doorstep, he loves her and she knows it. To feel loved is all any of us can hope for, surely? And she did. *Does.*

'Right, come on then, Annie. We've another eight to go I'm afraid.'

'Yes, alright. Coming, Mother.'

As she turns away from her young love for the first time, she sees the thin glow of the rising sun on the horizon.

'That's our sun, I think. Don't you?' she says now. 'I know I didn't say that. At the time, I mean. But I think it's true, don't you?'

He smiles at her, confused at first, but then she remembers that he understands her completely.

'Yes,' he says. 'I think that's our sun.'

'Oh good. I'm so glad.'

Her mother cannot fail to notice the glow radiating from her daughter, as the two of them continue off down the old lane.

'Well. He seems nice.'

'What's that?'

'Very handsome.'

'Oh, was he? I didn't notice.' But she glances at her mother as she says this and the smile they share holds all the words they do not say, as their shoes clip-clop under a moonless sky.

The nothing hour fades into warm sunlight, Annie remembers.

We are standing on a table, my brother and me. In a room of our grandparents' house, beneath a bulb that glows a nostalgic orange.

'Faster, faster!'

'Mine's nearly there.'

'McDonalds or Wimpy?'

We are as one, he and I.

'I hope you two aren't on that table again?' my grandma calls out, from somewhere that may as well be a thousand miles away. We look at each other and giggle like the schoolboys we are.

'No, Grandma,' we answer, as one.

'Mine's there too now!'

'Show me.'

'OK. Go!'

We hold the bowls to our faces and drink the melted ice cream down in one gulp. The bowls are a light brown ceramic with two stripes of darker brown on the inside. Dormant, now reawakened. Evocative far beyond the inanimate. We both finish at the same time and look at each other with thick ice cream moustaches. Behind us, the television glares. Top of the Pops; neon and coiffured.

'A new entry at number three!'

My brother's eyes widen. 'It's Bananarama!'

We jump down from the table and begin to dance manically around the room, as the music plays. We roll on the floor, jump on the sofas and sing along; gloriously out of tune. And then the chorus. We raise our arms in triumph.

'*I'm guilty. Guilty as a gum-gum tree.*'

We laugh at our own comic mastery and collapse onto the sofa. A misheard lyric; an opportunity for ridicule that's instead turned into a joke only we share. We are as one, he and I. It will always be so, for the rest of our lives. Or rather, the rest of mine.

'What actually is a gum-gum tree?'

'It's where bubble gum comes from.'

We laugh again.

'Great big bubble gum trees that grow along the side of Cherry Coke rivers.'

'Radical!'

I look at us both. I step outside this cherished narrative and see the two brothers sat in the warm orange glow. Pudding basin blondes in matching corduroy trousers and Spiderman socks. Their world is so beautifully small. Its freedom is in its confinement. They know why the caged bird sings. There is *no* world; not really. They're surrounded by love and days that never end.

'I love you, baby brother,' I say, although he cannot hear me. Neither of us can. For a second, I see the men we will become; jaded but still laughing. Still sharing jokes only we are in on. Separated by time and circumstance, responsibilities and forks in the road. But still as one. Along crackling phone lines, on drunken nights where the band plays our song and simply in the choices we make. We are these children still. We shaped each other. Without him, I could not have been me. From New Wave to Britpop, from Rik Mayall to Alan Partridge. He is my Christmas morning. 5am, full of innocent anticipation and wide-eyed excitement. He is the voice in my head that whispers, *You've got this*. He's the brat who broke my X-Wing and the man who held my baby daughter in his arms, as tears rolled down his cheeks. He's the first person I was ever proud of. A pride that never waned. Secret worlds and wellington boots in muddy puddles.

We are as one, he and I.

I watch as he picks his nose, rolls it up into a ball and flicks it at me.

'Bogey bomb!'

I chase him round the room, both of us laughing as the scene fades away.

In the seconds before the threadbare blues, there is nothing beyond my thoughts. I think of a clock striking midnight. How many New Years will they see without me? My brother and the others. How much of me will they forget? How much have I already forgotten? All I have is nostalgia. All I *am*. I'm their nostalgia.

'Raise a glass for me, baby brother. When the band plays our song.'

TWENTY-TWO

'Are we really going to do this again?' asks Percy.

'Eating into your busy schedule, are we?' Bessie enquires.

'But, really? The meaning of life?'

It was inevitable, I suppose, given our situation, that we would return to this sooner rather than later. My grandma looks at her father inquisitively.

'Well, you brought me up as a Calvinist, Daddy. So surely the meaning of life is straightforward?'

'Well... indeed. My point exactly, my sweet.' He's looking at the floor as he says this, refusing to meet his daughter's eye.

My grandma continues, seeming not to have noticed. 'To earn our place in the kingdom of heaven. God grants us free will, we must use it to live a life of goodness. In His name. It's as you always said to me, Daddy: death is certain, tomorrow is not. Tomorrow is ours to write. So, you see, as far as I'm concerned there is no great mystery to the meaning of life. Be a good person; earn your place in God's kingdom.'

'Well, quite. Well said, my love.'

'You don't sound certain, Percy,' says Bessie.

'Well... no, it's...'

'Is the kingdom of heaven not as you'd imagined, perhaps? A touch disappointing? Dull, even?'

'Why do you all keep saying that?' cuts in Clara. 'I've sat here and listened over and over again, as you've spoken of being trapped or even that we're in hell!' She looks at me and I shift uncomfortably in my seat. 'I didn't always share Percy's faith in life, I must confess that now. But here we are. Well, we are, aren't we?' She looks around at each of us, as if daring us to disagree.

'I don't think,' begins Bessie, 'given our predicament, that anyone is denying the existence of an afterlife, but I struggle to see how being sat in this compartment for all eternity can be equated to heaven.'

'Whyever not?' asks Clara. 'I'm here, with all the people I loved most in the world. I am in their company forevermore. There is no pain, no aging, no hunger or illness. Just me and the people I love, together forever. And I get to dream of happy times. All the most significant moments from life, floating by over and over again as we sit and talk and laugh. What is it that you find so lacking in that, Mother dearest?' There is an undercurrent of frustration in her voice.

'*I'm* not,' I say.

Clara looks at me, startled.

'With my loved ones, I mean. I'm with my grandma, of course. But I'd never met any of the rest of you until I woke up here.'

'Yes, but you're an unscheduled stop, my dear. Your loved ones will be with you again before you know it.' She smiles at me with those thin shapely lips.

'The point of it all is to be happy,' Algie speaks for the first time.

'A typically hedonistic interpretation, Algie,' retorts Bessie, rolling her eyes.

'Not at all,' he says. 'The key to happiness is gratitude. And love, of course.' The compartment falls silent as Algie continues. 'Every night, for my entire life, I'd take a moment to feel grateful for all I had. Sat in my favourite armchair, in front of the fireplace, Dropsy at my side, whisky in hand. I'd think about Bessie, the love of my life. I'd think of my darling daughter and how proud of her I was. I'd think of little Jack, and how lucky I was to have known him. Of sweet Dropsy, a true and faithful companion. Of our perfect little house, so full of us. I'd sit and think and all else would melt away. Lost in the warm orange flames. I was in heaven my whole life, you see? And I took a moment to appreciate that every night.'

Clara and my grandma are both wiping tears from their eyes.

'Oh Pops, did you really do that?'

'Of course. Still do. Whenever I remember to, that is. Minus the whisky and faithful mutt, naturally. Oh, how I miss that hound.'

Bessie takes her husband's hand in hers. 'You silly old fool.' She smiles one of her best at him and I can see the warmth and love he has for her bloom across his face like a cherry red flower.

'What about all the other religions?' I ask, conscious of my grandma's eyes suddenly on me. 'Or atheists, for that matter. I'm an atheist. I didn't live my life in His name, and yet here I am, same as the rest of you.' My grandma opens her mouth to speak but I continue, 'And my partner's family are Hindu. So, what happens to them? Where will they go? Hell?' I finish the thought with a flourish, expecting a stunned silence, but Bessie answers immediately.

'Well, we've *all* asked ourselves those questions many times, obviously.' I'm visibly crestfallen as she continues, 'Clara's lack of faith in life came from her parents, I'm afraid.'

'Personally, I think it comes down to morality,' begins Clara. 'Each religion, for all their differences, has the same basic set of moral values. Do unto others and so on.' She waves her hand, somewhat dismissively, as she says this. 'And our societies, through the various religions, were built around those values. Hence even those of us without faith will live our godless lives with the same basic sense of right and wrong.'

'And murderers?' Bessie asks. 'I mean, if I'm understanding you, what you're suggesting is essentially the same as Annie? Live a good life, according to the aforementioned set of moral values, and you get to spend eternity on a train?'

'Well, I wouldn't put it quite so flippantly, Mother dearest, but… yes.'

'So, what of murderers?' Bessie persists. 'Your theory requires judgement. Whether it be from God, Vishnu, Zeus or Bodhisattva—'

'Bodhisattva isn't actually a god,' Clara cuts in.

'Nevertheless!' Bessie continues. 'Someone or something needs to be casting judgement on your life, in order for your theory of morality to hold up. So, as judgement is a double-edged sword, and as your notion of heaven is apparently being locked in a small train compartment with your family, there must also be a hell? And what of memories?'

'Memories?'

'As we know, we must be remembered in order to be here, yes? Hence.' She gestures towards the Unremembered. 'And where was your daughter in the time between her death and that of her grandson? Do the lonely not qualify for your heavenly train?'

Finally, the silence.

'It's a bit like all that *Día de los Muertos* stuff, isn't it?' says my grandma.

We all look at her uncomprehendingly.

'The Mexican Day of the Dead. That's all to do with memories, isn't it? I watched a documentary on it once. It's something like, you only exist in the afterlife for as long as you're remembered on Earth. Something like that.'

'What happens when you're no longer remembered?' asks Algie.

'I can't remember.'

We all laugh at this, and the tension is broken. It's Percy who speaks then. Those burdened hazel eyes.

'I must confess, my faith has been tested since arriving here. There's an irony to that that's almost comical, isn't there? I saw my fair share of horrors in life and I never wavered in my belief that the Lord was watching over me. Yet, Bessie is right. This isn't what I imagined.' He looks at his wife then. 'You put me to shame, my dear. And you, Algie.'

'What's that, my boy?' says Algie, who had been dozing off.

'With your gratitude. Both of you see the beauty in all we have here. To be together, with those you love. What more do any of us have the right to want?'

'Don't be hard on yourself, Percy,' says Bessie. 'There's more to this than we yet know.'

'Your puzzle, Bessie?' he asks. 'Well, perhaps. But until your plans come to fruition, I think your husband and your daughter have the answer to my own existential quandary. Be grateful. All I ever valued in life is here with me now. I am truly blessed.'

PERCY

Strange, Percy thinks, that he should be so nervous. A funny thing, perspective. To keep a cool head in the face of enemy fire and to go to pieces at the prospect of walking your daughter down the aisle. Mind you, 'going to pieces' is a bit strong. But he is nervous, no doubt about it.

He appraises his reflection in the full-dress mirror. When had he gotten old, exactly? Grey at the temples, thinning on top, the moustache almost white now. And in need of a trim, if not mistaken. No time for that now, he supposes. Besides, not a bad show, all things considered. Cuts rather a dashing figure, if he does say so himself.

The image of a younger man flashes before his eyes; skin and clothes stained lyddite yellow, flecked with patches of dark mud and ugly cherry red. A reflection in the broken window of another world, where the dead live. Unshaven and unrecognisable, save for the burdened hazel eyes.

Then, just as quickly as he appeared, the young man vanishes. In his place in the mirror, Clara stands smiling at him with thin and shapely lips. As beautiful as she ever was and ever would be.

'Oh darling, look how handsome you are.'

Percy puffs out his chest and stands taller. 'You think?'

'You'll do her proud, my love.' She kisses his cheek, their eyes never leaving each other's in the mirror's reflection. 'Although, that tie needs straightening. Allow me.'

Percy looks at his daughter.

'Hello, Daddy.'

And his nerves disappear. A vision in white, smiling the same smile he's seen a thousand times. The smile of "read me a story, Daddy" and "look at me, look at me". Of rocking to sleep and carrying on shoulders, of look when you cross the street and respect your elders. Of boats across oceans and cold Christmas mornings. Of glowing school reports and tea parties with friends, of don't be late home and summers that never end. His little girl, now a strong and handsome woman. She needs her daddy this one last time. Needs him to be strong and true. Her ship through stormy waters, steadying her nerves as only he can do.

'Are you ready, my sweet?'

'I'm ever so scared, Daddy.' Almost a whisper.

'Take my arm, I'll lead. One step at a time, alright?'

The church is full on both sides. Although many of the faces, Percy realises, are lost to him now. Echoes of people he once knew but are now unremembered. Confetti in his hair… no, that's not right. For a second or two the years fall away like landslip. It's his young wife on his arm and the cheers are ringing out so loudly that they almost obscure the bells. The right church, their church, but the wrong memory. *How easily it all blurs into one*, he thinks. Life as a quiet explosion. He steadies himself, takes a breath.

His daughter looks up at him and he meets her inquisitive eyes with a reassuring and fatherly smile. They move slowly past the people they love. Family and friends and all those other shapes. Billy's family; the Murrells. From London, but decent sorts, really. Stanley and Marge. A little fond of the sauce, perhaps, but we all have our vices.

Percy would've liked *his* family to be here. Perhaps they were? They would be, after all, surely? Unless… what year is this? He tries to recall the information but cannot. He supposes it doesn't matter.

The Clarkes, the Wallaces, the Richards and the Skinners. Names and faces, faces and names. Almost there now. Algie and Bessie, beaming smiles and Sunday best. So vivid amidst the blurred figures of this faraway place. And yet Bessie can't have been there, of course. No matter; she is now. Clara, with tears rolling down her cheeks as she gazes adoringly at the two loves of her life. And then, they're there. Billy is smiling, nervous and in love. Percy kisses his daughter on the cheek and then… steps back. One small step for man.

'And now, ladies and gents, pray silence for the father of the bride!'

'Thank you. I'm not really that good with words but…'

'A man of action!'

'Yes, thank you, Stanley.' Percy pauses as the laughter subsides. 'Luckily, there is so much to say about my wonderful daughter that I might just go on all night.'

'Lucky Clara!'

'Oh, for heaven's sake… yes, thank you, Stanley.'

Marge slaps her husband's arm and shushes him as Billy's face reddens in embarrassment at this father's outbursts. Percy, unphased, continues.

'I could not be more proud of the woman my daughter has become. Neither could her mother.'

He goes on with a time-honoured list of sincere platitudes. Some of those opening sentences are forgotten now. Something about Annie the angelic, well-behaved child. Hard working and sensible. Doubtless the customary welcome to the family for his new son-in-law. None of it would do, really. None of it was even close to adequate. And so, Percy remembers, he goes off-script. He stops mid-sentence, calmly folds the piece of paper in his hand and slides it into his blazer pocket.

'The truth is, this is both the happiest and the saddest day of my life. Without this woman, Clara and I are incomplete. Our souls are better for having her in our lives. I remember my daughter, every single second of her. She is the very best of us. She is all our lives, every thought we've ever had. All our achievements, our failures, our fears and our dreams, made flesh. She is the reason I breath in and out. The *effect* of her, you see? Of her existence, has altered everything. She has changed the very fabric of our world. Of what it means to be. The love we feel for her is beyond time and space and reason and logic. She flows through us, disassembling and rebuilding. She is the answer, for her mother and me. Our explanation for existence itself.'

He looks at his daughter then. He looks into her watery eyes and for just a second, they are alone. In that vast empty place. Silent and at peace.

'I love you, Annie. Completely. From the moment I first held you in my arms until the day I slipped from this life. I love you. I wish you only happiness and love for each blessed day. It will be yours, for you have chosen well. He is a good man. There will be moments of darkness along the way. I've seen them. But, know this; the sun will rise. For you, my darling daughter, the sun will always rise.'

The room is quiet. Percy picks up his glass and holds it aloft toward his daughter.

'To the happy couple.'

Long has paled that sunny sky:
Echoes fade and memories die:
Autumn frosts have slain July.

Still she haunts, phantomwise,
Alice moving under skies
Never seen by waking eyes.

Lewis Carroll

TWENTY-THREE

The twisted metal of the car; an ugly cherry red. Is that a phone ringing? A tinny rendition of some nineties indie song. I can see her name through the pain. Through the blood. It's Ela. But I can't reach the phone. I know it. I can't even try. It's already too late. But I speak to her anyway, don't I? Yes, I think so. But I can't remember the words.

It strikes me that the urgency I feel then, isn't life slipping away. It's something else. Something worse.

'Did you hear that?'

Percy and Clara are both sat bolt upright and alert.

'It sounded like the engine firing.'

'Are we getting moving again?' asks my grandma.

Everyone is alert now. A silence pulsing with excitement and tension. And then… nothing. No engine, no motion. One by one, we slump. Surrender to the threadbare blues. We are static, like a finished story:

The End.

We are what remains once the book is closed. We are the afterthoughts; futureless and inert.

'Well, it's something though! A good sign, eh?' Ever the optimist, Algie is smiling encouragingly at us. 'We'll be off again in no time, I should think.' His emerald eyes search for confirmation in the faces of his dearly departed. Indulgent smiles and affected contemplation. Except for Bessie. She's staring at me.

'Do you remember what you were just dreaming about?'

'Sorry?' I reply.

'Just before the engine sounded. You were sleeping.'

'Was I? I don't remember.'

For a second to two, her eyes burrow into me. I feel my face redden, but have no idea why.

'Oh well,' she continues. 'Probably doesn't matter.'

In the corner, the Unremembered is squirming.

ALGIE

As Algie makes his way home, the storm rages on. He cradles the silent mutt, wrapped both in blankets and in Algie's large woollen overcoat. In these rain-soaked moments, as the wind howls through his bones, Algie shows the animal the same level of love and care that he has always done, every single day for the last seventeen years. It never went hungry or cold, its whole world was love. Its own recollection of its troubled beginning had long since faded and all it had understood of the world was love. Algie has tied a pink ribbon into a bow around its neck. The pair arrive home, one drenched to the bone, one warm and dry. Algie places the mutt gently down on the front step, raps loudly on the door, runs and hides behind the bush in the front garden, where once roses bloomed. Lights come on; familiar irritated footsteps pound the wooden staircase. The door swings open.

'Algie you—' Bessie stops mid-sentence. There's no one there. And then she sees it. And…

She screams.

Eight months earlier, Algie and his faithful old hound, Dropsy, were making their way home from the Red Lion. Their pace was slow and laboured, as had been the case for many a starry evening. If a young artist wanted to capture the essence of our Algie, to see inside his soul, this would be the scene they should paint. Algie and Dropsy, side-by-side, wandering down the old lane that connects the Red Lion to the place where they hang their hats. Two best friends together in a world that makes sense. Timeless, happy and in love. And yet, as we all know, time is the cruellest of all our creations. And it takes its toll.

Dropsy panted at the effort it took his arthritic joints to carry him down the old lane, where so often he had run and played with tail wagging. Algie swayed from side to side, chatting away to his loyal companion, just as he always had.

'And as for Rascal, the man's an absolute rotter. Did you hear him, Dropsy, old thing? The temerity of the swine. Still, never mind, old thing, eh? We showed him in the end, didn't we, my sweet? Eh?'

He stopped, suddenly aware that the mutt was no longer by his side. He turned his ample frame in confusion, to see the beloved creature sat in the middle of the lane, a few yards behind him.

'Well, come on then, old thing.'

But Dropsy remained seated.

'What's this then?' Algie enquired, as he walked back towards his dearest friend. 'Eh? What is it, my sweet?'

Still the dog sat motionless, save for its continued panting. Algie sat down on the lane beside it, wincing at the sound his creaking bones made as he did so.

'What's wrong, old friend?' His voice was quieter now and laced with concern. He gently patted the animal's head, tickling him on his favoured spot, under the chin. Dropsy looked at Algie then. His old glassy eyes full of something that might have been an apology.

'Shall I carry you, old boy?'

And he did. He cradled his old friend in his arms, as though he were the most precious thing in all the world. Which, of course, he was. And they walked on like this down the old lane; one man and his dog.

When they arrived home the house was silent but orange embers still flickered in the fireplace. Algie placed his precious cargo gently onto the rug in front of it and then relit the fire. He sat on the rug beside his friend, patting his head with a tenderness that said more of the love between them than any words could ever do. Dropsy panted still, but slower and shallower now. Weakly, he placed his paw onto Algie's arm. Understanding, Algie picked him up again and placed him in his lap. The fire warmed their aching bones and lit the room with a nostalgic orange glow. Dropsy raised his glassy eyes to Algie's and then closed them. After a short while his panting stopped and he was gone.

Algie's tears were silent at first. Great droplets that fell onto his friend's fire-warmed fur. Then slowly he began to sob. It's impossible to know exactly how long they sat like that, two best friends together in a world that would never make sense again, but when Bessie found them there the fire was once again only flickering embers. Her husband seemed not to notice her. He sat cradling his beloved pet, his face a study in anguish. Silent howls and screams as the tears endlessly fell. She'd only really seen him cry once before in all their years. She sat beside them on the rug. She offered no words, for there were none. Instead, she wrapped her arm around her two boys one last time and the three of them sat there for as long as it took.

The following morning, Algie told Bessie about a patch of long grass, beneath a gnarly old tree, where Dropsy and he would often sit. A spot on the old lane that links the Red Lion to the place where they hang their hats. He told her he'd like to bury his friend there, so that he could stop there still, of a starry evening. So that he could sit a few minutes with his old friend, until he too was done with this life.

Bessie thought this might be the most beautiful thing her husband had ever said. She told him that she'd make them breakfast and then go with him – with them. But Algie protested:

'No. No, my love. This is something I'd like to do alone, if that's alright? You understand?'

And Bessie did understand. She understood this new, vulnerable and heartfelt incarnation of her husband better than at that any point in all their years together. She felt a deeper connection with him and it were as though, perhaps for the first time, they were truly a partnership.

A pity, then, that it was all a lie. Well, not quite all of it. There was a place beneath a gnarly tree where Algie and Dropsy, Dropsy and Algie, would often sit. But that wasn't where Algie was going to take his old friend. Algie had plans.

'Course I can do it, Algie. I'm just asking you if you're sure is all. The little fellow's still warm!'

'I'm sure, Willy. Never been more so. Work your magic.'

'And what about your Bessie? What does she say about it?'

'It's a surprise.'

'Yes… it'll be that alright.'

After kissing his wife goodbye, Algie had carried his beloved Dropsy, wrapped lovingly in blankets, down the old lane. But instead of heading for the gnarly old tree, he turned off the lane and marched to old Willy 'the dabbler' Donaldson's house. Willy, as the name suggests, dabbled in many things. One of which was taxidermy.

Algie missed his best friend for every single moment of the eight months that followed. He walked alone down the old lane, sat alone beneath the gnarly old tree and dozed off alone in front of the orange glow of the home fire. All that knew him – family, friends and neighbours alike – agreed that he was no longer *their* Algie. The red-faced belly laughs, the mischievous glint in his emerald eye and even the insatiable appetite for food, drink and life itself, were all absent. He was a shell of the man he'd once been. The new connection that Bessie felt with her husband slowly, and inevitably, faded as the months rolled on. To her surprise, she eventually found herself missing the loveable buffoon she'd tolerated for so many years. Irresponsible and immature, yes, but kind and good as well. They all missed their Algie in the end. And all hoped for his sake, but also theirs, that his period of mourning would someday pass. But he wasn't simply mourning, of course. He was waiting.

'I done the best I can, Algie.'

'Oh, Willy. He's… well, he's… he's back!'

Algie, much to Willy's embarrassment, then began to cry. He hugged his old friend and looked into his glassy eyes.

'Hello, old thing.'

Willy shuffled awkwardly, not knowing where to look. But Algie didn't care. He had his friend back. He knew he didn't, of course. He understood that this wasn't really Dropsy. And yet… it also was, wasn't it? Literally, in part, but in some other way as well. Algie wasn't a religious man, but neither was he not a religious man. He simply never thought of such things. But he felt and believed, somehow and in some way, that something of his friend had been returned to him and lavished praise and thanks upon Willy. This was too much for the old dabbler to bare, and so he ushered the great blubbing man and his motionless companion out into the night.

'The storm's going strong, Algie, so you make sure you wrap the thing in blankets and keep it dry, alright?'

'Indeed, indeed. Just wait until Bessie sees him!'

'Yes… I'm sorry I won't be there to see that, Algie. It'll be quite the sight, I fancy.'

Algie took the faded pink ribbon he'd kept for seventeen years and tied it into a bow around Dropsy's neck. He wrapped him in blankets and then in his own old woollen overcoat and headed out into the storm. As the two of them travelled together down the old lane, Algie chatted away to his loyal companion, just as he always had.

'I've got you, old thing. Together again at last. These months have been… well, it doesn't matter now. You're here. Oh, I can't wait for Bessie to see you again. It'll be just like the night I first brought you home. She won't believe her eyes!'

With Bessie mid-scream, Algie emerges from his hiding place.

'Ta-Dah! Bessie, my love! Look what I got for you. He's back!'

Bessie, her face contorted in horror, looks at her ridiculous husband and then back down at the prone figure staring lifelessly up at her. Words fail her… almost.

'Algie, what have you done? This is… this is… what *is* this?'

Eventually she came round. Well, sort of. As with so many things that had happened in her life with Algie, she simply learnt to ignore it. To ignore the fact that her husband went everywhere with a dead dog under his arm. And it was *everywhere*. And all that knew him agreed, it was a very strange thing. Eventually though, they *all* learnt to ignore it. Because *their* Algie was back. Red-faced belly laughs and that cheeky emerald-green glint.

If a young author was writing a book about Algie's life, this would be a very important and character-defining chapter. It would capture something of his soul. The simplicity of his heart and his inability to accept the inevitable sadness of life. In some ways, I suppose, this is a weakness. But in other ways, Algie is stronger than all of us, isn't he? And much more interesting. For a start, his memories are like storybooks. We occasionally hear the thoughts of the other characters, perhaps more than even his own. Empathy or delusion or both. Because, really, they're all *his* thoughts, aren't they? He understands how others perceive him, even those he loves. So, in actual fact, he must understand all too well the sadness of life. This knowledge and his uncanny ability to remain grateful and happy in the face of it, may yet stand him in very good stead for what's to come. Of all the sacrifices yet to be made, his is the greatest.

TWENTY-FOUR

'Do you think there's an animal train?' asks Algie, his eyes glazed over, as if part of him is somewhere far away.

Bessie, understanding him, squeezes his arm. 'Yes, I should think so. Although it won't be a train.'

'What will it be, my love?'

Bessie ponders this a moment. 'A lane,' she says.

Algie smiles at this. 'Yes, of course. An old dusty lane in the summertime.'

'Yes, full of smells and accommodating tree trunks.'

'He'll like that.'

'Yes, he'll be very happy.'

'What is out there?' I ask.

We all look at the black window, straining our eyes but knowing it will be to no avail. My grandma stands and steps toward the glass. She runs her hand across its smooth surface.

'It's too smooth, isn't it?'

'What do you mean, my sweet?' asks Percy.

'Well, this is an old train."

'Is it?' Percy enquires, looking around the compartment. 'It's definitely a bit tatty, I suppose.'

'Yes, but the design is old,' my grandma continues. She looks at me. 'Nineties?'

'Yes, it's the design they used when I used to travel to school.'

'Yes.' She returns her gaze to the glass. 'But this glass is... newer. It's not quite right, is it? What if it's not a window?'

This gets everyone's attention.

'What if it's a one-way mirror? Or a screen?'

'What, you mean someone's watching us?' asks Algie.

'I don't know, but they could be, couldn't they?'

'Pull the curtains, dearest,' says Clara with an anxious expression.

'It's a window.' It's Bessie who says this. Calm and quiet, almost uninterested. We all look at her with wide eyes. She sighs, stands and with one swift downward motion, opens the window. We sit mute and useless.

'Most of us, although you'd never know it to listen to you all, have been on this confounded train for a very, very long time. We've seen this compartment in many reincarnations and opened many, many windows.' She looks at us all, as if waiting for something. When it doesn't come, she continues. 'It's just a memory. Like everything else.' She looks at me. 'In this case, yours. If the window is wrong it's because you remembered it wrong. That's all.'

This doesn't quite make sense, I think but don't say out loud.

'So... what is out there, then?' my grandma asks.

Bessie falters at this. She looks suddenly confused. 'I don't remember. Nothing, I suppose. A void.'

Percy stands and leans his head through the open window and into the blackness beyond.

'Percy!' cries Clara.

'Daddy!' cries my grandma.

He pulls his head back into the compartment. 'Nothing,' he murmurs, with resignation in those burdened hazel eyes.

I stand then and lean out. Stillness and silence beyond the natural world. Nothing. I strain my eyes again. Nothing. The blackness is thick, not hollow and empty, as I expected. It's not like being in a cave, it's more like being in a painting… no, a simulation. Like wearing a VR headset. Dislocated and without… feeling? Not tactile. There's no sense of space or anything of the endlessness that is suggested behind the closed window. I look left and right but can't even see the rest of the train. Only blackness.

I pull my head back into the compartment. 'Well, I'm going out there,' I say.

'No, you are not!' protests my grandma.

But I am, and I do. I climb, almost leap, through the open window.

I wake with a start. The threadbare blues of the daily commute.

'Well, I could've told you that would happen,' says Bessie. 'But well done. Very brave of you.' She smiles and I feel safe.

Everyone takes a turn at leaning out of the window.

'Yes, I think I do remember this, actually,' says Clara, as she stares out into the void.

'I just want to go home,' I say, perhaps only in my head.

'This place isn't important,' says Bessie. 'I don't think so anyway. Certainly not as important as the other places.'

'The other places?' Percy asks.

'The memories. They're the key. They're the places we can escape from, I think.'

My grandma closes the window and we stare again through the glass. There's an unnatural calmness about us all, I think. It's always there, no matter what we're talking about. The meaning of life, where we are, how we died. These are conversations that should induce panic or nausea or, I don't know, something. But the compartment is always calm and slightly drowsy. Like Boxing Day afternoon. Comfortable but with a low simmering boredom. Perhaps not boredom, exactly. An itchiness, just inside the skull.

'Oh, must we talk of escape again, Mother?'

'What would you rather we speak of, my dearest?'

'Oh, I don't know. How about the future?' She looks at me and then at my grandma. 'Tell us more of life beyond the New Age.'

Algie perks up at this. 'Good idea. I have some questions for you, as it happens. Now then—'

'Just one more thing before we do that,' cuts in Percy. He turns to face his mother-in-law. 'Escape to what, Bessie?'

Bessie looks at him appraisingly.

'You say escape, but to what and where? What are you hoping for? Where would you go?'

We must look in the place where we will be, Bessie thinks to herself. Then out loud she says, 'To the seaside.'

BESSIE

The rising sun and the ethereal full moon share the Christmas morning sky. The house is full of life and love and laughter.

Like it used to be, Bessie thinks.

Clara and Percy and their new daughter, Bessie's granddaughter, are here.

Five souls captured for all eternity; round and round they go. Except, of course, that they don't. Not really. One soul. Only one.

Carols on the wireless, tinny and faraway. The oversized tree, adorned with wooden shapes that blur and fade a little more with every go-round. It sits a little too close to the roaring open fire, that glows a nostalgic orange.

Algie is on his favoured chair, threadbare and worn, his loyal Dropsy curled up at his feet. He smiles and laughs and regales.

He's so happy, Bessie thinks, *so... untroubled.*

Clara is radiant, babe-in-arms and handsome husband by her side.

Perhaps Bessie had wanted different for her daughter. She can't be certain as it's all so, so long ago. But it would make sense, wouldn't it? Such a clever and vivacious soul, her Clara. Her mother's daughter; full of adventure and stubbornness. She could've... well, what does it matter now? She too is so vividly happy. She has chosen her path and that's the end of it. Or at least it would be, should be. But it never really ends, does it? Would we make the same decisions in life if we understood that we'd be damned to replay them for all eternity?

Bessie wouldn't. What a terrible acknowledgement that is. To carry that knowledge forever and ever. But then, it's far more complicated than that. She doesn't regret a thing, really. How could she? She looks at her wraiths and she smiles a smile that would make them all feel safe, if only they were real. No, it's not regret, it's something else.

Gifts unwrapped; tankards and lipsticks, knickknacks and delicate trinkets. Parlour games and nutcrackers. A make-believe world that runs like clockwork in a place beyond time. After the feast; bountiful and splendid.

'See, Percy, my love? I told you Mother makes the best gravy in all the world.'

They snooze. At the precise moment that she always does, Clara looks at her mother with a smile full of mischief and love.

She whispers, 'Come on, let's give Pops a bit of new look, shall we?'

She holds up her gifted make up kit and gestures towards the snoring Algie. Bessie knows how this goes, and in the end, it's what breaks her. It was such a happy day, wasn't it? Not surprising that it made the final reel, really. And this particular moment, a mother and daughter, so much love. He must've known; their Algie. But he decided not to wake; he chose to let them do their work and be the butt of the joke. So much love.

'I say, Clara, you didn't tell me you had a pretty sister?'

Bessie remembers Percy's smiling face as he says this. Just for a moment those hazel eyes don't seem so burdened. Only Dropsy doesn't appreciate the jest. He barks and growls at the sight of his master's ridiculous face. So much love. But not this time. Not again.

'Stop!' Bessie cries. 'Enough!' She stands and addresses the shocked visions in the pretend room. 'This isn't real. This was a glorious day, joyful and full of love. But it was so long ago, do you see?' She surveys the vacant cast. 'No. No, you don't. And that's the point. You aren't here, any of you. You're all on a train somewhere. Or maybe not. Maybe you're just all dead and gone. But something of you is on a train. A stopped train. Something sentient that remains when we're gone. And you're stuck there and I think... I think it's because of this. Of all this. We're wallowing, you and I. In memories of days like this. But every time we do this a little bit more of that day is lost. The happiness it gave us, gave me, fades a little further. So, I'm going to leave now. Because I know how this goes. Unlike you, I *was* there and it was beautiful; you were beautiful. I loved you all. But that was then and this is now. I am now. And I am leaving.'

'But where will you go?' Curiously, Bessie decides it's Percy who asks her this. Because he did.

'You've already asked me that, Percy. The seaside, I'm going to the seaside.'

But what will the seaside be like? That's the tricky part, isn't it? Because it never was, not exactly. *Go to the place where we will be.* All well and good, but it doesn't leave much margin for error, does it? Perhaps a little diversion might be in order? To look into those emerald eyes and take from them the confidence this will require.

Neatly arranged tables, covered in cloth so white it glows. Ornate and delicate things. Silvers and embroideries. Sipping tea and chattering inaudible words to recognisable rhythms. Queen Victoria, above the unused fireplace, forever staring into the unseen distance. Regal, enigmatic and captured. And the grasses. Arranged in wild displays that hang and sit and grow from every surface. Far too elaborate for such restrained days. Bustle, volume, drape. Traditional in description. But not on *her*. The Naughty Nineties and the New Age. Strutting and defiant. The ladies who do not tea.

'Dear Heart,' says Bessie, rising from her seat.

'Beloved!' smiles Effie. She takes her hand and kisses it. The ladies who tea stare.

'Have you been waiting for me for a long time?' Effie asks.

'Forever.'

'Oh, I am sorry, Beloved.' She removes her gloves from hands that will never age.

'I have news,' Effie says.

'Yes, I know your news all too well, Dear Heart.'

'You do?'

'I do. And, for whatever it's worth, I did like him. He was the best man I ever met.'

'Oh.'

'But that was then and this is now, Effie. And we have plans.'

As Bessie says this, something in Effie's face changes. Surprise gives way to understanding.

'Oh, I see.'

She smiles and Bessie feels safe.

'Indeed. We must talk of the seaside.'

'Yes, it is time then?'

'It is.'

'But, well. You do realise that I'm not…'

'Yes, Dear Heart, I realise all too well that you're not.

But you're all I have. I must find you, the real you… or what remains of the real you. I must go to the place where we will be. But, well, as we never did. Go there, I mean, it's tricky, do you see?'

'Yes, Beloved. I can see that.' Effie looks around the room. 'What a strange memory to burden with this, if you don't mind me saying so?'

'Yes, I thought that. The first few hundred times, at least. But then, every time I see you walking across this room, I understand. It is… quintessential.'

Effie laughs at this. 'I see! I'm a vision.'

'Indeed. A vision that lasts a thousand lifetimes.'

They clasp hands across the table and Bessie allows herself to wallow in a shared moment of twinkle-eyed adoration.

'But, enough of this. The seaside, Dear Heart.'

'Yes, Beloved. Now, I always imagined a little hotel in Worthing.'

'Worthing?'

'Yes. But perhaps with a bit more sun?'

TWENTY-FIVE

The orange lights flicker. That's new, I think. For a second, we are enveloped in a darkness as thick and black as that beyond the window. And then it settles, this scene in which I now am. I wonder how long it's been? I understand that time isn't really a thing anymore but, well, I still wonder. I can still count. What if it's longer than I was ever alive? What if I died a thousand years ago? No. That can't be the case because Ela and Annie would be here with me, wouldn't they? But what if they don't remember me? What if Annie remembers Ela and Ela remembers her mother or father or if she finds someone else and then remembers them? My replacement. What if I'm not the love of her life? What if I never see them again? What if this is all there is, forever? Or perhaps I died a second ago? Or less even. Perhaps all this is the instant of my death. Who remembered me, I briefly wonder? A thought that should penetrate and explode but doesn't, not yet.

'Algie?'

'What's that? Yes, Percy, my boy?'

'Where's Bessie?'

'What's that now?'

We all look at the spot where Bessie should be sitting.

'Erm. I don't know, my boy. She was here… wasn't she?'

'Do you think she's gone to meet someone?' Clara asks. 'Someone new?'

'Like when you came to meet me, Mumsy?' asks my grandma.

'Yes!' Clara's excitement is palpable.

'Someone new!' cries my grandma. Both women and Algie are bouncing in anticipation. I feel a surge of excitement rise in me, but then I look at Percy. And he looks at me.

'That can't be right though, can it?' I ask him.

'No. No, I don't see how,' he replies.

The others look at us and all fall silent.

'What do you mean? Why can't that be right?' Clara asks us, a hint of concern creeping in behind her fading smile.

'Because I'm here,' I say. 'And Bessie died long before I was born—'

'I don't follow you,' Algie cuts in. But I can tell that the others do.

'Oh,' my grandma begins, 'yes, I see now.'

'Who would she be meeting?' Percy explains. 'I mean, it's not impossible. What year was it when you died?' he asks me.

I have no idea, I realise. But Percy doesn't wait for an answer in any case.

'They'd have to be in their nineties, I think.'

'Well, that's doable! I lived into my nineties,' Algie offers, with some of the excitement returning.

'Yes,' begins Clara. 'But who would it be, Pops? There's nobody I can think of.'

'Well, now. Don't be too hasty, let me ponder this for minute or two, will you?' Algie sits back and begins to think. I almost laugh out loud as he does so. I've never seen such a visual expression of someone deep in thought. It's as though I can actually see his brain cells firing.

'Could there be any other reason for her absence?' I ask. 'Do any of you remember anyone ever leaving this compartment before for any other reason?'

'Didn't you?' Clara asks. 'Something to do with marshmallows?'

I look at her blankly.

'Alright, I have it!' Algie exclaims. 'She's moved compartments.' He folds his arms in triumph, awaiting his plaudits.

'Sorry?' says Percy.

'You remember, my boy. We move compartments as and when more people arriv... oh. No, wait, that doesn't make sense either then, does it?'

'Perhaps she's gone to the seaside?' Clara says.

I watch a solitary tear run down her cheek and wonder what it is. What it's made of. I think about Bessie; her smile that keeps us all safe. Who will keep us safe now? There is a train, in the middle of nowhere, amidst the endless blackness of a forever night. Ordinarily it speeds along, although I have never known it to. I have only known this one room, this unscheduled stop. The blackness of a night that isn't really night at all. But now this. A change. Bessie is gone. There are only five now, and the Unremembered, of course.

'The seaside?' asks Algie.

'Perhaps she's worked it out, Pops. That puzzle of hers.'

CLARA

There was a time, some years after her mother's death but before she had to make the decision to put him into a residential home, when Clara's father was truly happy. She believes that not just because she wants or needs to, but because it's true. None of them ever fully recovered from Bessie's death, certainly not her Pops. But they found a way, together, to be happy again.

Clara became the matriarch. A role she'd never imagined herself playing. She became the hostess; the lighthouse guiding her ships back home. Not just for her father but in time, for Annie and Billy as well. And then much later, for Charlie and his family.

But that is yet to be. Lifetimes lie between these markers and here and now, in this memory, it's Christmas Day. The orange sun and the crescent moon share the sky above and all is well. Percy and Annie have decorated the customary oversized tree and her Pops is regaling them all with tall tales around the fireplace.

'And do you know what happened then? She kicked me! Hard. In the posterior. I wailed like a banshee, and she said to me: "if I ever hear you using language like that in my house again, I'll cut out your tongue with a pair scissors, cook it in a stew and feed it back to you".'

'Oh, Pops, I'm sure she didn't say she'd cut out your tongue!'

'What's that? Ha! The Snarling Tigress wouldn't have hesitated, let me tell you, my girl. God rest her soul.'

'So, wait,' said Annie. 'Napoleon lived in your village?'

Algie chuckles at his granddaughter's question. 'Not that one,' he assures her.

'Well,' Annie continues, 'I think your mother sounds like a bit of an ogre.'

'Now, Annie—' begins Percy, but Algie interrupts.

'That's your great-grandmother, remember. And ogre doesn't cover it. She was a hellcat!'

Clara watches on as her family huddles around the fire. She knows why this day is in the final reel. This is her time.

She remembers how she felt this day and the significance of it. It's difficult to say, or even think, but the presence of this memory is important. You see, when you are the daughter of a woman like Bessie, it's impossible not to remain in her shadow, to some extent. An enlightened woman in unenlightened times. A smile that made the whole world feel safe. But a restlessness as well. A sense of chances lost and sacrifices made. Sacrifices Clara was never trusted with. Her mother never confided in her, not really. But she did expect of her. She expected her not to make those same sacrifices. It was always very confusing. And the difficult truth is that after she passed away, and once the grief had stabilised, that confusion lifted. That restlessness calmed. And another thing; the guilt. Clara only realised that she'd felt guilty once that guilt disappeared. She loved her mother so completely, so unconditionally, but it was a heavy love. She knew that her mother could and should have been someone else. That she never really had *her* time.

With understanding comes peace. Not a revelatory peace; a slow and lasting acknowledgement and contentment. Unlike her mother, this was all Clara really wanted. She had seen something of the world, lived something of the high life, and then… she settled. Not for second best; this was no compromise, not at all. To her mind, it was all about gratitude. Such a powerful word. She'd looked at her lot in life and been overcome with a profound satisfaction. An understanding that the future had arrived. That life, the one she had been waiting for, was in fact happening now. She was in it. The past and the future are constructs; imaginings. The present is all that matters. And at present, in this memory from so, so long ago, she loves and is loved.

The feast is bountiful. She doesn't make gravy quite like her mother, but Percy says it's the finest he's ever tasted. Gifts unwrapped, tankards and lipsticks, knickknacks and delicate trinkets. Parlour games and nutcrackers. A perfect world full of joy and family. Her family, together and strong. Clara thinks to herself that if this scene were to last for all eternity, that would be fine.

Later, as Algie snores, stuffed Dropsy forever standing guard beside him, and Percy does the dishes, Clara and her daughter are alone.

'Mumsy, I've something to discuss with you.'

'Yes, I thought you might have, my love.'

Annie glances at her mother and the smile they share holds all the words they do not say.

'He's asked me and I think I want to say yes.'

'You think?'

'I mean, I know I do. I just want to… I mean, I can't very well say yes without talking to you, dearest. Well, can I?!'

'Certainly not!'

And so, they talk. For the love between Clara and

her daughter is not a heavy love. It's complete and unconditional, and uncomplicated and nurturing. They share everything, always, and on this day, in this memory, Clara tells her daughter to go with not just her heart, but also her head. Love should not be a sacrifice, she tells her. Compromises must, of course, be made along the way, but in the end, love should be a completion. A puzzle solved. Yes, this was Clara's time and she was so grateful for it. And she was brilliant.

TWENTY-SIX

'Oh, Pops! Will you please sit down?!'

Algie is pacing up and down the compartment, wringing his hands and muttering incoherently. 'What's that now? Oh, yes. Alright, my girl.' He rests on the edge of his seat for a second and then stands again and resumes pacing. 'But what if someone, or something, has taken her?'

'What on Earth are you talking about?' pleads Clara.

'Well, that's just it, isn't it? We aren't on Earth, are we? So, what if all your mother's talk of escape and puzzles and whatnot, what if it's got her into trouble? Why did she always have to be so dashed enlightened?'

'Isn't it more likely that Clara's right?' suggests Percy. 'That she's solved her puzzle? That she's escaped?'

Algie ponders this for a moment. 'No. She wouldn't have left us here. She wouldn't have left Clara.'

'Well,' begins my grandma. 'Mumsy has been saying quite clearly that she doesn't want to leave, hasn't she?'

'What's that?'

'I mean, it's true, Mumsy, isn't it?'

'Yes, my love. It is true, Pops. I've no wish to escape and I've said as much. So, perhaps… oh, I don't know.'

Algie finally sits down. His daughter holds his hand tightly and he calms. Clara then reaches across and takes my grandma's hand in her other.

'It will all be alright. This is Mother we're talking about. She has plans, we know it, and we will understand as soon as she needs us to. So, until then, we do what we've always done, alright? We stick together.'

She smiles and I sense that both Algie and my grandma feel safe.

I look at Clara and see that something is different. There is a gravitas about her that hasn't been there until now. Handsome and angular, the star in a silent movie or a beautiful stranger staring back at you in a black and white photograph from the 1920s. Yes, she's still all that, I suppose, but something else as well. A thousand other things. She gives Percy a knowing nod that alludes to an understanding so deep and intuitive that I almost shed a tear at the completeness of their partnership. They are as one.

'Besides,' Percy begins, 'I'd doubt there's anything or anyone in heaven or Earth that could *take* our Bessie anywhere she didn't want to go.'

A knowing chuckle ripples around the compartment. Even I feel the truth in his words. Bessie has not left us, or been taken against her will. She will return and we will become. I don't know what that means yet, I don't think any of us do, but I sense that we're all thinking essentially the same thing. Bessie has plans, we are a part of them, and they are happening now.

ANNIE

The pink sunset is a radiant strip along the horizon, above the ghostly silver ocean that mirrors the sky above. Jagged rocky cliffs, torn by time, are contrasted against the lush green, daisy-strewn grass upon which they sit. Young lovers at the very beginning of an adventure.

Two adventures, as it happens. This one and life itself. This is day five of what will be in the region of sixty days spent on this path. Reality paused so that a fairy tale can play out. Packs on their backs and blisters on their feet. Trailblazers; literally. They are ahead of their time and young enough for time to be of no consequence.

'What will it be like?' Annie asks.

'What will what will be like?' Billy replies.

'Our life.'

'Like this, I should think.'

'Oh, I do hope so.'

From this cliff edge Annie feels as though they are the only two people alive in an empty and beautiful world. The pink strip is darkening to cherry red. It's funny, she thinks, life was so long and she's forgotten so much. But she remembers every step of this adventure, not just this moment. The forever summer, with the most handsome man in the world. Twisted ankles and insect bites, rain-soaked climbs and sun-kissed sandy beaches. Drama and tranquillity, laughter and aching limbs. The endless vistas; the scale of it all. So much space, so much time. The burning embers of youth, the end of a chapter, signed off with a flourish. And the beginning of a new one. It's all in this memory, she supposes. Superimposed in retrospect.

A memory built from memories. So many nights they'd reminisce, adding the knowledge of what came next to the original adventure. Finding new meaning, rewriting and reimagining. An origin tale. Where love is born and a partnership forged on the rolling waves and the inescapable horizon.

For a moment, Annie considers staying here. No more go-rounds, no more threadbare blues, just this. Him and her walking on the very edge of everything, toward a sunset they never reach. But it's too much, isn't it? Annie is not her grandmother, or her mother for that matter. Life is not a postcard. This is one moment of many. And it's fun, she remembers. This adventure really was tremendous fun.

'Hey, watch this!' Billy calls. He tears off a corner of his sandwich and holds it in the hand of his outstretched arm. The gull that's been circling the fading blue sky above them dives and grabs the offering in its beak in one seamless manoeuvre. Billy turns to her, his eyes wild with shocked delight. They laugh a laughter free from the burden of retrospect.

'Those things fly better than the Hawker Hunters!'

'My turn,' Annie exclaims.

She tears a piece from the sandwich and holds it out. The gull dives again, but this time he comes to a stop, perched on her arm and stays there as he eats. Annie and Billy are both catatonic. The gull swallows and stares deep into Annie's eyes. It cocks its head slightly. For a second, she thinks it might attack her; peck at her face as if in some ghastly horror novel. But it just stares with its beady black eyes.

'Billy,' she whispers. 'The camera.'

'Already doing,' he whispers back. But it's too late. Having realised no more morsels are coming, the gull flies away with flapping wings that bring momentary chaos to the world.

Annie and Billy look at each for a second or two and then collapse into fits of laughter.

'You've got the knack!' Billy cries.

Annie holds out her arm towards him and he rests his smiling head on it, as though perching. She feeds him a piece of sandwich. He eats it, stares at her and then pretends to peck at her face.

The sun dips behind the ocean and their world turns an ethereal grey. Tomorrow, they will build a sandcastle and Annie will attempt to carry Billy over its tiny threshold. And they'll laugh. They'll meet an old and wizened Cornish fisherman and ask him for directions to a tea-shop. He'll be wearing a threadbare blue jumper, and trousers tied up with string. And they'll both nod along appreciatively as he answers. Then, as they walk away, Billy will turn to Annie and ask, 'Did you understand any of that?'

'Not a word,' she'll reply. And they'll laugh. It will rain and the wind will howl but then, by the evening, all will be calm and dry. They'll sit on the daisy-strewn grass, several miles from here, and look out at the pink sunset above the silver ocean. They'll talk of things to come and the days already behind them. And they'll laugh. But all of that is tomorrow and, as Annie knows, it's a tomorrow that has already come and won't come again now. And that's fine, isn't it?

And then the mourners. So young and raw. The pregnant swirling clouds above us unleash and never really stop. Mingling with hot salty tears. *I want her back*, I think to myself, as I stand there in my ill-fitting suit; I want my grandma back. My brother places a caring hand on my shoulder and I wipe the tears away with the back of my hand.

'Who are all these people?' I ask him as we stand in the grey lifeless morning of a world that will never be the same again. We're stood outside the crematorium, waiting for the previous mourners to leave. A timeslot for our grief.

'Don't know,' he begins. 'Look, here they are.' He nudges me and I turn my head to see my grandad, my dad and my stepmum walking sombrely towards us. *There's a strange smell to this place*, I think to myself. I can't be sure if I've added it to the memory or if it was really there that day. Pungent and unnatural, a gas leak? They don't usually cry, my father and grandfather. They aren't unemotional men, per se. They're kind and giving and honest and they radiate a pure and uncomplicated love for their family. They just, don't really cry. That makes it even harder, doesn't it? When you see them in tears? When you see them fighting them back, losing and collapsing into sobs. Puffy red eyes and a sadness so hopeless that it sucks all the air from the world. There is nothing in this life, or any other, as truly awful as seeing the people you love weeping, I don't think. Only grief itself comes close. But that's your pain, isn't it? Your loss. Theirs is always worse.

I'm struck by a thought. What will my funeral be like? Or, what was it like? One thing I never got to see was the tears of a parent burying their child. I suppose I should be thankful for that, but I'm not. I think of Ela then. Of the strength she'd have to have found. She was always the stronger of us. She was always the man of the house. Enlightened in enlightened times. But this? To explain it to our daughter, to push aside her own grief and keep our Annie safe from this moment. From these mourners. I snap myself out of it.

'Hey, Pops.'

I call my dad Pops. Strange, isn't it? Family. Round and round we go.

'You OK, my boys?' He gently cups his hands beneath our chins. 'Heads high. She's watching.'

My stepmum smiles warmly and squeezes his arm.

'You OK, Grandad?' I ask.

He looks at me and smiles a smile that will stay with me far beyond this life. A smile where love and sadness merge and are as one. I put my arm around him and, together, we walk.

The speakers are tinny and old. The service is ordinary and lost in time. It's difficult for them, I suppose. The people who organise our mourning. How can you ever do justice to a life with words? Besides, I don't really hear anything said. My brother puts his arm around me and we both weep. I can't take my eyes from the coffin. It's so small and yet it contains so much. So many years. Its cargo is so precious, so fundamentally essential and important. I watch as, in front of me, my father bows his head, his shoulders silently heaving. I reach out my arm and rest my hand on his shoulder.

'Head high, Pops,' I whisper. He holds my hand tight then and the love and pain we feel flows between us, through us. We share it.

Later, once our allotted time has passed and our diminished ranks are leaving this strange and quietly terrible place, I spot my grandad talking to his sister, Mary. As I make my way over to him, they embrace, she departs and he is momentarily alone. A gull lands on the wall beside him and, for some reason, I stop. The sorrowful din coming from the mourners that separate us fades into static. Like losing reception on a radio that's quietly playing in another room of the house. The air thickens. I watch as my grandad holds out his arm to the bird. It cocks its head at him, appraising him with its beady black eyes. Then, with a chaos-inducing flap of its wings, it's gone. And he's alone. I carry on walking toward him and the static clears. But he remains frozen in that spot, lost in thought and staring at the place where the gull once was.

TWENTY-SEVEN

'Now then. The pier is a great long thing, isn't it? Let's say, what, one thousand feet? Ornate and a touch frilly. Oh yes, and those rather grand art deco entrance kiosks, I remember. But wait, is that right? Or is that too late? A band must play, of course. And chairs must line up on the decking for the ladies who tea.'

She remembers that the sky is a cornflower blue; a summer's day in mid-July. Almost cloudless, except for a few fluffy cumuli slouching lazily above the horizon. The sun is crayon yellow and, although she resists it, it may as well have a smiling face. Hip-hip-hip-hip-hooray. The beach is smooth with pebbles of pastel reds and browns and greys. Fossils and rock pools and other signs of life. There is a strip of yellow sand, doubtless carried here from some faraway place, and laid like turf. Sandcastles and wooden kiosks that sell cockles and eels and ice creams and anything, really. There must be room for them all to choose for themselves, she supposes. To some extent, at least. And shells, of course. There must be augers and banded wedges, limpets and oysters, periwinkles and piddocks. And they must all sound like the sea, mustn't they? And what of the sea, then? That great lumbering beast. It must be blue and silver, gentle and alive. It must dance and sparkle and snooze beneath the crayon-yellow midday sun. Gulls! There must be gulls. Endless squawking monsters that prowl and bob with beady black eyes and wings of chaos. What other birds? Do sparrows visit the seaside? Or robins?

This will take time, she thinks. All the time there ever was, perhaps. There is so much to remember and so much she can get wrong. There are moments when she doubts herself. She thinks of Clara's words: 'floating by over and over again as we sit and talk and laugh. What is it you find so lacking in that, Mother dearest?'

And she doubts her plans. But then she remembers that this will work, it will, it will, it will. Because this isn't just for her. It's selfish, yes, but not only that. She must smile and make them all feel safe, just this one last time and then… all this will be theirs.

PERCY

Percy sits on the wooden bench in their pretty garden, shelling peas into the wooden bowl he carved himself a thousand lifetimes earlier. He's wearing a suit and tie because, well, because he always wears a suit and tie on a Sunday. And this is the most Sunday of all Sundays. The quintessential Sunday, you might say. Clara and he attended church in the morning, as they always do, and now she was stood in their modern lime green Formica kitchen peeling and basting and whatever else it is she does in there. It was all something of a mystery to him. But he could shell, oh yes, he could shell. Percy loves nothing more than a good ritual. He fills the twilight years of a life that seems both exhaustingly long and to have passed by in the blink of an eye, with rituals. Reliable markers that keep the chaos at bay. And on a Sunday morning, after church, he sits on the same wooden bench and shells peas into the same wooden bowl.

He turns and smiles at Clara, who's smiling sweetly back at him through the kitchen window, just as she always is. Annie and Billy and young Charlie will be arriving in a while to share in the bountiful Sunday roast. *Sometimes*, Percy thinks, *memories aren't about anything in particular, are they? They aren't remembering an event but rather a sense. A feeling.*

A sparrow sits atop the neatly preened hedge that separates the garden from the lane. It sings its solitary song, as though it were performing especially for Percy. The air is thick with evocative smells. Honeysuckle, cut grass and orange marmalade. There are flowers, nestled in their springtime beds, quietly bursting with vibrant pinks and yellows. And ugly cherry red lotus flowers.

'Should they be there?' Percy wonders out loud, but then he forgets. Because this is a memory about a feeling. He can't remember the church service or the dinner he'll soon share with those he loves more than words can express. They pulse and fade into one warm and happy vision. But he remembers this moment, although nothing happens. He has seen both too much and nowhere near enough. He has won and he has lost. Yet, in the end, and the end isn't too far away now, he knows that he has won. He knows this because of this very moment and this is why it makes the final reel. The feeling he feels, that sits alongside love and happiness and warmth and familiarity, is contentment. Such an ordinary sounding word. So easy to mistake it for something lesser than it is. But Percy is old enough to understand that contentment is the biggest and most beautiful word in the whole world. It is the only word, or rather the only feeling, that carries peace and love and all those other things, in its outstretched arms. Perhaps gratitude comes close, but for Percy it isn't quite the same thing. One can be grateful and not content, after all. Contentment is the absolute, as far as he's concerned.

He nicks his finger with the old pocket knife that's travelled the world with him, across oceans and over mud and mangled remains. He watches as a small spot of ugly cherry red appears on his fingertip.

'Should that be there?' he wonders out loud, but then he forgets. He thinks of Clara, the strong and handsome girl, the beautiful and intelligent woman, the fierce and loyal matriarch. He thinks of how much more a partnership can be than the sum of its parts. Without her, he is a broken thing. Officious, upright and starched. Troubled, weakened and skin deep. But with her, and because of her, he is a husband, a father and a grandfather. He is selfless and strong and loyal and compassionate. And then he thinks of Annie, his kind and courageous Annie. The light that shines the way. The proof of a life lived well. Because life isn't a series of moments, not at all. It's an accumulation of decisions and mistakes and the kindness and cruelties you show to others.

'How are those peas coming along, my love?'

'Almost there, my darling wife.'

A long and bumpy road full of magic and loss. And it comes to this: contentment. Such a big word.

How I love you all, Percy thinks.

Far away, in another time and place, Percy remembers his mother and father and all his brothers and sisters, for there were many. Seated together around the family table on a quiet Sunday afternoon, much like this one. The room is dappled in sunlight. Warm rays filled with swirling dust. Heads bowed in prayer; be thankful for all we are about to receive.

'And dear Lord, please watch over our Percy. Please keep him safe from all the horrors he faces in that place. Please return him to us so that we can be complete once again. And if that cannot be, then please keep him with you and allow him a long and happy life. Please give him contentment as we give you our eternal gratitude. Amen.'

The cancer that kills Percy is already inside him at this point. He didn't know that at the time, but he realises now, here, in this memory. He finds, much to his relief, that it makes no difference. His contentment is unimpeded by any knowledge of what's to come. It remains absolute. Although, absolute isn't the same as infinite, of course. He takes a deep breath, inhales the fresh spring. He looks at the wooden bowl, full of vibrant green peas, and he smiles. He gets to his feet, with creaking bones and painful echoes, and slowly walks through their pretty garden, to find his wife. His Clara.

'This isn't the last. But it's not far off. And then, I suppose, we'll do this all again, won't we? You and I. Perhaps, my love… perhaps your mother is right, after all. Perhaps there is another way? We were beautiful then. Perhaps we can be again, in some new place and some new memory?'

He doesn't understand these thoughts and he doesn't say them out loud to his Clara. Because, of course, this isn't his Clara.

TWENTY-EIGHT

'Well, yes, but they aren't really telephones. Not as you remember them. They're miniature computers that are small enough to carry around.'

'Like pocket calculators?' asks Percy.

'Yes, a bit.'

'You remember them, don't you, Algie?'

'Oh, yes. I saw much of the New Age, Percy, my boy.'

We're trying to distract Algie from the absence of his wife. It's proving less difficult that I'd assumed.

'So, you're saying that, in the future, everyone carries pocket calculators around with them?'

'Well…'

'And that these calculators can also make phone calls?'

'Yes, I suppose so. But their primary purpose is to give you connection to the internet.'

Blank faces.

'Which is, erm, well. As I tried to explain before, it's kind of a network that connects together all the computers in the world and enables them to share information with each other.'

Blank faces.

'Like a giant and ever-expanding library of information. Everything that's ever been written, theorised, filmed, painted, discussed or dreamt of is accessible via the device in your pocket. And you can connect with anyone and everyone in the world.'

'Fascinating,' says Percy.

'Amazing,' says Algie.

'How utterly appalling,' says Clara.

We all turn to look at her.

'How cheap and wonderless the future sounds.'

'I think you're missing the point a little, my girl,' replies Algie, with more than a touch of condescension.

'Is that what brought about the end of the New Age?' asks Clara, ignoring her father.

I think about this. 'Maybe. That and a series of existential threats and our collective inability to respond to them.'

'So, mankind is now, what? Wallowing without direction? Sat staring at screens, basking in its own past glories, incapable of anything more than nostalgia and self-congratulation... or self-pity?'

'Kind of.'

If Bessie were here, she'd doubtless offer a retort along the lines of: 'Does that sound familiar to anyone?' But, as she isn't, she doesn't.

'Come, come,' interjects Algie. 'What rot is this? What of equality and peace? What of knowledge as strength and education for all? What a great leveller this Inner-net must be?'

'Well, it is whatever we make of it, I suppose. I'm

of a generation that remembers life before and after its invention. As such, I guess I'm well placed to see the good and the bad of it—'

'And I'm of a generation who sees it for what it is,' cuts in my grandma. 'A lot of silly fuss about nothing.'

I'm taken aback by this at first and then find myself smiling broadly at how very *my grandma* it is.

She continues, 'We already had libraries, if you remember? And we could already talk to anyone around the world, couldn't we? It's all just an excuse for being lazy, if you ask me. We are being infantilised.'

'Well, I mean, there's certainly some truth in that, but then the potential it has to do good is really quite staggering,' I offer, somewhat half-heartedly.

'And what does humankind use that potential for?' my grandma asks, rhetorically. 'I'll tell you: to be nasty to each other and watch filth.'

'Filth?' enquires Algie.

'Filth!' confirms my grandma.

Everyone looks at me, the defender of the future. The internet's last hope.

'I've got nothing,' I say.

'So, let me get this straight,' begins Algie. 'Beyond the New Age, the world is dying, everyone is arguing and watching... *filth*?' He glances at my grandma for confirmation and she nods. 'Filth... on their pocket calculators, and there are *no* flying cars?'

'I'm afraid so.'

Algie puffs out his cheeks and theatrically leans back on his seat. 'Well, I mean to say. It's difficult for a chap not to get a case of the morbs, isn't it?'

ALGIE

Algie stands at the bottom of the wooden staircase. He looks down at Dropsy and meets his lifeless glassy stare, then looks back up at the door to the bedroom. His daughter and son-in-law's words ring in his ears once more.

'You can't put it off forever, Pops. If you won't let us do it, or even help, then you have to do it yourself. It's too morbid; all just sat there gathering dust.'

'She's right, Algie. It's time, old chap.'

Bunch of poppycock, if you ask Algie. Which, apparently, no one intended to. Still, he had been avoiding it, no doubt about that. Why wouldn't you avoid such a thing? It's not the sort of task one sets about doing with relish, is it? He tentatively takes the first stair, and then the second.

'Hang on,' he says out loud before retreating from the staircase, 'you needn't think you're getting out of it, my boy.' He picks up the ever-ready Dropsy and places him under his arm. Together they climb the wooden creaking stairs and push open the door that has remained closed for too long. Algie has been sleeping, when sleep has been possible, in the bedroom that was once his daughter's, wearing only the clothes that were left hanging on the washing line. What an eerie sight that had been. As though she'd be back at any moment, carrying the old wicker laundry basket in her arms. That had been the first of many tasks he'd carried out alone for the first time. The strangeness of loss was, in his mind, almost as dislocating as the pain of it.

And it had been strange, hadn't it? Why the seaside? Why had she insisted that only he be there at the end? It was as though she'd meant to tell him something. But she hadn't. She just… slipped away. And the secrecy. How long had she suffered in silence? Carrying on as though nothing was wrong, as if she wasn't… the whole thing was bizarre. A puzzle with a missing piece.

He gently places Dropsy on the rug beside him and surveys the room. Where once there had been… what, love? Yes, he believes she had loved him. And his love for her was…

'I say, would you like a game of I spy?'

Bessie laughs at this and as she does – in that very moment – Algie falls in love. And from that very moment until the very moment he dies, he will always love Bessie. And then, after the very moment he dies, he will go on loving Bessie, forever and ever. Never for a single second, in this life or the next, will his love falter. From that very moment onwards, the darkness will never again smother the light.

…everything.

He smiles then. A small and complicated smile that holds a lifetime spent with the one you love.

'Right then, let's get the thing done, shall we, my sweet?'

And so, he does. He folds things, empties things and piles things up. Separates, wraps up and casts aside. Lipsticks, knickknacks and delicate trinkets. And then, as he was always destined to do, he comes across the letters. The letters hidden in drawers. Desperate declarations sprawled in spidery ink.

Algie has always known. It's important to clarify that, I think. From the very beginning, when he found her in tears by the graveside of his dead fiancée. But then, knowing something and acknowledging it to oneself, aren't the same thing at all. And as has already been said, melancholy didn't suit Algie. Life was a rich pageant of possibility, after all. As he reads the letters now though, the faded pen strokes of the lost, all that lies buried in him is unleashed. More feelings than he had thought it possible to have, all exploding in his belly at once. To his surprise, chief among them is guilt. He assumed it would be sadness, betrayal or even anger. *I'd rather it was sadness*, he thinks to himself. A simple and passive sadness would be something he could cope with. But not this. Not guilt. For all her enlightenment, for all her strength and brilliance, was she no more than a caged bird? For all his clumsy good intent, for all his pure and simple love, was he no more than her jailor?

That Algie didn't realise these letters weren't from Effie doesn't really matter. In fact, if anything, it's probably better that way. He tries to remember Effie, but cannot. They had the same eyes, he remembers that. But he never really knew her, nor she him. Only Bessie really knew him. The light and the dark and all the grey spaces in between. What is love, if not that? Knowing every dusty corner of a soul and staying with them anyway. He thinks of his father then.

'*Life isn't too complicated if you've got your wits about you.*' Poor old Pater. Algie wasn't sure he'd been right, in the end.

In another box, Algie finds the rubbings. *Here lies Mary Upcott. Born 1723, fell asleep 1787.* He vaguely remembers these. From some faraway place in his memories. A hidden drawer of a different kind. There are piles of them here. Names and lives forgotten; the unremembered. As though his wife had been collecting them in an attempt to save them from the fragility of memory. He looks at each one of them but really, they're just names to him. Less even. Just words. They hold nothing of the souls they commemorate, nothing at all.

And then he sees it. *Here lies Jack Algie Knighton, forever our baby boy.* His tears are silent at first. Great droplets that fall onto the paper and mix with the marks once made by Jack's mother. And then he sobs. For all that has been lost. Bessie and Jack and Dropsy. Mater and Pater and even Leopold. *Life is far too long*, he thinks. *And far too short to be doing this alone.*

He takes the letters and the rubbings, picks up Dropsy, and leaves the room, closing the door behind him. Perhaps he burns them all on the fire that glows a nostalgic orange. Or, perhaps not. Perhaps he keeps them in the belief that one day, in some other time and place, he will be able to return them to his wife.

Later he will tell Clara and Percy that they will need to finish sorting out the room without him. What he doesn't tell them, and what they will never know, is that he will not go in there again, from this day until the day he dies.

TWENTY-NINE

The houses lining up behind the promenade and looking out across the ocean of blue and silver must be perfect. Brick for brick, they must be the homes they all know, reassembled in this new place. She will leave hers until last, for it is something beyond the physical and she doesn't think she can do it alone. But really, the others should be easy, shouldn't they?

Clara and Percy's must smell of honeysuckle, cut grass and orange marmalade. With neatly preened hedges where sparrows sing, and flowers bursting with pinks and yellows. And that ghastly green kitchen of theirs, that she can never have seen, she supposes. She smiles at this realisation and all that it means, and the house nestles into place.

And what of Algie? Should she assume he'll still think of that old house of theirs as home, once all this is done? It's quite an assumption to make. She thinks on this. She knows Algie, the light and the dark and all the grey spaces in between. The warm orange glow of the fire, where he and Dropsy sit. The wooden staircase and the rosebush in the garden. *But not the bedroom*, she thinks. He won't want the bedroom anymore. And so, their old house, minus the bedroom, nestles into place.

As for Annie, Bessie has never seen the home she built with her husband, of course. Not even in shared memories on a train going nowhere. So, she will leave it to her to fill in the details. A welcoming canvas to be painted as her granddaughter sees fit. And the makings of the house nestle into place.

Now then, what of her great-great-grandson? That visitor from beyond the New Age. That is more complicated because she senses he may not be alone. A story as yet unfinished. She sees much of herself in him. That pleases her. She doesn't give any credence to blood. Ugly cherry red. So, it makes her happy to think that something of her has survived in the attitude and teachings of those she left behind. And those that they left behind. This man, who she never met and who lived in a world far beyond her understanding, who carries something of her in his outlook. Yes, it pleases her. And so, she creates something new for him. Using all that binds them to guide her, all that they share that reaches across lifetimes and dreams. And as the house nestles into place, she smiles.

Will there be others? Yes, she thinks there will be. The train has many compartments with lives that were once connected. She will leave them room. Space to find this new thing. Guests as well, she supposes. Word will travel, after all. She realises something then, perhaps for the first time, although it seems obvious now. There will be, can be, no memories here. No affectations of those who once were, seen only through the eyes of those who remember. All who call this place home must be originals. This, too, pleases her and with a deft flick of her thoughts, several more houses nestle into place.

It's beginning to take shape, isn't it? And then she must find them, all of them, and bring them home.

They must all go to the place where we will be.

CLARA

The house is full of life. *As a house should be*, Clara thinks. She knows in her heart that, before too long now, it will be as quiet as her own thoughts. But not yet. Not in this memory.

'Billy, where's that television?' she calls.

'On its way.'

Young Charlie, who really isn't all that young anymore, she supposes, sits beside Percy's bed in the makeshift bedroom. How long does a space have to function in a certain way before you can no longer reasonably refer to it as makeshift? Perhaps this will always be Percy's bedroom now. Forever and ever.

He is diminished, her love. The cancer has taken so much of him from her already. He always had those burdened hazel eyes, of course. As though they somehow saw this coming. He looks so withered, so many years older than he is. Gaunt and discoloured… frail. Yes, that's it. That's the worst of it, isn't it? Her husband is many things, but never frail. How cruel that is. Let there be no misunderstanding, her love for him is undiminished. When she fell, she fell completely and with absolute abandon. In fact, she's never stopped falling. Even now, he amazes her. Sweeps her off her feet. He's spinning his grandson the same yarns that the boy's been asking his grandad for his whole life. A soldier's tales. But they're still as though new and Charlie is as spellbound as he always was.

Annie is in the kitchen making the tea. Clara can see that she's already becoming the matriarch. She wonders if she'll live to see that. If she'll meet Charlie's wife and children. There are moments when it's all too fast; the dizzying cycle of their lives. When it feels as though she's only just begun. She's heard it said so many times that life speeds up the older you get. A sentiment as cliched as the realisation that it's true. Hadn't she read something about it once? It's all to do with memory. You remember your youth in more detail because you're experiencing things for the first time; the endless summers, the gayest parties and all the love and laughter. It's brand new, so your memory captures it with vIvid clarity. Then, as you get older and settle into the inevitable routines of life, your memories too become routine. Repetition blurs events into one unchanging period of time. The details of an unremarkable day aren't required and so aren't saved. So, when we look back over our lives, at those captured reels, time seems so much slower and more detailed when we're young and so fast and formless when we're older.

How strange, Clara thinks, *that it's our memories in charge of us. Slaves to the things we remember and the things we forget.*

There is an empty chair in the room, of course. Where her father should be sitting. Sometimes it feels as though there's an empty space in every room. A sensation that began when her mother passed away, many lifetimes ago now, it seems. And the space is so much larger now. And will soon be larger still, she realises. It won't be all that long before she herself is part of the space. A ratio of life and loss that can only move in one direction. How like them both she is, and yet how different they were.

'Right then, here we are.' Billy wheels the television set into the room, wires trailing in his wake. 'Just give me a few minutes and we'll have it all set up.'

'How exciting!' exclaims Annie, entering the room, laden with a tray of teas.

'Why haven't you used the teapot, Annie dearest?' Clara asks.

'Oh, Mumsy, nobody uses a teapot these days.'

'How cheap and wonderless the future is,' Clara says, but she's smiling at her daughter as she speaks.

'What does it look like when someone dies, Grandad?'

'Oh, Charlie! That's enough of that, thank you very much. Now leave your grandad alone and watch the television.'

Charlie looks at his grandad, who winks at him, then turns towards the television that displays only static and white noise.

'That should do it,' says Billy in triumph, as the picture flickers into life.

'Is that Cliff Mitchelmore?' asks Annie.

'No, that's James Burke,' replies Billy.

'Oh dear, I thought it was going to be Cliff Mitchelmore?'

'I'm sure he'll be there as well, my love.'

'Oh good! I do like Cliff Mitchelmore.'

'Will you please stop saying Cliff Mitchelmore, Annie dearest, and sit down? You'll give me a headache,' Clara enquires pleadingly. Her daughter perches on a chair next to Billy, and Clara moves to stand beside her husband. She clasps his hand in hers and smiles down at him with those thin and shapely lips.

'What about this then, my love?' he says, smiling back at her.

She feels herself wanting to cry but instead simply squeezes his hand a bit tighter. Beyond the window, the summer day is dawning. They hadn't stayed up all night, as many had. They were early risers anyway, so had simply set their alarms. There were rumours that the men wouldn't venture out straight away, that they were scheduled to sleep first. But Percy had said that this was nonsense.

'Could you sleep in those circumstances? No, mark my words, my sweet, they'll be straight out to explore.' And he was right.

'*There is Armstrong,*' the clipped tones announce, and the room falls silent. The family stares at the screen, totally rapt. '*There he is putting his foot out.*'

'My goodness,' says Percy. 'Look at that.'

Clara thinks of memories again. *This is certainly something new, I hope you're recording this*, she thinks.

'I'm going to be an astronaut,' announces Charlie.

'I should think so too,' replies Billy, smiling affectionately at his son. 'You'll be landing on Pluto in a few years, my lad.'

Clara looks at her family. She leans over and kisses her husband on the lips. *You are my moon and stars*, she thinks. Each of you. *Life is a series of moments*, she says to herself. And some moments are worth more than others. Frail or not, her husband is here with her to share in this one. She realises that, were he not, this would mean so much less to her. This event, like no other, is only so great and significant to her personally because she's able to share it with him. That's really something, isn't it? To have lived your life with a person who makes the world a better place. No, not *the* world, *your* world.

'*It's one small step for man...*'

THIRTY

Time has passed and has not. We have spoken and spoken some more. We have distracted and put at ease and now we have run dry. Hope has left this place. Time has passed. The air is stale now. The conversation has boiled away in the heat of this slow burning fear. Where is she? We all try to rest but it's no longer possible.

Algie sits, then stands and paces; a never-ending and self-unaware ritual where anxiety has taken full control of all other emotions and characteristics. He is only worry now, there is nothing else. Percy and Clara shuffle in their seats. Heads in hands, legs that jiggle uncontrollably. My grandma huffs and puffs beside me as she tries in vain to settle. To be calm is beyond us now. The compartment itself has changed as well. The warm orange glow is now an ugly cherry red. It seeps into us and picks at our remains. Everything about us and our prison cell evokes one thing, points to one thing:

We are left behind.

Characters of a chapter ended. Written out of someone else's story. We are the afterthoughts and we do not feel safe.

I think of Ela and Annie. Of Mum and Dad and my brother. I think of my stepparents and my dear old grandad. It's as though I'm only realising now that I'm the one who's missing. Understanding for the first time that I'm gone whilst they remain. Understanding that this is what it feels like to be gone. To be dead and lost and forgotten and nothing.

To be nothing. Where am I? Is this heaven or hell or the final desperate thoughts of a dying mind? Is this the dream of a lifeless body connected to tubes and machinery? Is this not my story? Am I the whimsy of a woman I never met? Are my memories no more than her flights of fancy? Imaginings from beyond the New Age. And where is she?

'Did you hear that?' Percy asks.

We all strain to listen. The Unremembered is frantic, glitching and writhing in untold agony. Silently screaming at us. And then we hear it. The low rumble of the engine.

'Is that? Is… it is!' my grandma exclaims.

And it is. The engine splutters and coughs and then erupts into life.

'Move,' I mutter. 'Come on, move.'

But we don't. We remain stationary, but where there was silence there is now the constant roar of… hope.

'What does it mean?' Clara asks, when enough time has passed to be certain that we are staying in place.

'It's her. It has to be,' Algie whimpers. 'She's come back for us.'

'There's no way of knowing. But it's something. Something is happening. We aren't forgotten,' says Percy.

Then, all of a sudden, the carriage shakes. We move, not forward but side to side. The scraping of metal, the clunk of machinery. Then stillness. We hold our breath. The engine fires once more and then the sound of movement. The sound of it but not the feel of it.

'Wait,' begins Percy. 'Is it? It's getting quieter.'

We listen as the sound of the engine begins slowly to fade away.

'It's the rest of the train, isn't it?' I ask. 'The rest of the train is driving away and leaving us here.'

'Yes,' says Percy, his hazel eyes frantic now. Darting around the compartment, as if the answer lies in the threadbare blues of this lost place. 'They've unclamped us.'

'No,' cries my grandma. And then the ugly cherry red lights go out. We are in darkness. 'No,' my grandma says again, as a cold rises. A cold like nothing we've known in this place or in life.

I start to shiver as Algie starts to sob.

ANNIE

'Alright, try this,' says Annie, as she walks into the dining room with another jug. She pours a small quantity of the steaming liquid into each of the three mugs and takes a step back. She watches with bated breath as the assembled diners take a sip.

'By Jove, I think you've got it!' cries Algie.

'It's very nice, my sweet,' says Percy.

Annie waits as her mother swirls the liquid around her mouth, as if sampling a fine wine. The tension in the air is palpable.

'Nearly,' Clara declares, with a consolatory smile. 'A touch too fruity.'

Annie walks back into the kitchen, where Billy waits for her, nervously stirring the pot on the stove.

'Well?' he asks.

'Too fruity.' Annie sighs.

'Oh, for heaven's sake.'

'I know, I know. But we're nearly there now, I'm sure of it.'

'It's only gravy, after all. We've been here for hours.'

'Ssshh, they'll hear you. This is important. You know that.'

And it was important. Important enough to be the one thing Annie's grandfather had said he'd like for his birthday.

'There must be something you want, Pops?' Clara had asked.

'To taste Bessie's Sunday roast gravy one more time.'

The request had silenced them all at first. He hadn't spoken of his late wife for a long while and the suddenness of the wish seemed to hint at a quiet and hidden sadness. Annie didn't think of her grandfather as sad or nostalgic. He was Grandpa; jolly and kind with twinkling emerald eyes that hinted at a boyish mischief. Simple and constant. She'd been moved by his request and had overridden her mother on the matter.

'Oh, Pops. I've tried, but it simply isn't possible.'

'I could give it a try?' she'd said, almost without realising she was speaking. And so it began, the day of the great gravy tasting. A day that would become legend and be spoken of at family gatherings forevermore. A tale that would span four generations.

'Perfect as ever, my sweet,' her father would say.

'Perfect as ever, my darling,' Billy would say.

'Perfect as ever, Mum,' her Charlie would say.

'Yes, it really is fantastic, Annie.'

'Oh, thank you, Jennifer, dearest.'

But all that is the future. Today, on this day and this memory, it had turned into something else, hadn't it? Something more. In truth, her grandfather had declared it a triumph on the second attempt. Percy and Billy had long since lost interest. It was all about her and her mother now, wasn't it? For her mother to declare her efforts successful would mean the passing of something from one woman to the other. Annie both understood and didn't, not fully at any rate.

'Alright, try this one… I really think it's there this time.'

'That's it! That's the one,' exclaims Algie.

'Oh yes, that's it alright,' agrees Percy.

'A touch salty.'

Time melts away and the orange sun is drifting into sleep. Annie is finally ready to concede defeat; Billy already had, several attempts earlier.

'That's it, you're on your own,' he'd said, before kissing her on the cheek and joining the others at the table. He'd then refused to sample any further attempts. 'No, that's me done with gravy for this century, thank you very much. I never want to see another blasted gravy. My world is now totally devoid of the stuff, and all the better for it.'

Then, at the very last, when all hope is lost and the day of the great gravy tasting is set to become a failure, Annie realises what she must do.

'Mumsy, I need you.'

The room falls silent.

'It's the only way. I can't do this without you, but together, I know we'll get it.'

All eyes are on Clara now. Minutes seem to pass in this suspended state.

'Very well. Let's get to it, daughter of mine.'

A collective sigh of relief sounds out.

Mother and daughter chop and sprinkle, strain and stir.

'What do you suppose she'd think of all this, Mumsy?'

'Your grandmother?'

'Yes.'

'What would she think of the two women slaving away in the kitchen all day as the menfolk lounge around waiting to be served?'

They both laugh.

'Yes, I see what you mean. Most unenlightened.'

'She'd probably ask what we were doing in here when we could be flying a hot air balloon.'

'Or swimming the channel.'

They laugh again and embrace, beside the steaming pot of gravy, in the kitchen of a home far, far from the sea. This is the memory, of course. The connection between Annie and her mother. It's only gravy, after all. Within a few months of this scene, Annie would be pregnant. In not much time beyond that, Algie would move into Sunny Pines, the care home he would eventually die in.

'Damn silly name.'

They couldn't have known it then, of course, but this moment between mother and daughter bridged the gap between two chapters. It would retrospectively stand as testimony to the strength of their bond. Their resilience in the face of whatever life throws at them.

The gravy they present together is, Annie knows but doesn't say, all but identical to the second attempt she'd made. How long ago that seems now.

'A triumph!' declares Algie.

'Bravo!' agrees Percy.

'Don't let it anywhere near me,' pleads Billy.

'Is there a dinner to go with it?' Algie smiles.

'Cook it yourself,' Annie and Clara say in unison. 'We're off to swim the channel.'

Many years later, by which time only two living souls remember that day, the family is assembled once more.

'Grandma, you are the Michael Schumacher of gravy making.'

Annie looks at her grandson inquiringly.

'Relentless perfection.'

'Hear! Hear!' cries Billy, raising his glass.

'It's my grandmother's recipe,' Annie begins. 'You know, I hadn't noticed until now, but I can see her in you. That smile of yours, maybe.'

Billy squints at his grandson, as Annie goes on.

'I could teach you it, if you wanted?'

'What, the gravy? Really?'

'Well, I won't be around forever, you know? It's survived three generations. It would be a shame if it died with me.'

'Tell him about the day of the great gravy tasting!' Billy smiles.

'The great what? I'd be honoured, Grandma. Although, I'm absolutely certain you'll outlive us all.'

A chemical surge. Sweat and neon. The crowd is a writhing mass of heat and limbs. Odorous and animalistic as it howls and whistles with teeth bared in a grinding nihilistic grin. The music is a never-ending crescendo of fireworks. A bomb that counts down and then explodes, over and over again. I see him, the boy I'm looking for, towering above the flailing beast.

'Can I get another five, Danny?'

He gurns at me, black pools for eyes, all pupils and ravaged gums. His sodden sandy hair is stuck to his forehead with sweat and his logo-laden clothes glow, flicker and reflect. He starts counting out loud as he drops them into my open hand:

'One Mitzy, two Mitzy, three…' But then loses his train of thought.

'Thanks, man. How much do I owe you?'

He waves a dismissive hand in the air, smiles like a crazed Cheshire cat, leans over and kisses me on the cheek, and then disappears; melts into the pulsing mass of creature.

I spot my friends huddled in the customary corner, chain smoking and passing around a bottle of water; the elixir of life. Take a sip, pass it on. I head towards them, never once flowing against the tide. A slow unfocused and swaying zigzag beneath electric pinks and reds and blues and greens. I'm carried to them by the night itself. They see me and erupt into grins and whoops. We embrace as though I've returned home from war, as though I hadn't been with them ten minutes ago. We are a sub-beast, a mobile chillout zone. This is our movie, man.

'Hey, man. We were just… oh, nice one!'

On the tongue, swig and swallow.

'Hey, man. We were just saying… erm. Oh, man, I've forgotten.'

Hysterics, arms round shoulders, it doesn't matter. Words don't matter. Nothing matters.

'Oh, yeah, that's it. You fancy checking out Pollen on Victoria Street? Kenny Ken's on.'

The night outside is warmed by our brains' crossed wires. The lights, metal and skin are a carboard film set. We are so willingly vulnerable. Let's be this forever, man. Useless and envied. This hedonistic sweet spot, independent but without responsibility. We are the end of the century; we are the party that ends all parties. There is us and then there is the aftermath. We are the end of the New Age.

'Oh, man. There's a queue. Eff that.'

She's standing in a kebab shop when I see her; the woman I will love until the day that I die. I see her through the glass, one life viewed from another. The future viewed from the past. I'm unsure if she's real at first or simply a vision. We don't meet, this night. How can we? I can barely stand now. In fact, if we had it would have been the end before the beginning. A life lost. She's laughing and I realise I can hear her. I know that's not possible from where I slouch, but I can. Because it's a laugh I know and love to my very core. I can hear it because this is my memory. The first time I saw her, she didn't see me. I couldn't have known, of course, that we'd ever meet again. That circumstance would throw us together within weeks of this broken dream. And that makes it all the more strange, doesn't it? That she was the catalyst for change; the death of the twentieth century boy. My Ela, who was just a girl I saw in a kebab shop, laughing. It was a laugh that made me feel safe, I think. That made me yearn for sunlight and summer and meaning.

Of course, to project on to someone before you know

them is not the foundation for a love to conquer worlds. And ours doesn't – didn't. It was a spider's web carrying an elephant. But it held. Someone once said to me, I forget who now, that people who stay together their whole lives aren't soulmates. They're just people who decided not to split up when others would have. I think that's true. And really quite beautiful, actually.

'What are you looking at, man?'

I gaze clumsily up into the black mirrors of my friend's eyes and then point across the traffic choked street, at the kebab shop. It's empty now and I wonder, for just one frozen second, if it always had been. If any of this is real. Can such a lost thing be so easily found? It seems improbable, in retrospect. But it's something to believe in and that's important, I think. I believe in her. In Ela. In the girl across the street.

'Gross, man. Kebabs are like… gross, man.'

'Do you want to hold her?'

And then her. Our girl. Our beautiful girl. Pure and untroubled, fact and fiction. The light that shines the way. The three of us, tired and happy and burning so, so bright. I hold her in my shaking arms as salty tears run. I kiss Ela, so radiant and shining, on the forehead.

'Is this real?' I whisper.

'It bloody better be, given how I feel right now.'

This is the moment, I think to myself. *This is the moment that will flash before my eyes when I die.*

'Hello, Annabelle Chakrika Murrell. I'm your dad.'

'Hey, who said anything about Murrell?'

I perch on the bed next to Ela and we stare at our daughter. At this thing we made, slimy and vulnerable.

'She's so tiny,' I say.

'That's what you think,' says Ela.

I kiss her forehead again. 'You're amazing.' She is.

'You're a bastard man and I'll never forgive you.' She smiles that smile of hers. 'But I love you.'

'Well, I am loveable.'

A puzzle completed. I am a whole person for the very first time. Because she needs me, this slimy and vulnerable little thing. She needs us both and I feel… ready. Grown up, I feel like a grown up.

We nearly didn't make it, Ela and me. Once that initial fierce orange flame had inevitably burned itself out, we were found wanting. I remember feeling that she was somehow better than me, and that somewhere deep down inside, in a dark corner, hidden away from her kindness and inherent goodness, she knew it. I was a needy and anxious thing, then. And she was a cold and lost thing. But we had made each other those things, and I guess at some point we just decided to understand that they weren't the truth of us. That we were better than that. And so, we simply tried harder.

Someone once said to me, an old friend on a strange neon night before the New Age ended, that people who stay together their whole lives aren't soulmates. They're just… well, you know.

There are so many off-ramps and forks in the road. One single wrong turn and the world would never know her; our beautiful girl. She looks at us then, I swear it. Focuses for the first time in her little life. She sees us, like no one has ever seen us. We are hers.

Ela's crying as well now. She speaks to her daughter for the very first time.

'Hello, my beautiful girl. Where did you get those emerald eyes, my love, eh?'

THIRTY-ONE

It is a café on the seafront, Bessie remembers. *Bessie & Effie's?* Or *Effie & Bessie's?* No, neither will do. *The Place Where We Will Be? Of course*, Bessie thinks. *The Place Where We Will Be* café on Worthing seafront. Perfect. It's a sunny spot, naturally. Chairs and tables adorn the promenade at the café front, which is brilliant clear glass from top to bottom. With ornate gold lettering and a chalkboard menu.

Inside, the shiny floor is black and white chequers and the table clothes are pastel pinks, yellows, blues and greys. English ivy, ferns, grasses and herbs festoon the walls and ceiling. A small but ornate chandelier hangs in the centre of the room and colours everything a nostalgic orange... no! That's not right. There is no nostalgia here. It colours everything a warm, rich yellow. There are spaces left for pictures. Frames that will be filled with photographs of new memories, not old ones. Mementos from this life, not the last. The music that plays is a viola sonata by Rebecca somebody. Clarke? It plays and plays and never ends;

elegant but not sombre. Ushering in the New Age. Cakes and pastries are displayed in all their glory on the counter top. Iced fruit and Genoa, Madeira and Bristol, jam tarts and a giant American devil's food cake.

'Aren't you forgetting something, Beloved?'

The sound of these words fills the space a thousand times. A chemical surge. Bessie closes her eyes, squeezes them tight, and then opens them again. She slowly turns to face her. She's removing her gloves from hands that will never age. Her emerald eyes twinkle and shine.

'Is it… really you?' Bessie whispers. 'The *real* you?'

'It is, Beloved. You did it. You found me. In the place where we will be.'

The two women slowly walk towards each other and meet in the middle of their new world. Bessie is trembling as salty tears silently run down her face. A face that is young again. Effie places a delicate hand on Bessie's cheek.

'Is it alright?' Bessie asks, gesturing with her eyes to the room in which they stand.

'Of course, it's perfect. Everything is perfect, Beloved.'

And then they kiss. Their very first kiss, in this life.

'I'm so cold.'

My grandma and I hold each other for warmth, but there is none. This isn't a natural cold that can be reasoned with. The same goes for the darkness; it is absolute. Hopeless. It doesn't cloak us, it is us.

'But we can't… I mean, we can't die, can we? We're already dead, so nothing can really hurt us, can it?' Clara asks. But it's not a question that can be answered.

'You're awfully quiet over there, Algie. How are you bearing up, old chap?'

'Oh, fine, fine, Percy, my boy.' But he isn't fine, not at all. 'I just… well, I just thought she'd come back for us.'

Silence. Deep and heavy and cloying.

'Look, we don't know what's happening,' I say. 'We don't know where Bessie is. We shouldn't just write her off, should we?'

'Quite right,' agrees Percy. 'This may be nothing at all do with Bessie's plans and, even if it is, she certainly won't have abandoned us here. The very idea is absurd.'

Algie lets out a long sigh upon hearing these words. 'There's… information I have.'

'What information?' Clara asks.

'Things I know about your mother that she, well, that she doesn't know I know, if you follow me? It isn't that she didn't love me, I don't think… it's just…'

'Oh, that,' begins Clara. 'Oh Pops, I hadn't realised you knew about all that.' She reaches out to her father in the darkness.

'What's that? You mean, you know it too?'

'Well, she never told me, of course. But, yes, I knew it.'

'The love that dare not speak its name,' Percy says.

'Oh, for heaven's sake!' begins Algie. 'You mean everyone knew it?!'

'Poor Bessie. To be born into such unenlightened times,' says my grandma.

'And how in the blazes did you know, granddaughter of mine?'

'Well. Things Mumsy has said and, well, I sort of guessed, I suppose.'

'Well, that's just splendid! Everybody knew. I suppose you knew as well?'

I assume he's looking at me. 'I didn't know,' I say.

'Well then, it seems you and I are the only idiots on board, my boy.'

'We just assumed you knew, Pops.'

'And… well, you did know, Algie, didn't you? You just said so,' points out Percy.

'Well, yes. I knew. But you didn't know that I knew, did you? It would've been nice to know that you all knew and to have known I wasn't the only one who knew.'

'I'm losing track of things,' I say.

'Oh, Pops. You do know she loved you though?' says Clara.

'Indeed,' agrees Percy. 'Bessie was no shrinking violet, Algie. She spent her entire life with you. She'd only do that if she wanted to. You do realise that?'

'Yes, yes. I suppose so. I am inherently loveable, after all. But, well, I'm not Effie.'

'Who?' we all ask. All but Clara.

'Effie?' she begins. 'Wasn't that the girl you were once… oh, goodness.'

'Well, quite,' confirms Algie.

'So, wait?' I begin. 'You think she's left us here to find this Effie?'

'Absolutely not,' Clara cuts in. 'My mother would never leave us. *Any* of us.' She puts an emphasis on the any and I sense another consoling hand being placed on Algie's.

But Algie obviously doesn't agree, I think but don't say out loud. So, what of Bessie? *That* face. A face that glows with the light of life itself. Kindness and wisdom. Forgiveness and strength.

'I agree,' I say. 'Bessie hasn't left us. She'll be back for us.'

'Unless,' my grandma whispers. 'Unless she can't. Unless she wants to but can't reach us. What if once you've left this place, there's no going back?'

Silence and the darkness. I'm so cold.

PERCY

Silence and the darkness. Percy is awake, he supposes. As much as he is ever awake nowadays. Somewhere deep down, he understands that this is a memory and, more importantly, what that must mean. Because you wouldn't remember a painful and sleepless night, in amongst all the other painful and sleepless nights, unless there was a very good reason to do so, would you?

He listens to the darkness for signs of life but finds none. His love, his dear Clara, is sleeping soundly in their upstairs bedroom. The only moments of rest she ever really gets now. Should he try and wake her? How can he possibly know the answer to such a question? Would it give her more pain to miss it or to witness it and remember it always? There is no correct answer and, in the end, it doesn't matter. Because how could he wake her, really? He has no energy to call out and certainly none to move, bang on a wall or suchlike. No, let her sleep. Give her that, at least. A few hours of peace before the truth shatters everything.

Yes, it must be time, he thinks. This night is the night that will not see the sunrise.

'The sun will always rise, sir. We can be sure of that, if nothing else.'

'Hello, private.'

'Hello, sir.'

'I did wonder if you might show up. How are you?'

'I'm good, thank you, sir. All the better for seeing you, sir.'

'You'll forgive me if I don't return the sentiment on this one occasion, old friend?'

'Of course, sir. But you have nothing to fear.'

'Will it be the Plains of Asphodel, private?'

'Oh no, sir. Nothing so grand as all that, sir. For you, a train, I believe, sir.'

'A train?'

'Well, it's supposed to be a train. But things have changed, sir.'

'For better or worse?'

'It's difficult to say, sir.'

'I did my best, private.'

'You did all you could, sir. And…'

'And?'

'And you were wonderful, sir.'

'Thank you, private.'

'You'll see them again, sir. Your loved ones.'

'I will?'

'Oh yes, sir. My Alice is here with me, sir. She sends her regards.'

'Send her mine back, won't you?'

'Yes, sir.'

'Private?'

'Yes, sir.'

'Is it done? Am I dead?'

'That's a very difficult question, sir. Is there pain?'

'No. Not any more.'

'Then yes, sir. It's done.'

The dream is lucid and fragmented. Silence like spilt milk; rancid and cloying. A place where only useless panic obscures an acceptance as quiet and devastating as the end of everything. Time stops. Silence and the darkness and the letting go. And no pain. Or a pain beyond sense. A quiet pain that smiles and waves goodbye. No embers, no afterthought, no meaning.

Colour and fragrance. A family seated together around the table on a quiet Sunday afternoon. The room dappled in sunlight. Warm rays filled with swirling dust. Heads bowed in prayer; be thankful for all we are about to receive. The longest night. And then the dawn. Mud and mangled remains. Ethereal figures on a desolate landscape. 'Fix bayonets, prepare to move.' Noise like nothing I've ever heard. And I'm screaming then, as the bombs rain down and the world is torn apart.

Legs and head, I think. *Legs and head.*

I'm screaming. Odd, I think, that I hadn't registered this at first. Then someone is with me. Calming and clean and tender. Is it Bessie? No, that's not possible. Then nothing. Blissful and wretched. Painless and lost. The void.

'You didn't make it, did you, private?'

A boat on a river. The delivery of something precious to a soul almost lost forever. An errand for an old friend.

'If I did not believe, I should think the darkness would swallow me whole.'

A knock at the door.

'Your alarm call, sir.'

The sepia-tinged dining room is absurd in its pomposity. And then, there she is. A girl from another world. Elegant and youthful, handsome and angular. The star in a silent movie. Cocktails in nightclubs and stories captured forever in the pages of books I've not yet read. Skin like pearl and eyes that I could lose myself in. Distant echoes of safety and warmth but laced with something more exciting. Our eyes meet then, and she smiles at me with thin but shapely lips.

I'm pacing nervously. Clutching my cap in my hands, my thumbs rubbing at the cloth, kneading it like dough. The midday sun is relentless. The air is thick and sticky like honey or boiling flesh. I avert my eyes from the ugly cherry red lotus flowers that pepper the garden. Another scream rings out.

'Sir.'

'Judith!'

'You have a daughter, sir.' I follow her back inside the house, my legs are jelly beneath me. And then her. Our girl. Our beautiful girl. Pure and untroubled, fact and fiction. The light that shines the way. The three of us, tired and happy and burning so, so bright. I kiss Clara, my Clara, and we look down at our daughter. This perfect thing that we have done. And the light that shines on the three of us is that of a movie set, or a dream.

'Hello, my darling. You are going to be quite, quite exquisite.'

'Hello, Daddy.'

And my nerves disappear. A vision in white, smiling the same smile I've seen a thousand times.

'I remember my daughter, every single second of her. She is the very best of us. She is all our lives, every thought we've ever had. All our achievements, our failures, our fears and our dreams, made flesh. She is the reason I breath in and out. The *effect* of her, you see? Of her existence, has altered everything. She has changed the very fabric of our world. Of what it means to be. The love we feel for her is beyond time and space and reason and logic. She flows through us, disassembling and rebuilding. She is the answer, for her mother and me. Our explanation for existence itself.' I look at my daughter and for just a second, we are alone. In that vast empty place. Silent and at peace. 'I love you, Annie.'

'How are those peas coming along, my love?'

'Almost there, my darling wife.'

A long and bumpy road full of magic and loss. And it comes to this: contentment. Such a big word. How I love you all. The garden is quiet now. Peaceful and still. Honeysuckle and orange marmalade, Sunday roasts and sparrows in hedgerows on country lanes. I am at peace. In the stillness of this dark and final night. Alone but not alone. The dream is lucid and fragmented, and peaceful.

ALGIE

Algie sits in his wheelchair, in front of the fire, in the living room of Sunny Pines.

'Damn silly name.'

Dropsy by his side, the two of them positioned so as to have the best view of the orchard in the fading autumn light. Ugly cherry red fruit hang from the trees.

Should they be there? Algie thinks briefly, but the thought doesn't linger. Algie is not one for dwelling on things. Although, on this particular evening, he *is* in a reflective mood. This is most unusual for Algie and he wonders what it might mean. But the thought doesn't linger.

'Where did all the years go, eh? One minute you're

bounding about the place, full of joie de vivre, the wind in your hair and the world at your feet. Then before you know it, you're confined to this blasted wheeled contraption in some chintz-covered purgatory with all the other miserable dribblers. Food pureed to within an inch of its life, legs as much use as a bicycle on the ocean waves and if I want to use the lavatory, I have to ring a *bloody* bell. Pardon my French. But, I mean, a bell! If it wasn't for darling Dropsy here, I'd probably go stone cold bananas. Wouldn't I Dropsy, old thing?

'Perhaps 'miserable dribblers' is a touch cruel. I mean, as octogenarians go there are worse sorts than old Mrs. Parsonage-Mead over there, I'll concede. She's a good old girl. The problem is she has the memory of a goldfish. Not a young virile goldfish, mark you. Oh no, I'm talking about the scatter-brained and distinctly long in the tooth category of goldfish. A goldfish renowned for being forgetful, even in goldfish circles. Every time I meet her, which is every blasted morning, she hasn't got the foggiest idea who I am. I may well have spent the entire of the previous day with her but as far as she's concerned, we're complete strangers. I spy's a nightmare. I mean, it's not entirely without its advantages of course. So far, I've introduced myself as her husband, her long-lost son, the late Lord Kitchener, the president of the United States of America and the archangel Gabriel. Still, she's a good old sort.

'Not like that horrid Nurse Crochett. Po-faced old crackpot. The way she looks at you, Dropsy, old thing. I don't like it one bit. *I do wish you'd get rid of that horrid thing. Staring up at me like that all the time, it's enough to give anyone nightmares.* Mark my words, if she ever lays a finger on you,

I'll… well, you get the gist. She's forever obsessed with getting me in the bath. I swear, I have two baths a week more often than not. It's absurd. And without warning, oh yes! There you'll be, sitting minding your own and, bang! Suddenly you're being wheeled off by a bath-crazed old thornback, armed with a sponge. I've lived through five monarchs! The invention of the motorcar, the wireless and the tele-whatsit. Look at me now. It's enough to give a chap the morbs.

'Still, I can't grumble, really. It's been a bit of a life, hasn't it, Dropsy, old thing? I should write my memoirs! There's an idea. What a romp that would be. Not one of those stuffy old tomes where the author whines on endlessly about how much better things were in their day. Not a bit of it.'

Algie thinks of his mother and father then, and of his long-departed brother. He thinks of Bessie, of all the years they were together. Will he see her again? He doesn't know. Isn't sure. The letters, you see? He did think he saw her, didn't he? Beneath the apple trees with their cherry red fruit. She smiled at him and he felt safe. But perhaps that was a dream. Algie loves Bessie, will always love her. His is a love that transcends time and space. A love that, in the end; the actual end, will prove itself as pure and strong as any love has ever been or ever could be.

He thinks of little Jack. He remembers him now. A little cherub; their little cherub. Innocent and forever young. Algie leans down and absentmindedly runs his hand over the worn-down fur of his beloved Dropsy. He thinks of Clara. Algie loves Clara, will always love her. She is proof of a life lived well. She is the moon and the stars. He thinks of his son-in-law and his beautiful granddaughter and he is happy. He is at peace.

'Yes. Memoirs,' he whispers. 'That's the thing. We'll get on that as soon as, Dropsy, my love.' And then he fades away. His hand rests forever on the worn-down fur of his faithful old friend.

'Algie.'

'Bessie, my love. Is that you?'

'It's me, Algie.'

'Am I… is this?'

'Do you remember my death, Algie?'

'What's that?'

'When and where we were?'

'I… I…'

'It's important, husband of mine. Very important.'

'But it's all too tangled up, you see?'

'You must remember it. I know you don't want to, but you must, darling. And it must be now. You must force yourself. It is *very* important.'

Outside the window, in the fading autumn light, the bare and colourless apple trees cast shadows across the fires of the New Age. He is remembered; his place on the train is assured. She does love him. But there is so much yet to come, isn't there?

The dream is lucid and fragmented. Laughter like spilt milk; rancid and cloying. A place where only useless panic obscures an acceptance as quiet and devastating as the end of everything. Time stops. Fading and reflections and the worn-down fur of old friends. And the loss. A pain beyond sense. A fragile pain that stands in the shadow of an apple tree. No embers, no afterthought, no meaning.

I have plans: a summer that never was and Pater's mystery sweeties. From America.

'Mater, Leopold has eaten Pater's sweeties even though you said he wasn't supposed to.'

The Snarling Tigress and her angelic second born. And my tummy aches. An immaculately kept parlour room, on a dreary afternoon. The death of a Frenchman and Mr. Pike overheard. She kicked me! The pain is lucid and deep purple. And poor old Pater. His dark blue tunic with shining brass buttons. Several sizes too big for him and it seems to swallow him up.

'Mater kicked me, Pater.'

'Yes. I've been hearing all about it. Does it hurt?'

'Yes.'

'Life isn't too complicated if you've got your wits about you.' Poor old Pater, I think you might be wrong.

'Algie! Answer me this: should I simply engrave your name on this cane, boy?'

But it's all too tangled up, you see? The darkness always smothers the light, in the end. And so, I don't remember. The loss and change, I choose not to.

And then her.

'Got the morbs? Did you know her?'

'Yes,' she says, in a voice that sounds the same as a harp does, when plucked upon by an angel. 'She was very dear to me.' She smiles then. And I feel safe. She folds the paper delicately and places it into a satin chatelaine.

'I'm Algie.'

'Good day, Algie. I'm Bessie.'

'Ahoy, Bessie!' I search for something to say. She loves me, she loves me not. 'I say, would you like a game of I spy?' She laughs. Isn't that wonderful?

A single bulb that glows a nostalgic orange. A table of

friends on a dark and stormy night. A wager made. And then… I melt. I'm smitten. The storm rages on and I cradle the whimpering pup. In these rain-soaked moments, as the wind howls through my bones, I make a promise. I will show it love and care for the rest of its life. Never again will it go hungry. Its whole world will be one of love.

'Algie you—' Bessie stops mid-sentence.

'Bessie, my love! Look what I got for you, what a beauty, eh?'

'Algie, you fool. Come here, you great lump.'

And then him. Our beautiful little boy. How can a father forget?

'Dropsy.'

'Dropsy?'

'Dropsy.'

'I'm not sure that's… how about Scamp?'

'Dropsy.'

'Or Trigger?'

'Dropsy.'

'Dropsy it is.'

The faithful hound, by my side as we wait for Percy. The boy with the burdened hazel eyes who wants to marry my daughter. My beloved Clara.

'Now, then. Let me look at you, my boy.'

'Algie… Mr. Knighton, sir. May I have your permission?'

Two best friends walking down the old lane. I've never been good with loss, old thing. I can't imagine how I'll go on without you. My tears were silent at first. Great droplets that fell onto my friend's fire-warmed fur. Then the sobs. I don't think I've ever cried so much as that night. But now here you are, back with me. Bessie looks down, and screams.

But it's all too tangled up, you see? The darkness always smothers the light, in the end. And so, I don't remember. The loss and change, I choose not to. And then she's gone. No… wait. There is something. The seaside. Why the seaside, Bessie? And she tells me something. Yes, that's it. I'm leaning over and placing a kiss on her cheek and she tells something very important. And then she's gone. The letters and the empty house. The darkness always smothers the light, in the end.

And then the rest. The half-life.

'Time for your bath, Algie.'

The dream is lucid and fragmented, and very important.

CLARA

She wakes with a start. Images of Kenya; a handsome young man in uniform with kind but burdened eyes. It slips away like sand and is gone.

The house is quiet and empty, as quiet as her own thoughts. No house should be so quiet and certainly not this one, where once there was so much.

She needs the bathroom. When was the last time she got through the night without needing the bathroom? What is it, exactly, about the process of aging that renders one incapable of getting through the night without using the bathroom? Does the bladder age at a faster rate than the rest of you?

She sighs, lifts the covers and manoeuvres her tired limbs. As she slides twisted toes into threadbare slippers, she feels a sudden twinge of pain shoot up one arm. It fades as quickly as it came.

'That's new,' she says out loud.

She switches on the bedside lamp and begins the slow trek to the bathroom. The floorboard nearest the door creaks, as it always does.

'I must ask Annie to send Billy round to take a look at that board,' she says, as she always does.

The bathroom light flickers and splutters to life, pouring a warm orange light over the darkness. The pain in her arm returns and her muscles spasm and lock involuntarily.

'Must have slept funny.'

But then it happens again and this time it doesn't fade.

'Oh,' she says, as she realises the truth. 'Oh, my.'

The pain spreads into her chest and she clutches and staggers and slowly falls to the floor. It can only have been a few moments that she lay there, but a thousand thoughts run through her mind, before the final reel plays. Mundane at first; the floral-patterned tiles. Ugly cherry red on yellowing white. *Do you know, I can't remember choosing those tiles? I have no memory of it whatsoever.*

And then, inevitably, she thinks of them. Clara had never learnt to cope with loss. She carried it like a great weight from the day her mother died until this very moment, lying on the bathroom floor in her slippers. She missed Percy and her parents every single second of every single day. She wept for them still and the pain of losing them never seemed to dull.

'I'm ready,' she says. And she means it. She feels so old and left behind.

She thinks of her darling Annie and her beautiful grandson and she smiles through the twisting knife of pain.

'I love you all.'

Her daughter is strong. Much stronger than her. She will be devastated at losing her mother, but then she will be strong. She will focus her love on her husband and son and they will hold each other as the tinny speakers play.

She thinks of Percy. Sees every line on his perfect face. Young and old and everything between. *He* faced this moment alone as well. She slept through his last and it has haunted her ever since. What were his final thoughts? Were they of her, of them? She thinks so. He loved her as she loved him, as she still loves him. She reaches out a hand, or least she thinks she does. She closes her eyes tight. Darkness pours over the warm orange light and she wills it. A tear rolls down one cheek and with the last breath in her body, she calls his name.

'Percy!'

The dream is lucid and fragmented. Grief like spilt milk, rancid and cloying. A place where only useless panic obscures an acceptance as quiet and devastating as the end of everything. Time stops. But lost faces flicker and distant laughter rings out. And the pain. Endless loss. A hopeless pain that dances on the broken bones of every sunny yesterday. No embers, no afterthought, no meaning.

My childhood is a whirlwind of rich colour. Sunshine and roses and them. They smile and love and I feel safe.

'It's really the opportunity of a lifetime, Pops.' Rosy cheeks and twinkling emerald eyes. My teddy bear. My rock.

'Thank you, Mother. I knew you'd support me on this.'
'I'll do nothing of the sort.'
'What?!'

'I agree with your father, you mustn't go.'

'Mother. I have to say, I'm really rather aghast. I had considered you to be a modern woman.' Strength and truth, enlightened in unenlightened times. My guide. My champion.

'Daisy, dearest, at least half of that lurid concoction is pooling at your feet.' Smoke-filled dancefloors and the ushering in of a New Age. Faces in photographs at parties long forgotten. Those halcyon days. Arched eyebrows and promises whispered. Every second was a life being lived. I wonder where you are now. I wonder about the lives you lead. One last dance and a glass raised to the future. Hanky-Pankies at the Blue Lagoon.

'To Clars!' Glasses clink, music plays and laughter sounds out across the vibrant echo of youth.

Sweat and screams and poor young Judith, wide-eyed in fear. And then her. Their darling Annie. But it flashes past in a fog of exhaustion and faraway heat. More like a dream than a memory. Percy's tears of happiness; had that been the first time I'd seen him cry?

'Westbury 4291, the Clayton residence.' The call that marked the end of innocence on the eve of war. A corner of the world that would never be the same again.

'Pops? Is that you? Where are you?'

'Worthing.'

'Pardon?'

'The seaside. Your mother, she wanted…'

Four wretched and sleepless figures sit on a bench, on a windswept and all but deserted promenade.

'It feels significant, doesn't it? This place, I mean.'

'As though we're meant to be here,' Percy replies.

'Yes, exactly. As though we're… linked to it, somehow.'

Then, I am the hostess, the lighthouse guiding my ships back home. Not just for my father but in time, for Annie and Billy as well. And then much later, for Charlie and his family. Christmas Day after Christmas Day. The orange sun and the crescent moon share the sky above and all is well. Percy and Annie have decorated the customary oversized tree and Pops is regaling them all with tall tales around the fireplace. They are mine. My family; my reason. There is a hole where my mother should be, but her light shines on us and we are happy. Truly happy.

'Mumsy, I've something to discuss with you.'

'Yes, I thought you might have, my love.'

'He's asked me and I think I want to say yes.'

'You think?'

'I mean, I know I do. I just want to… I mean, I can't very well say yes without talking to you, dearest. Well, can I?!'

'Certainly not!'

The love between my daughter and me is not a heavy love. Complete and unconditional, uncomplicated and nurturing. We share everything. I tell her, 'Go with not just your heart, but also your head. Love should not be a sacrifice. Compromises must, of course, be made along the way, but in the end, love should be a completion. A puzzle solved.'

Yes, we are truly happy and we shine like sunlight.

The house is full of life. As a house should be.

'Billy, where's that television?'

We gather, it's what we do. There are two holes now. Dark and ever present. They weigh on me. But we're still here, Percy and me. He is slowly fading, I know it. But only on the outside. And, really, what does that matter? They are mine. My family; my reason. Annie is in the kitchen making the tea. She's already becoming the matriarch. My baby girl, all grown up. There are moments when it's all too fast, the dizzying cycle of life. It feels as though I've only just begun.

Life seems to me to speed up the older you get. Didn't I read something about it once? It's all to do with memory. I look at my family. I kiss my husband on the lips. You are my moon and stars. Each of you. I love you all. Life is a series of moments and some moments are worth more than others. It's really something, isn't it?

'It's one small step for man…'

The floorboard creaks, the pain shoots and twists. I love you all. Darkness pours over the warm orange light. The dream is lucid and fragmented and I am gone to find them.

ANNIE

The strip light flickers, almost in time with the beeps and background whirl of this place. Wires and tubes, groans and distant chatter. The pulsing electric green lines that speak of life, but not life as Annie considers it. A facsimile of life where those who can no longer rage against the dying of the light hide in plain sight. In clean rooms and soiled sheets; a sterile space where unread stories peter out. No unexpected plot twists or action-packed finales. Endings by numbers, formulaic and familiar. Haven't we read this one before? Fade out. Starched uniforms and disposable aprons stride purposefully; attentive and numb. Young minds with just enough space between them and this to maintain the paper-thin mask of denial that most beyond these four walls wear in waking hours. Yet, Annie supposes, they must see themselves lying here, surely? These administrators of the end. How can they not? Poor souls.

Billy is snoring quietly on the really quite unnecessarily uncomfortable chair beside her bed. He must've been there all night again. Annie knows what it means, that they've turned a blind eye to this, those poor souls, attentive and numb. Small acts of kindness that go against the protocol of death. He's always been a light sleeper, her darling husband. So, she also knows what it means that the flickering strip lights and purposeful strides of the young enough have not woken him from his uncomfortable slumber. He is exhausted. These long months have taken such a toll. This is eating away at him. And at Charlie, who'll no doubt arrive within the hour. And her grandsons, who'll not be far behind. They'll sit at her side with smiles and watery eyes. They'll speak of other things. Work and weather, shopping and old friends who send their best. Anything but this.

She isn't fighting. She knows, can see, what this is doing to those she loves. This lingering, it's just happening. How does one simply give in? If she could will it, she would, but that doesn't seem to be how it works. Every time her eyes close and her thoughts dissolve into the void, she wonders if that's it. The end of everything. Of every thought and every moment spent. All the love and laughter, the dreams and the plans. The gardens and the holding hands. The holidays and wedding hats, the bubble baths and falling snow. Hedgerows, birdsong, Sunday service, marmalade, new car smell, television, teardrops, talcum powder, pasta bake, wristwatches, a lie of kindness, engine sounds, wagging tails, daffodils, piles of ironing, the feel of him beside her, ice cream, wellington boots, afternoon sunlight, headaches, motorbikes, kisses on lips and cheeks and foreheads and hands, a good book, a bad book, athlete's foot, petting zoos, platform waiting rooms, strangers, friends, perfect gravy, writing letters, blue cheese and the two of them, sitting in a comfortable silence. Together. On their chairs. Knowing where everyone is and that the sun will rise in the morning. But then she wakes up. She always wakes up. The beeps and whirls and flickering lights are still there. Should she say goodbye; heartfelt and sincere? Or make future plans; transparently hollow declarations to sooth and ease?

'What would you like for breakfast this morning, Mrs. Murrell?'

'Oh, whatever's going.'

He stirs, opens his eyes, squints and groans as his aching bones remember. He sees her and he smiles. 'Good morning, my love. How are you feeling?'

'Oh, tiptop. I'd expect they'll let me out today.'

They both smile. Not quite a laugh but enough. He leans over and kisses her on the cheek. The tenderness of it almost breaks Annie.

'I've just got to nip off and spend a penny. Be back in a moment, alright?'

Annie watches him walk away and it almost happens then. A pain, a sound and a sudden rush of colour and limbs. She tries to let go, to slide into the darkness like a warm bed on a winter's night. But then it passes. Porridge oats and margarine on thin-sliced brown bread. Curtains pulled across in a futile attempt to maintain dignity. Visitors and acts of kindness. Loud beeps from somewhere in the room. Running footsteps and routine panic. One less story in the building. Cheese sandwich, ready salted crisps and raspberry yogurt. Billy, always Billy, by her side. They face this together.

'You go and get a change of clothes, have a rest at home. I'll be fine for a few hours, my love.'

But he won't. She knows he won't.

'Charlie brought me in some clothes. I'll go for a wander outside in a while. Get a spot of fresh air.'

But he won't. She knows he won't. More visitors, more acts of kindness. Flowers and magazines, mints and a photo in a frame. Pie and mash and soggy peas. Lemon meringue, still frozen in the middle. Television, familiar theme tunes. Billy snores quietly in the really quite unnecessarily uncomfortable chair beside her bed.

And then, in the evening, it does happen. The dimming pink light beyond the window turns an ugly cherry red.

'That's strange,' she says, perhaps out loud, perhaps not. Then a quiet pain floods through every inch of her. 'Oh.' She understands. 'Billy. Billy.'

He wakes with a start and is by her side.

'I love you, Billy. I love you so much.'

'I love you, my darling. I'm here, my angel.'

His face seems to fold in on itself with sadness. She can see he understands beyond any doubt that the moment has come. He kisses her on the lips, the cheek and forehead, as nurses and doctors appear; far, far too late.

The last thing she feels is a teardrop. It falls from his face onto hers. A tiny splash that makes no sound. And then she's gone.

The dream is lucid and fragmented. Falling tears like spilt milk; rancid and cloying. A place where only useless panic obscures an acceptance as quiet and devastating as the end of everything. Time stops. Honeysuckle, cut grass and orange marmalade. And the pain. A pain beyond any doubt. No embers, no afterthought, no meaning.

Palm trees line the busy streets, full of cars tooting their horns and bicycles ringing their bells. Big tall buildings of different colours and bright blue skies full of fluffy white clouds. Days that never end. A beautiful garden where my mother tends to roses. Cucumber sandwiches and Judith, whose secret name is Makena, combing my hair.

'That's a funny name.'

'In my home, it means "one who brings happiness".'

Daddy and me, green-faced and heaving. He lifts me up so I can be sick over the edge, as the endless ocean rolls on forever.

'Daddy?'

'Yes, my sweet.'

'I want to go home.'

He reaches across and puts my tiny hand in his. 'I know, my darling. But we *are* going home and it will only be a few more days now.'

Home. I lightly drag my fingers along the smooth plastered wall. The dark green carpet is dappled in afternoon sunlight. I can hear their voices, happy and excited, coming from another room of the house. Beyond the pane of the window, a sparrow sits atop the neatly preened hedge that separates the garden from the lane. It cocks its tiny head to one side as it registers movement behind the glass. The air is thick with evocative smells. Honeysuckle, cut grass and orange marmalade.

'What do you think, my darling? Should this be your room?'

'Yes, Mummy, I want this one. It's beautiful.'

Just before the dawn, there is a dullness to the world. As if everything is in the background, starless and grey. Still asleep but no longer dreaming. Mumsy and I are on morning delivery duty. Our breath rises in the cold air. There's a new family; the Murrells. From London.

'Hello, Annie Clayton.'

'Hello, Billy Murrell.' And there he is. Handsome and backlit. The sun, that will always rise, washes away the night with light and warmth.

'That's our sun, I think. Don't you?'

'Yes. I think that's our sun.'

'Oh good. I'm so glad.'

Reality pauses so that our fairy tale can play out. Packs on our backs and blisters on our feet. Trailblazers, ahead of our time.

'What will it be like?' I ask.

'What will what will be like?'

'Our life.'

'Like this, I should think.'

'Oh, I do hope so.'

From this cliff edge I feel as though we are the only two people alive in an empty and beautiful world. Our forever summer. Twisted ankles and insect bites, rain-soaked climbs and sun-kissed sandy beaches. Drama and tranquillity, laughter and aching limbs. The endless vistas and the scale of it all. So much space, so much time. And, oh my, that gull.

'Billy. The camera.'

'Already doing.' But it's too late. Flapping wings that bring momentary chaos to the world. We look at each other for a second or two and then collapse into fits of laughter.

'You've got the knack!' Billy cries. I hold out my arm towards him and he rests his smiling head on it, as though perching. I feed him a piece of sandwich. He eats it, stares at me and then pretends to peck at my face.

'Alright, try this.'

'By Jove, I think you've got it!'

'It's very nice, my sweet.'

I wait as Mumsy swirls the liquid around her mouth, as if sampling a fine wine. The tension in the air is palpable.

'Nearly… a touch too fruity.'

'Mumsy, I need you. It's the only way. I can't do this without you, but together, I know we'll get it.'

'Very well. Let's get to it, daughter of mine.'

Family is all that matters in the end, isn't it? Tall tales and Sunday roasts. Generations of smiling faces that blur and merge into one happy day.

'Grandma, you are the Michael Schumacher of gravy making. Relentless perfection.'

'Hear! Hear!'

'It's my grandmother's recipe. You know, I hadn't noticed until now, but I can see her in you. That smile of yours, maybe. I could teach you it, if you wanted?'

'What, the gravy? Really?'

'Well, I won't be around forever, you know? It's survived three generations. It would be a shame if it died with me.'

'Tell him about the day of the great gravy tasting!'

'The great what? I'd be honoured, Grandma. Although, I'm absolutely certain you'll outlive us all.'

Oh, how I love you all. Pulsing electric green lines; a

facsimile of life. The sunset an ugly cherry red beyond the window. A teardrop falls. A tiny silent splash to carry me from this life to the next. The dream is lucid and fragmented and I will it.

BESSIE

The smiling yellow sun shines down on the sparkling silver blue ocean. The cornflower blue sky is vivid and clear. Gulls bob gently on the water and glide gracefully above; silhouettes on the endless horizon. The pier and promenade shine fresh and vibrant. A familiar jumble of houses stand in line. Hedgerows bursting with life, rose bushes in bloom, honeysuckle and orange marmalade. Beyond or beneath the sounds of the gently lapping shoreline and the distant squawks, music plays. A viola sonata by Rebecca Clarke. Chairs and tables adorn the promenade in front of *The Place Where We Will Be* café and a chalkboard menu lists the treasures therein.

But at this moment, Bessie is nowhere to be seen. In fact, she lies in the bed of a building that will very soon be erased from this place. It stands separate and isolated, with cherry red letters above the entrance and a cast of half-formed ghosts wandering its corridors. Memories soon to be forgotten.

'Algie.'

'I'm here, my love. Fancy a game of I spy?'

'Is that you?'

'It's me, my dearest.'

'But is it… the *real* you?'

Algie seems to consider this for a few seconds before smiling a smile that makes Bessie feel safe. 'It is.'

'It worked?'

'Yes, my darling Bessie. It worked. I don't know how, mind you, but there we are.'

Bessie clasps Algie's hand as tightly as her strength allows and a surge of relief passes through her.

'Do you remember this day, Algie? You know what happens here?'

Algie's smile fades then. 'Yes. I remember.' He pauses before continuing. 'Although it seems a bit cheerier than I recall. And you've got the weather wrong, my sweet. It was kicking up a storm that day. Enough to give a fellow the morbs.'

Bessie smiles at him. 'It really is you. I have to tell you something.'

'Yes, I rather thought so.'

Their eyes meet.

'It will be… difficult for you to hear.'

'Effie?' Algie says, in almost a whisper.

Bessie's eyes widen in surprise. 'How?'

'The letters.'

Confusion spreads across Bessie's face until, through the fog of time and space, she realises her husband's misunderstanding.

'Oh. I see. I'm sorry, Algie.'

'I know, my love. I'm sorry too.'

'But I do love you. And we had a wonderful life, Algie. With a beautiful family.'

'We did.'

'But now. Now I must follow my heart, Algie.'

'She's here?'

'She is. We have a café on the seafront.'

'I see. So, this is goodbye then?'

'No. Or at least, I hope not. That's up to you, Algie. We are in the place where we will be, but what this place will be exactly is up to you.'

And so, they talk. Husband and wife, in a memory that's fading, in a world that's new. A New Age is coming. And Algie decides. He decides and then he watches his wife slip away. The tears that fall are different than those he remembers.

The dream is lucid and fragmented. And Bessie has no time for it. The sun is shining and Effie is waiting. She dismisses the final reel. The ladies who tea, the loss of love, those twinkling emerald eyes. Both sets. A puppy with a bow tied round its tiny neck. The loss of a child and the birth of another. Love and family and Christmas Day. Chance meetings and letters hidden away. She dismisses the reel but keeps the memories. Holds on to the love and loss and happiness and pain that they hold. Holds on to them, but on her own terms. They are her memories to wallow in or repress. She will call on them when she needs them but they will not define her. Love is not the past and her husband will not fail her. He never could.

THIRTY-TWO

We're huddled together in the cold darkness of this place, on the floor between the seats; the four of us. At some point Algie, too, disappeared. I thought then that we all would, eventually. One by one we'd be removed from this place and taken somewhere else. But that was a very, very long time ago. Now, I suppose this is where we'll remain? For all eternity; cold, silent and blind. What a fate. How very cruel. What have any of us done to deserve such a punishment? We are the forgotten. No embers, no afterthought, no meaning.

I *say* a long time ago, but of course, that's not really true, is it? Time doesn't exist here; I know that now. At some point we stopped speaking. Ran out of words and the energy required to say them. Since then, we've been this strange collective thing. Limbs and chattering teeth. Not individuals any more, but one shivering mass. And then, of course, there's her. I do think it's a her. The Unremembered. I sense her still, writhing and silently howling. We are five, not four, and it chills me even in this cold, cold place. And then the lights flicker on.

We squeeze our eyes tightly shut, blinded by the harsh suddenness of sight. We untangle and the first sounds any of us have made for so long crawl out of us like wounded animals. Groans and desperate questioning whimpers. A once great beast waking from a thousand-year slumber. The temperature's rising as well. Warmth spreads through us. We *see* each other. Percy is the first to return to his seat, followed by Clara and then my grandma and me. A sudden sense of absurdity washes over me then. It's as though we'd always been sat here and the darkness had never come. The threadbare blues. Then, the footsteps. We turn to the door in time to see it sliding open.

'Good day,' Algie says, with a vast and knowing smile beneath those bushy white whiskers. 'Room for one more?'

We flood him with questions and love and relief.

'I told you all she wouldn't leave us here. My Bessie has plans and they're under way, by Jove!'

Beyond this, he's maddeningly vague about our predicament. Bessie has come to save us; he has a job do – to get the train moving. We're off to the seaside! Rejoice, one and all.

It's Percy who asks the question first, once the hubbub has subsided.

'So, when will we get moving then, Algie?'

'What's that? Oh, any moment now, my boy. Patience, patience.'

But we don't move. For a long while, none of us are particularly troubled by this. We're still basking in the light and warmth and the passing of all that was. The cold and the darkness. But slowly, the fear creeps in.

'Pops?' asks Clara tentatively. 'We're still not going anywhere. Is… is there something wrong?'

Algie ponders this. 'Perhaps… well, it could be you, my sweet.'

'Me?!'

'Well, now, don't excite yourself. It's simply that I do recall you saying you were happy here? You had all you need, and so forth?'

'Well, yes but…'

'So, perhaps we all have to really *want* this. To believe in your mother's plans, or something like that, before we can lift off, as it were?'

Clara is angered by this, but restrains herself. 'My opinions on the matter have been somewhat altered by the previous episode, Father. And in any case, I was simply pointing out that I wanted to spend my eternity with my family and was not looking to escape them.'

Algie does not fail to clock the use of 'Father' in his daughter's response. 'Erm, well yes, quite right. A noble sentiment, my dear. In which case I'm rather afraid I'm a bit stumped. If we're all on board… figuratively speaking, I mean. Then we should be on our way. All loose ends are good and tied, no?'

'No,' my grandma answers. 'Not quite all.' She glances in the direction of the Unremembered.

'Ah,' says Algie. 'Yes. That's a good point, my dear. Anyone happen to know who it belongs to?'

We look at each other, but no answer comes. Then, the voice.

'Remember.'

A quiet whisper full of forgiveness and sadness. I jolt upright and the others turn look at me in startled surprise.

'Did you hear that?' I splutter.

'Hear what?' Percy asks.

Then it comes again. 'Remember.'

It's Bessie's voice. I look at my fellow passengers and know beyond doubt that I'm the only one who can hear her.

'Remember.'

And then I do.

Colours and screams and metal and skin, rush and bite and sob. The twisted metal of the car; an ugly cherry red. Is that a phone ringing? A tinny rendition of some nineties indie song. I can see her name through the pain. Through the blood. On the cracked screen. It's Ela. But I can't reach the phone. I know it. I can't even try. It's already too late. But I speak to her anyway, don't I?

'I'm sorry, Ela. I'm so, so sorry.'

There's something else. The urgency I feel; it isn't life slipping away. It's something else. Something worse. Focus.

'I'm so, so sorry.'

I fade away and then lurch back into the pain. Focus on the pain.

'Sir?! Sir, can you hear me? If you can hear me, tell me your name.'

Hands and arms reaching through twisted metal and mangled remains. Lights that blind and sounds that deafen. There's something else. I can't answer him; it's already too late. But there's something else. Focus on the pain.

'Sir?!'

Answer him. Say it. Say the words that hold the truth of this. The coldness and the darkness and ugly cherry red. The end of everything. Time stops. *Say it.*

'My daughter.'

'Sir?'

'Please. My daughter, Annie. She's in the back. Please. Help her... go to her!'

THE UNREMEMBERED

'So, what did you do in nursery today, sweetie?'

My name is Annabelle Chakrika Murrell and I have green eyes.

'I drawed you a picture, Daddy.'

'Did you! Oh, that's awesome. You'll have to show me as soon as we get home, OK?'

I nod. My daddy's looking at me in the mirror. Mummy says he has sad eyes, but I think they're nice. Our car smells of milk from when I spilt some ages and ages ago.

'It's a Mr. Man.'

'Hooray! My favourite. Is it Mr. Stretch?'

I laugh at Daddy, because he's being very silly. Daddy is always silly.

'No, silly. It's Mr. Tickle.'

Nanna Jennifer says I look like Mummy and that's very lucky. I *do* look like Mummy but I love Daddy as well.

'Oh, of course it is! Silly old Daddy. And do you know what Mr. Tickle does?'

I do know what Mr. Tickle does.

'No, Daddy. What does he do?'

My daddy smiles at me in the mirror and I know he's going to try and tickle me.

'Well, he… tickles and tickles and tickles!'

I giggle lots and lots as Daddy's arm reaches out to the back of our car to tickle me. And then there's a very big bang. The car goes upside down and round and round very, very fast and I can't remember anything after that.

Everything hurts but not for a long time. My name is Annabelle Chakrika Murrell, I have green eyes and my daddy remembers me.

I wake with a start. The threadbare blues of the school commute. And then her. Our daughter. Our beautiful girl.

'Annie!' I cry out and throw myself at the Unremembered. I reach through the writhing pain and glitching limbs and I find my daughter. Small and fragile and perfect. The others gasp and cry out. My grandma reaches out to us. I hold my daughter in my arms as she emerges from the blur. She is formed. She is remembered. She is finally recognised. She cries tears that both break me into a thousand pieces and lift me up to heaven. She buries her perfect face in my shoulder, and weeps.

'Daddy. Daddy,' she sobs.

'I've got you, baby girl. Daddy's got you now.'

'Look!' calls Clara. 'The window!'

The darkness beyond the window has lifted. Even the longest night has a dawn. The smiling yellow sun casts a warm and vibrant glow over a New Age. The sky is blue with fluffy white clouds. A gull flies past the glass and squawks, taking us all by surprise.

'Did you see that?!' Algie cries.

'Can you smell it?' Percy asks. 'The sea. I can smell the sea.'

I hold my daughter; I never want to let her go.

'My baby girl. I love you so much. How could I forget?'

My grandma places a consoling hand on my shoulder and whispers tenderly. 'It's not your fault. The pain of it, my boy. You blocked it out, it's natural and, besides, it's this place. It does that. Makes you remember and makes you forget.'

I reach out and fold her into our embrace.

'It was my fault. The accident. It was…'

'Sssshh. It's done, my sweet. The past is gone. We are here now and so is she.'

'Baby girl,' I say softly to my perfect daughter. 'You remember how Mummy and Daddy always told you that you were named after your Great-Grandma Annie?'

Her sobs are slowly calming, and she looks up at me, into my eyes, and I melt.

'Well, my love. This is Great-Grandma Annie. Annie, meet Annie.'

My grandma looks down adoringly at her namesake and smiles the biggest and sweetest smile there's ever been.

'Hello, Annie, my angel. You look like your mummy, don't you? Apart from those eyes of yours.'

And then, the engine roars into life.

'Here we go!' Algie cries out in triumph, punching the air as we begin to move. 'Here we go, family of mine! To the seaside!'

The dream is lucid and fragmented. Chaos like spilt milk; rancid and cloying. A place where only useless panic obscures an acceptance as quiet and devastating as the end of everything. Time stops. But colours and screams and metal and skin, rush and bite and sob. And the pain. A pain beyond sense. A hopeless pain that dances on the broken bones of every repentant tomorrow. No embers, no afterthought, no meaning.

A lightning flash of something past. A sepia-tinged garden where my mother tends to roses that fade and scowl. Her eyes are a colour that lives inside me. Developmental. Vibrant and cognitive. She smiles as she sees me. A warmth that might be literal rises up in me to lace the pain with a sweet and yielding poison. A plastic cup with a tiger's face printed on it. Unforgotten now. Dormant all these years. Silently waiting for this moment, and only this moment, to resurface. The garden dissolves and I'm lying in a bed that was once my own. My father kneels beside me and gently strokes my hair with his giant hand. An action so tender it dilutes the pain with soothing resignation.

'Mummy's all better now, my boy. And in the morning, you can meet your new baby brother.'

'I want a story, Daddy.'

We are stood on a table, my brother and me. In a room of our grandparents' house. We're holding bowls of Neapolitan ice cream up to an electric bulb that glows a nostalgic orange. We stir frantically, a competition to see who can turn their desert into milkshake the quickest. We are the same, he and I. For this captured reel, we move and laugh and think as one. And then the mourners. So many. They age at triple speed as lines of sadness spread across their faces. Scars left by a silent whip that flogs us all. But in this scene, they are young and raw. My grandmother was the first of us to leave. The pregnant swirling clouds above us unleash and never really stop. Mingling with hot salty tears. *I want her back*, I think again, so many lifetimes later. I want my grandma back.

A chemical surge. Sweat and neon and the faces of friends who own a part of me long gone but fondly remembered. Tactile, messy, glorious and so willingly vulnerable. Innocent and exposed. Those halcyon days. And there she is. Love of mine. All the warmth of an endless summertime. A beauty that boils blood and severs veins. Slowly the coldness creeps as we write our story. But our hands remain clasped together, even in the darkest nights. There are years in the wilderness, yes. Knots that will take us forever to untangle. But untangle them we will. We do. We did. And then life. Full and true and kind. And then her. Our girl. Our beautiful girl. Pure and untroubled, fact and fiction. The light that shines the way. The three of us, tired and happy and burning so, so bright.

And the pain. She is here with me, our beautiful girl. I'm so, so sorry, my love. We will wait for you always in the place where we will be. The dream is lucid and fragmented, and I remember.

EPILOGUE

'Will Jack be there, Daddy?'

She doesn't remember it. Any of it. In her memory, we were in the car and then she woke up on the train, with my arms around her. I'm so thankful for that. I think of the writhing and the glitching and I'm so, so thankful for the strangeness and fragility of memory.

'Oh, I should think so, sweetness.'

We hold hands as we walk along the picture postcard promenade. The yellow sun is smiling down on us and the sky is cornflower blue. Gulls bob up and down on the gently rolling water, their distant squawks are the only sound at first. But then, as we near *The Place Where We Will Be*, a viola sonata plays.

'I hope so because I want to show him my drawing.'

'The one of Mummy?'

I'm so, so sorry.

'No, silly. The one of our new house.'

The chairs and tables that sit outside the brilliant glass

café front sparkle in the afternoon sunshine. The three figures adorning them slowly come into focus as we approach. It's my grandma who sees us first and waves enthusiastically.

'Great-Grandma Annie!' My daughter runs into the waiting arms of her namesake.

'Hello, my darling girl!'

Percy and Clara both stand to greet us with warm smiling faces. Clara embraces me and Percy holds out a hand, but I ignore it and pull him into an embrace as well.

'Quite right,' he says.

They look well. The handsome man with the neatly trimmed moustache and the weightless hazel eyes and the movie star with thin and shapely lips. But then, we all look well. It's this place; it brings out the best in us. We take our seats as Bessie and Effie appear, laden with trays of cakes and tea.

'Aunty Effie!' my daughter cries in delight. She has taken to dear Effie, we all have, and the feeling is mutual.

'Good day to you, Miss Annie. And could I perhaps interest you in a slice of chocolate cake this afternoon?'

'Yes please!'

'I thought as much.'

She kisses us both hello as she places the sumptuous slice in front of my daughter's wide eyes. Bessie embraces us both and gives us a smile that would make us feel safe, if we didn't already feel safe.

'Is Jack here, Great-Great-Great-Grandma Bessie?'

Bessie laughs at this. 'I keep telling you, just call me Grandma Bessie, my sweet.'

And then Jack appears in the doorway. Little Jack, smiling and sweet and with no memory between falling asleep in one place and waking up in another. He pretends to be shy for a few moments, as he always does. He hides behind the sister he never met in that other place.

'Oh, come now, baby brother, you're not shy! Annie's come to play with you.'

My daughter climbs from her chair and hands Jack her drawing. He looks at it and grins from ear to ear.

'It's for you,' my daughter says. 'It's our new house.'

We talk then, of things trivial and new. We always do this now, in this New Age. We are the people who tea. We look forwards, never backwards. There is laughter and love and all the things that make a life. My daughter and her Great-Great-Uncle Jack draw pictures. Each trying their hardest to impress my grandma, who feigns amazement at their every effort. Effie and Clara dance to the music that always plays here. Percy and I make plans for the future; garden parties and cocktails on the veranda. And Bessie watches over us all, dipping in and out of conversations as it suits her. She could be anything from thirty to eighty. Almost improbably generic. Or at least she would be. Were it not for *that* face. A face that glows with the light of life itself. Kindness and wisdom. Forgiveness and strength. We are safe.

We hear them before we see them. It's always that way. The excited bark and the unmistakeable sound of running paws on the promenade.

'Dropsy!' cry Jack and Annie. The happy mutt appears with tail wagging. He jumps into the arms of my daughter and licks his hello before greeting each of us in turn, his excitement never waning. His master comes in to view through the afternoon heat haze and we smile and wave and feel that same sense of completeness that we feel every time we're all together.

'Good day!' Algie lifts his hat before he, too, greets us each in turn. There was an awkwardness the first time. As he greeted his wife, whom he loves forever and ever, and her new partner, who also happens to be his ex-fiancée. But the awkwardness was ours rather than theirs and we took our lead from Algie. Melancholy doesn't really suit Algie; life is a rich pageant of possibility, after all.

'Where's my Jack?'

'Pops!'

'Hello, my boy!'

'I drawed a picture with Annie.'

'Well, show me, show me!'

Algie takes his seat, Jack on his father's lap, Dropsy at his master's feet. Percy places a slice of lemon cake in front of his father-in-law's wide twinkling emerald eyes.

'What took you so long, Pops?' Clara asks.

'What's that?' Algie splutters, with a mouthful of cake. 'Oh, Dropsy wanted to explore a bit. So, we headed off down the beach in the opposite direction.'

'How far did you get?' my grandma asks.

'We're still going!' Algie chuckles.

'Yes, I see. I'd rather thought that would be the case.'

'Can we play I spy, Pops?' Asks Jack.

'What a splendid idea, my boy.'

In the middle of nowhere, amidst the endless blackness of a forever night, there is a train. But we are not on board. We are somewhere new. Are we in heaven? Yes, I think so. Well, what other explanation is there, really? Your guess is as good as mine. But it feels like heaven. There is a train station here that usually sits empty, but not always. We have visitors. There are many unanswered questions. But not all questions require answers, do they? One day, I believe there will be more of us. My grandad, my parents and stepparents, my brother and his family and, of course, her. My darling Ela. They'll arrive on a train and I'll be waiting on the platform to greet them. To welcome them home. I suppose I should hope not to see them *too* soon, but time isn't really a thing here. There are minutes and hours and days but not really anything beyond that. There is the smiling yellow sun and a happy moon surrounded by twinkling stars. But there are no days of the week, or months or years. Heaven, it turns out, is an endless summer by the seaside. In our case at least. For others it may be a daisy-strewn meadow or a roaring open fire on a cold winter's day. Or a train full of memories and loved ones, I suppose.

It was all about family in the end, wasn't it? I try not to think about it too much, if I'm honest. Not everyone has a family, after all. Although family, in its true sense, has nothing do with names or ugly cherry red blood. It's just love, really. Family, I mean. It's just the people you love, isn't it?

'Right, come on then, sweetness.'

'Are we going home, Daddy?'

'We better had; we've got a visitor coming.'

My daughter's eyes light up. 'Nanna Martin!'

'Nanna Martin.'

'Hooray!'

'And you know what that means we'll be having for our tea, don't you?'

'Marshmallows!'